# Tallie's War

## Jan Webster

Woman's Weekly Fiction

**A Woman's Weekly Paperback**
TALLIE'S WAR

First published in Great Britain 1993
by Robert Hale Ltd
This edition published 1995
by Woman's Weekly
in association with Mandarin Paperbacks
an imprint of Reed Consumer Books Ltd
Michelin House, 81 Fulham Road, London SW3 6RB
and Auckland, Melbourne, Singapore and Toronto

A CIP catalogue record for this title
is available from the British Library
ISBN 186056 020 2

Printed and bound by
HarperCollins Manufacturing, Glasgow

# One

She always tried to prolong the time she spent in the wood gathering sticks for the fires, because she could sit down sometimes, maybe sucking at some wild strawberries she'd found, and think about how she could get away from the house and her mother, and become a nurse.

It was never going to be easy. Her mother needed her and being needed was something. But she also exploited her, knowing hers was the willing back. Her sisters Kate and Belle had an easier time of it. Kate, who was older, was a teacher in the village school and dubbed the Clever One. Belle, the youngest, was still a pupil-teacher, but the family paid for her piano lessons and agreed she had to keep her hands nice. She was also the Pretty One. So where did that leave Tallie (which had somehow evolved from Belle's lisping version of her christened name, Tabitha)? Pig in the middle. At everybody's beck and call. 'You're the nice one,' said old Mrs Beggs in the village. But where did being nice – which she wanted to be, at least most of the time – get you? Running the cutter, whatever that might mean, said Mrs Beggs, for everybody, including the brothers. Donald, the eldest in the family. Next to God in her mother's eyes. The only one who'd gone to university. Now 'in Shipping' in Glasgow. And Russell, the youngest, sixteen, who had chosen to go down the pit which had destroyed their father's lungs.

If she went away, who would wash the socks and hankies Donald sent home each week in a tin biscuit box? Who would tackle Russell's coal-grimed shirts and drawers? But

1

she felt often she was being submerged beneath the wash-house soapsuds and the routine of cleaning and cooking for the two boarders her mother had kept since her father's death. Why did she do it? Because she still wanted her mother's favour, to be more special than Kate or Belle, to have her mother's praise.

'God Almighty,' said a voice behind her. 'This is the year of Our Lord nineteen hundred and thirteen, Tallie: women shouldn't need to carry loads of sticks on their backs.'

She tossed down her load expertly and grinned at Toby Wilson. She had gone to school with him and it seemed to her he hung about the woods at a time when he knew she might be there on the pretext of walking his soft mutt, Algie. It seemed he could work or not in his father's grocer's shop, as and when he wanted.

'I quite like it,' she told him.

'You'll get a hump on your back.'

'They're not all that heavy. Just kindling.'

'Not away to the nursing yet?' In a weak moment, a moment of frustration, she had confided her ambition to Toby.

'We're due a new boarder today. How can I leave all the work to my mother?'

'She could get paid help.'

He had struck home. Her mother *could* get paid help. But it suited her to employ Tallie for nothing. Time and again an allowance had been promised but it was never forthcoming. You get your keep, her mother said. What more do you want?

'Who's the new boarder, then?' queried Toby, curiously.

She gave him an indulgent glare.

'Some old teacher starting at the boy's academy in Perringhall. I've got to go, Toby. I've to do the fire in his room.'

She surrendered the quiet of the woods reluctantly, as the only place where she could try to sort things out in her mind. She knew she had to get away from the house, Cullington Lodge, and her mother's unfair domination of

2

her. Maybe it had all started in childhood, when her mother had often been ill with bronchitis, and she, Tallie had been the strongest and most ready to help of the girls. Maybe she had tried the hardest for her mother's approbation. Whatever the reason for it, she had somehow got herself into the position of family scodgy.

Cullington Lodge lay behind much of it. After her father's death, her mother had been determined to get out of the Pit Rows and the Lodge with its six bedrooms and little field with room for a cow had been up for rent. It couldn't have been afforded without the boarders and help from Donald once he'd started work.

He'd brought the force of his position as head of the family to bear on Tallie. 'You'll have to give a hand,' he insisted. 'The old girl can't do it without you.' 'But why me?' she'd argued. 'I want to be a nurse.'

'Time enough,' he'd said. But her mother's possessive grip tightened daily. Tallie knew enough of what her mother had suffered to understand her desperation to underwrite their newfound family prosperity. The babies that had come, year after year, some dying before or after birth; the husband who became unmanageable in drink; the ill-health stemming from her own hard childhood as an orphan dairymaid; the ambition for her children, at least, for all of them it seemed, except Tallie. She had been cast in the not unusual role for that time of the Daughter Who Stayed at Home and Helped. Except that it wasn't what *she* wanted at all. She had once seen a hare caught in a farmer's trap and that was what she felt, that she was engaged in a desperate struggle for life itself. But all inside her head. For the outer Tallie still conformed to what people expected and asked of her. And had a desperate need to please and be liked.

'Come on, lassie,' her mother urged impatiently as she went in at the scullery door. 'Get the fires set and the tatties peeled.'

'Ma, say please,' Tallie addressed her parent in her head. 'Just once, ask me as though I have an option. Tell me you

3

appreciate what I do.' But it was useless to wait for anything other than an impatient wave of the hand to indicate she should get on. Smiles on that careworn, hardset face were saved for Donald's infrequent homecomings, or occasionally for Belle when she played one of her halting tunes on the shining new piano. 'I had no fal-de-rals when I was young,' her mother reminded her frequently. 'I had to do the work of two and none the worse for it.' It was as though she had to put Tallie through the trials of her own youth and at times there was an element of sheer malicious fury in it, in a determination to see the girl suffer. It was this more than anything that made Tallie want to get out. The hard work she was used to and did not greatly mind.

Wilfred Chappell took off the jacket of his brown suit and hung it up in the capacious wardrobe where it hung forlornly, then loosened the stud of his hard collar. Quel relief! The day had been warm and the train up from London to Glasgow busy, but every mile it took him away from the capital the more certain he was he had made the right decision.

It didn't make sense to go on teaching in the East End. After the spot on his lung the doctor had warned him of the need for more fresh air and less politics. He'd had his vision of the Western Isles, maybe Mull where he'd once gone hiking, but the Lanarkshire job had come up and Perringhall Academy had been keen to have him come to teach English and Latin. His own father had worked on the Kent coalfield, so he should feel at home here, with Glasgow and its fiery Socialist thinkers not far away. His lodgings were far enough out in the countryside to be agreeable and the girl who had shown him to his room had been friendly and helpful, even if there had been something cramped and shy about her manner. Nice to look at, too, with her dark hair and youthfully innocent, unformed features.

He must ask her about the name Tallie. But you're here to work, my man, he reminded himself with a half-grin, to teach those likely Scots lads how to decline the verb *amare*, not get into the complexities of *amo*, *amas*, *amat* yourself.

He glanced at himself in the long cheval mirror and thought how ridiculous it was he might be blushing. For God's sake, he must get more gravitas. He took a close look at his facial reflection. Questioning brown eyes, dark hair, thin cheeks. A mouth his mother had insisted was sensitive. Not an open face; perhaps too reflective for that. So, quench that sparkle at the thought of the girl with the odd name and the sideways look, and instead concentrate on the pleasant view from the window. The landscape was a bit featureless, except in the distance a glimpse of the Clyde and on the skyline a pit heap with its distinctive wheel and wires. But something was going out from him already, welcoming what he saw, feeling strangely and comfortingly at home. Maybe he was destined to find his teaching niche here, uplift the minds of the miners' and farmers' sons and show them the new Jerusalem. Sometimes he was a little ashamed of his idealism, tending to romanticism. But not today. Today was the start of a new era and he was full of the mission to teach, uplift and educate. An Englishman in the country that worshiped Education with a capital E. Nice wry touch, that.

He had already convinced himself it was a good thing to get away from southern cynicism and talk of a war, even while part of him admitted that what some of his friends said was true: Armageddon was coming. 'For I hear the steady drummer, Drumming like a noise in dreams.' Even as far back as 1896 Housman had been writing it. 'Dear to friends and food for powder, Soldiers marching all to die.' Maybe it could still be averted. Maybe sense would prevail. Yet Europe was arming to the teeth. Wilfred made a determined, conscious effort to thrust such black thoughts away. He had a new job, a clean bill of health – and now the girl with the odd name (he presumed) was tapping timidly on his door, with the supper he'd asked for on a tray.

Pretty forearms, he thought, taking the tray from her and placing it on the table with the aspidistra. It contained aromatic thick broth, beef, potatoes and a dish of creamy tapioca pudding, a not over-generous helping. She had unusual eyes, too, he added mentally, noting that they were almost more amber than hazel and the brows above them finely marked.

'Tallie,' he said. 'Is that your proper name?'

'I'm really Tabitha.'

'Thanks, Tallie. That looks great. I find I'm quite hungry.'

She suddenly lost her shyness and beamed at him. 'Then tuck in,' she said. 'It'll stick to your ribs.' He would have liked the conversation to go on but she suddenly lost her smile and looked haunted as a voice called imperatively from downstairs, 'Tallie, I want you. Come down here.'

He had eaten in his room on that first night, so that he need not wear a collar and tie, and jacket, but the boarders normally dined downstairs in a large room with a wood plank floor and thin carpet. The other boarder was a county council official, a small needling man with a swooping moustache, called Ernest Waters, who whistled a lot under his breath and went away at weekends.

The boarders were supposed to have the use of the front room if they wished, but were not encouraged to hang about downstairs after they had eaten in the evening. Their rooms were quite large, after all, and adequately furnished. But since the family joined them for supper (except for Russell who preferred to eat in the kitchen, only half-stripped of his coaly clothes, and sometimes for Mrs Candlish if she chose to eat with her youngest), the young men enjoyed chatting with the girls and often had to be shifted by a basilisk look from their mother.

It began to irk Wilfred that Tallie seemed to do most of the ferrying of plates and serving though the other girls were supposed to help. Belle with her gauzy mass of hair, pale eyes and small stature seemed to him a cool little madam, though she would sometimes get an endearing fit of the giggles with Tallie when they baited the self-important Waters, and Kate with her quelling school-

6

mistressy look was already a bit of a gorgon, he thought, though he liked to hear her musical voice and the lucid, no-nonsense way she could conduct an argument.

His conversations with Tallie were always scrappy and guarded, but it wasn't long before he realised the girl was bitterly unhappy with her lot.

One evening when he impulsively caught her hand as she was leaving the room, to ask her some routine question about his laundry, she pulled the hand away quickly, hiding it behind her back.

'What's the matter?' he demanded bluntly.

'My hands are a mess.'

'Show me.'

'Reluctantly she held them out. The knuckles were swollen, red and hacked. 'It's carbolic,' she said and ran away.

On another night when she brought his cocoa to his room where he was marking papers, she stayed to talk for a few minutes, her mother having gone to a woman's prayer meeting. She leaned against the open door, her hand on the doorknob, her face half averted to make sure she wasn't overheard from downstairs, but animated from the need to communicate. She half swayed against the door as if for support. '

'You tired?' he asked.

She shook her head but he took it for assent.

'You have to do too much. Or so it seems to a mere man.'

'Mere man?' Tallie suddenly burst out. 'Next time round, I'll be a mere man, I think.'

'Why do you think we are better off?'

'You can choose what you do. You get waited on hand and foot.'

'What would you like to do, Tallie?' he demanded curiously.

'Be a nurse.'

'From all accounts, that's very hard work, too.'

'But of my own choosing.' He looked away from the proud and vulnerable young face. He supposed girls didn't

7

have all that much to choose from – teaching, nursing, shops.

'Then you must do it. We only have one life, you know?'

'I wish – I wish I had the courage.'

'One day you will,' he said reassuringly. It was suddenly important to show he was on her side.

She looked as though she would like to say more; indeed as though she were about to launch on a great confiding spiel, when the front door opened and shut and she bolted downstairs. It took him ages to get back to his marking.

The next time it seemed to him Tallie looked more than a little tired and careworn, he protested to Belle on his way out to his room: 'Do you think you are fair on Tallie?'

'What do you mean?'

'She looks fed up tonight. She hates staying at home, you know, when the rest of you are out in the world.'

'It's Mother's wish.'

Wilfred looked round to make sure Mrs Candlish hadn't crept up the passage to sweep the dining-room with one of her heart-stopping glares.

'Mother isn't God,' he said mildly.

Belle had the grace to look uncomfortable, but soon rallied her quick-witted defences. 'Tallie will go, when she's ready,' she offered.

'But the rest of you should be more supportive, in the meantime.'

Belle flicked an imaginary piece of fluff from Wilfred's shoulder and gave him a flirtatious look.

'You're not family yet, Wilf,' she upbraided him lightly. 'How is it going at the Academy?'

'All right.' He wasn't going to admit to this confident little madam the problems he had with the thick Lowland accents or the teasing he had to put up with over his own London vowels. He was getting through and some at least were willing to learn.

Tallie brushed by him at this point, carrying a huge tureen that held their evening barley broth. He didn't know quite what happened to him when she came near him.

8

There was some kind of womanly scent that came from her, not from soap or lavender water but just from her tender young femaleness and tonight it had overtones of sweaty fatigue. She was asked to do too much. She was up before everybody else and he had seen her on her hands and knees, brushing carpets, washing floors and steps and with her arms steeped in suds in the wash-house across the cobbled yard or hoisting great lines of laundry on the green, battling against the stiff fresh winds that assaulted the little knowe on which Cullington Lodge sat in its stiff-backed Edwardian glory. He wanted to sit her down and put her feet up and wipe the damp hair back from her brow. He wanted to save her.

'Can I help?' he volunteered, gallantly but uselessly. Mrs Candlish would not allow boarders across the kitchen threshold. Tallie shook her head at him. But he knew he wasn't imagining it, the pleading in her eyes. She was like a maiden in a tower and he was getting to feel more and more like St George.

# Two

Janet Candlish watched her youngest daughter Belle hang up her flared serge jacket and the straw boater which had been sitting so attractively atop her mass of hair. As always, she felt her heart soften. Belle had always been the one most like her. If Janet's own life had been easier, she would have moved with that same easy grace and could have learned to laugh with that same joyful abandon. Belle was her own life made over again and made better. Janet brought out her special sultana cake to accompany the cup of tea she had ready and sat down to hear the latest of her daughter's doings at the village school.

9

'Tibby Robertson's got a new dress for the harvest soirée. It's cream ninon with the hem tamboured in pale green silk thread.'

'Your blue will look just as bonny.'

'She asked me if Wilfred was going.'

'If he does, see he dances with you and Kate, not with Tibby Robertson.'

'But it's Tallie he fancies.'

Her mother's face darkened. 'Aye, and if she's not careful—' She left the words unsaid. She took up the poker and fenced fiercely with the glowing cinders in the kitchen grate. Earlier that day, Tallie had used the emery paper to make the steel bits shine and blacklead to burnish the grate ribs. The fire gave off a cheerful glow that was not reflected in Janet's expression.

'I think it's you that's right for him if anybody is,' she said firmly. 'He's in the teaching profession and so are you. He needs a wife who'll smarten him up a bit with her ideas.'

Belle blushed furiously. 'Who's talking wife?' she demanded.

'I'm only speculating,' said Janet. She held out her hands to the fire. 'He must get a good pay and his prospects are good. You could do a lot worse.'

'But Tallie—'

'Tallie's not thinking about marrying yet,' said her mother shortly.

Belle looked at little uncomfortable. 'Mother,' she temporised, 'maybe you should let Tallie go to the nursing. Folk are beginning to talk—'

'What do they say?'

'That she doesn't have much of a life. That she's looking cowed and fed up.'

'Who said this?'

'Well, Tibby for one.'

'And who else?'

'Well, Wilfred for another. He thinks you should have a girl in to help her.'

'And he's going to pay her wages, I suppose?' said Janet

10

tartly. 'He should learn to keep his nose out of other people's business.'

'A minute ago,' said Belle, beginning to laugh, 'you were putting him up as a candidate for my hand.'

'Well, he needn't think he's coming in here and telling me how to run my house. And Tallie can think on about nursing. She thinks she's hard done by here. Wait till she gets on the fever wards. They'll run her off her feet and pay her five shilling a month for the privilege. Her head's full of a lot of nonsense from these silly books she reads.'

'He lends her books,' said Belle, meaning Wilfred, with a light note of censure. 'Proper books. He says she's got a good mind but it's untrained—'

'It's you he should lend the books,' Janet insisted. 'Or Kate. Instead of giving her false notions about herself.'

Sometimes in spite of everything Belle's notion of fair play asserted itself.

'She's entitled to make what she can of herself, Mother.'

'You'll be telling me you're turning into Sylvia Pankhurst next.' Janet's round-shouldered frame crouched angrily in its chair and she tapped the chair arm with thick fingers. 'Lasses nowadays don't know they're born. I was sent out to work when I was eight. Eight. I walked four mile in a snowstorm to start at my first farm and the weather was so bad they had to send the farmer out on horseback to look for me. I used to lie where the cattle had been to warm my feet.'

Belle began to wish this particular conversation had never started. She'd heard it all before. She wasn't sure yet whether she liked Wilfred Chappell or not. Sometimes he was nice and pleasant and sometimes he had a reproving edge to his tongue. At twenty-three he was a bit old for her. She liked larky men who knew the songs from the latest musical comedies and tried out new dance steps, not thin-jawed aesthetes who quoted Plato and insisted that a war to end all wars was coming. Sometimes at night, though, in bed, she recollected his large, dark, poet's eyes and got swallowed up in them, wondering what it would be like if he

11

kissed her. But in some almost relentless way, she felt Wilfred and Tallie were linked. There was a charge like that of electricity when they were in a room together and he became alive and all animated when she took him up on something or laughed at something he'd said, looking as though someone had just awarded him a medal.

Obscurely, Belle knew her mother wasn't fair to Tallie. From about the age of thirteen it had become noticeable, Janet's tendency to pick on her and make her the target for her uncertain temper. Not that the rest of them weren't in awe of their mother, too. She was a martinet who laid down the law for everyone, from parish minister to message-boy.

But because Janet had set the pattern in her implacable way, they all tended to pick on Tallie. Certainly to take her for granted. She was the one most like their late father, with something quiet and reflective and inaccessible about her nature. You did not really know what Tallie was thinking. Russell stuck up for her and deflected his mother's ire when he could, Donald regarded her as a skivvy, even making her run his bath for him when he came home, as though he were Lord Muck himself.

Belle tried to pick her way carefully through the confused maze of her feelings towards her sister. If she went away to nursing, not only would Tallie be happier but Belle would get to know Wilfred better. Maybe their mother would loosen her iron dictatorial hold on all of them. Belle took a surreptitious look at her parent now, filled as always with something like pity as well as resentment for the slight, indomitable form. If she was made of iron, it was because life had made her so. They would none of them have prospered if she had not risen above her husband's drunkenness, if she had not plotted and worked and politicked for them and demanded respect where there had once been contempt.

They'd had no shoes in the summer and parish boots in winter when they lived in the Rows. Not wanting to remember it, but assailed by the image, she had this sudden impactful picture of her mother sitting under the oil lamp,

12

sewing interminable unpicked hand-me-downs into trousers, skirts, coats for their narrow backs, followed by another of her turning the mangle to flatten other people's heavy sheets for twopence. Yet what had given her the right to command their lives the way she did now? She it was who had decided that with the aid of bursaries the clever 'lad o' parts' Donald should go to university. Only Russell, of all of them, had done exactly what he liked and that was because even his mother couldn't resist his good-natured insistence on taking life as it came.

But to get back to Tallie . . . Belle sighed. You couldn't, even with the best will in the world, always solve other people's problems for them. Compared to Kate, who was prickly and argumentative, determined to be superior, Tallie wasn't a bad sister. You couldn't get close to Kate. Belle remembered how patient Tallie had been when she'd had to take her to the outside cludgie when she was little and how she'd always seemed to be binding up Russell's cuts and bumps and bruises on his perilous journey through boyhood. She would make a good nurse.

'Finished your tea?' Janet's voice broke into Belle's reverie. 'Wash the cups, then, and get on with some darning.' Belle rose to do as she was bid. There was never time for slacking. Her mother kept them all up to scratch. Belle watched the frail figure, dressed in black from top to toe, cameo brooch at the neck of her high-necked blouse, rise to search out her own knitting. The fingers flews expertly over the grey wool, making yet another pair of grey socks for Donald, the apple of his mother's eye.

Wilfred had begun to think Tallie would not be joining them at the harvest soirée. He had danced a lively polka with Belle and a sedate veleta with the straight-backed Kate before the middle Miss Candlish put in an appearance, looking red-faced and a little dishevelled. She'd had to leave the kitchen spick and span before her evening out. But she's prettier than any of them, Wilfred thought, finding the way her soft hair tendrilled about her pale animated face quite irresistible. She wore a long grey dress of moiré silk and carried a small gathered bag – did they call it a Dorothy bag? – over her wrist, made from the same material.

'Tallie looks nice,' he commented to Kate, delivering her back to her seat with other young ladies after the waltz.

'She made the dress herself,' Kate responded. 'We put together and bought her the material, but as you can see, the hem dips where it shouldn't, at the back.'

'Perhaps it's meant,' he argued. 'I've seen dipping hems.'

'It's a bit homespun and unsophisticated,' said Kate disparagingly. She and Belle had their own dressmaker in the village, the skilled Mrs Baird, who also trimmed their mother's hats for church-going. 'But she gets points for trying.'

Wilfred determined to ask Tallie for the next dance, whatever it turned out to be, and to make a point of telling her the dress looked splendid. Now that she had come, homespun or not in her sister's eyes, the evening had assumed a different tenor for him. The country band, accordion, fiddle and drums, appeared suddenly to be leaving out all discordant notes. The hollowed-out turnips with candles lit inside them, the big green vases holding sheaves of corn and barley, the fruit and vegetables piled in baskets (that would later go to the fever hospital) seemed to present a more vivid and intensely colourful scene than London had ever offered. He had seen as he came in the supper laid out in the smaller hall and it was sumptuous – snowy tables decorated with chrysanthemums the size of footballs, with trailing fern and ivy, the plates piled with hams, pies, trifles and magnificent cakes. Lowland Scots might not attend all that many parties but when they did it seemed to him they knew how to enjoy themselves. The air of festivity and fun was almost buoyant.

Between dances, the girls and women congregated awkwardly at one end of the hall and the men and boys shuffled and guffawed at the other. Relieved of his pit grime and unnaturally pink and scrubbed in his navy serge

14

suit and white shirt, Russell and some of his pals indulged in the horseplay which passed for social intercourse among the younger men, while Toby Wilson, separated for once from his dog, gazed a shade longingly across the dance floor in the direction of the girls and, Wilfred thought possessively, in particular at Tallie. When the music started again, he'd have to make sure he beat him to the post for Tallie's hand.

'Not a bad do,' said a voice in his ear, and he turned to see Donald Candlish, who had come home from Glasgow for the soirée. They had been introduced at Cullington Lodge earlier.

Donald Candlish had dived straight in to the attack. 'As a career academic, you'll not find much material round here.'

'Boys are boys,' Wilfred had answered mildly. 'A lot depends on the way they are taught.' Faintly miffed at something patronising, even baiting, in the other's manner Wilfred had gone on, 'You went to university, after all, but are the product of these parts.'

Donald had acknowledged the rebuff with a raise of his eyebrows and a curl of the lip. Now he seemed to be annexing Wilfred's attention as the only one in the company of any intellectual stature apart from himself and the minister.

'I don't know why I bother to come to these things.' Tibby Robertson's bold, anxious gaze seemed to be boring into his back.

'For the attractive female company, perhaps.' Wilfred suddenly didn't want to fence and smiled instead at the other's transparency.

He could see why the sisters appeared to dote on this great shaggy-headed creature, with the skin taut-drawn over sharp cheek-bones. He had the same unusually-coloured eyes as Tallie, with a lot of white in them (someone had said you got that from Highland ancestors), a firm jaw and good nose, with a look of great intelligence and authority. But he also saw that no one had ever challenged Donald's excellent opinion of himself and that pride could be the undoing of him if he wasn't careful.

Donald turned his back on the prospect of the waiting girls and fixed Wilfred with an undeflecting gaze.

'All this Suffragism business,' he declared, 'is going to get them nowhere. Women are for breeding and raising children. And for pleasing the eye. End of story.'

'You don't think they should have the vote?'

'Certainly not. I've just been reading the *Glasgow Herald*. Creatures capable of stoving in shop windows and setting fire to sports pavilions don't deserve to be taken seriously. Did you see where they even attacked Asquith while he was playing golf? Biology is fate. They can't get out of the role nature has chosen for them.'

'So you don't think Tallie should be allowed to decide her own future?' Wilfred hadn't meant to start anything; the words had just come out because Tallie was never out of his mind.

'Tallie?' Donald appeared never to have given the matter a moment's thought. 'She's needed in the home, old chap. Mother being a widow needs all the support she can get.'

'But Tallie supports you all. She underpins the whole family.' Wilfred knew his latent anger was declaring itself in the rising note of his voice.

'We're into philosophical water here, aren't we? You have to think of the common good. No man – or woman – an island and all that.'

'But Tallie *is* an island at the moment. She's the only one who isn't finding any self-fulfilment. Can't you see it's sapping all her confidence in herself?'

Donald gave him a fierce and challenging look. 'Sounds like you could be a disciple of the filthy German Bernhardi.'

'I've read Bernhardi and I find it peculiarly insulting that you should even begin to associate me with his views. This is a man who thinks war a biological necessity—'

'And that the first and paramount law is the assertion of one's own independent existence. He thinks self-sacrifice is a renunciation of life—'

Without realising it, Wilfred had grabbed hold of the thick Harris tweed lapel of Donald's jacket. 'For God's sake, what's that got to do with members of a family having a care for each other? Christ said to love your neighbour as yourself, not negate yourself in the process—'

Donald brushed Wilfred's grasp away as he might a fly. Then pulling himself up with the realisation that they were in danger of making a spectacle of themselves, he laughed and patted the other's back.

'You'll not be the first Sassenach to think he can impose his namby-pamby ideas on us, Wilf. Suppose we shelve the philosophical arguments for another day and concentrate on having a good time?'

Wilfred took the hand extended to him and shook it, his face still betraying his uncertainty. But he was used to argument from his student days upwards and quite enjoyed the way Scots of all classes launched themselves into ethical and moral discussions at the drop of a hat. He'd take Donald on back at Cullington Lodge and try to make him see that giving women some ground, even learning to like them as thinking people, had nothing to do with German generals trying to impose their 'might is right' and 'survival of the fittest' views on the Western world.

He wasn't going to give up over Tallie. The Candlish family had to be made to see that what they were doing to her was damaging and unkind, even if he acknowledged that patterns of behaviour could grow up in families in a way that was inexplicable and hard to change because those closely involved did not see their own demeanour clearly.

The band were back in place and the fiddler invited everyone to take their partners for Strip the Willow. Toby Wilson started out towards Tallie but Wilfred was even quicker.

He lifted Tallie's hand. 'May I have the pleasure?' Full of his feelings for her, protecting, claiming, brimming with increasingly tender love his eyes met hers, those amber-hazel eyes held his momentarily, then her mouth turned up in acquiescence and she stood beside him, waiting patiently for the dancers to form their lines, her hand scrabbling in his like a little night creature waiting to come in from the cold.

Tibby Robertson had got tired of waiting and came forward to claim Donald as her partner. Once attached to him, she held on to him for the next few dances.

She was a big, full-bodied girl, as sturdy as one of the sheaves of corn on her father's prosperous farm, and as golden. Soft, downy golden hairs ran down her sturdy forearms and thick golden lashes embellished her bright, somewhat protruding eyes. Her near-red hair, cascading down her back, looked as though the sun rays had got netted in it. *Ceres*, Wilfred thought, glancing at her as they passed in the dance. That's who she is. You could put her straight into a Shakespearian masque as the goddess and hush the groundlings at a stroke. He caught Donald's eye and thought: the man's a goner and he doesn't know it. He can put women down all he likes; all that plenitude is not to be resisted. Maybe Donald did know. His grin back at Wilfred bore a certain resignation in it.

'Tallie,' whispered Belle across the narrow spaced between their attic beds, 'have you heard our Donald come in yet?'

'I'm sleeping,' Tallie protested.

'He was taking Tibby home.'

'He's probably slipped in without us hearing.'

'I would have heard.'

The two girls lay staring into the darkness, listening to the sound of Kate's even breathing in the bed under the window. Tallie scarcely gave Donald or Tibby a thought. Wilfred had managed to kiss her twice on the way home, despite Kate's best endeavours to keep an eye on them. She could still feel the warmth of his encircling arms.

# Three

After a midday meal taken without sitting down and a morning being assailed by her mother's litany of jobs still to be done, Tallie escaped into the woods while her mother napped, greeting the sight of blue sky and puffy white clouds with an almost pathetic gratitude.

The trees, which had been neither thickly nor carefully planted, and were none of them all that impressive or sturdy, being more of the scrubby sort, nevertheless lifted their branches in the summer breeze and threw down a jumbled tracery of shadows where she walked. She picked up twigs and small broken branches, discarding anything too green or sappy because it did not make good kindling. Absently she hummed, not wanting anything more for this moment than the sense of freedom, of being answerable to no one. When she reached patches of sunlight, she stood under the warming rays of the sun, feeling it on the skin of her face and her bare arms, beneficent and kindly.

If the weather kept up, there might be a picnic at the weekend, because Donald was home, declaring he could stay a few days after the harvest soirée. You'd think with the fields emptying of the corn and barley and days imperceptibly shortening and the nip of the cold lineoleum in the morning that the summer would relinquish its long golden tryst, but far from it. Tallie liked the season's romantic, lying insistence that it could go on forever. It was easy to think it might and if it did and winter never came, then perhaps the war everybody thought might happen, wouldn't, and she would get away to nursing and . . .

'You didn't save me the supper dance.'

Tallie jumped out of her unguarded reverie. Toby Wilson and Algie were regarding her from between two sapling trees. The little dog, with the mottled patch over one eye, wagged his tail at her but began a series of short, sharp barks as though he too were reprimanding her. Tallie looked down at him and laughed.

'No laughing matter,' Toby protested. He always tried to be nonchalant and urbane, a kind of fellow-about-town (what town? Perringhall was pretty one-horse), chaffing and sardonic. But they'd been in the same class and she knew that though he was quick at arithmetic and well informed about geography, he didn't spell all that well and his written work was always smudgy. Just as he knew she was good at composition but unreliable with figures. His great virtue in the eyes of his school fellows had been that he had an uncanny knack of playing on any teacher's weak spot. The good ones kept him in his place and the bad ones entertained by their exasperation. Their friendship, if that wasn't too strong a word for it, had always been easy-going; even, as when she'd told him about her nursing ambitions, occasionally confidential and trusting.

A part of her didn't want to acknowledge that Toby wanted something more, postponing the consideration of whether it might be possible. He was verging on the good-looking, almost tall, straight-backed, sandy-haired and candid-eyed with a lazy smile. She had not been fair to him at the harvest soirée, but then he hadn't been a match for the older Wilfred. Compunction made her nice to him now.

'You know how it is,' she offered. 'We were all together from the house, my brother—'

'The lodger *et al*. He's far too old for you.'

'Twenty-three,' she said swiftly. 'He's only twenty-three.'

'I suppose you think he's *soigné*,' he said offendedly. He pronounced the 'g' hard and she hid a smile.

'Look who's swallowed the dictionary. I didn't know you spoke French.'

'You don't know everything about me,' he said angrily, coming closer. 'I've known you longer than any johnny-come-lately to the teaching profession. I suppose my working in a shop isn't good enough for you. But the shops'll be mine one day.'

She said nothing. She didn't like to see the hurt on his face. She wasn't like Belle, leading boys on for the sake of snubbing them. Or like Kate, treating them as though they were some subspecies at the far end of a microscope.

Wishing to be placatory, she said, 'Nothing's changed, has it? We're still friends.'

'Depends what you think of him.'

She wasn't going to be bullied into revelation. So she said with a touch of Kate's quelling authority, 'That's my business.'

He walked further into the woods with her, picking up sticks as she did and then throwing himself down moodily on a fallen log whilst Algie tried to wrest a long stick from his hand.

'When this war comes, I shall join up,' he said. 'I want to get away from here. This small-minded place. I won't wait to be conscripted, either.'

'There might not be a war.' She hated to be made to feel guilty, almost as though she were a Beatty or a Fisher building up the navy to a point where the Germans would not be able to resist the challenge to take it on.

'You wouldn't miss me, for one.'

'I would. The last thing I would want is for you to go out and get yourself killed. Wilfred says the war can still be averted, if the workers can get their act together.' The moment she'd said it, she knew it was the wrong thing.

'I suppose he had the Prime Minister's ear. Or is he one of those rotten pacifist chaps who are too scared to fight?'

'I don't think so. He and Donald argue the toss but I think he feels he would fight under certain circumstances. If Germany attacked little Belgium, for example. He says then we'd have an inescapable duty to do something.'

Tallie felt a wave of real distress at the picture of Toby's wretched expression; she knew he really wanted a full-scale row as to why she hadn't danced with him at the soirée never mind not gone into supper with him as on previous occasions, and that he really wanted to find ways of criticising Wilfred Chappell yet couldn't because of his lack of knowledge of him. Yet pride could only let him reveal so much. He wasn't going to make himself vulnerable, in case what he suspected were really true.

Tallie was strung between allegiance to the kind of uncomplicated friendship she'd always had with Toby and the undefined turbulence of what was happening between her and Wilfred. There were all kinds of constraints back in the house, not the least her mother, that prevented her from any kind of open or straightforward definition of how she felt. Except that it was breath-taking, body-changing, overwhelming, frightening. And she wasn't going to call it love yet, because that would be too final.

In some ways, she was attracted to the straightforward path of a courtship with Toby. The known and familiar had their own appeal, though it seemed to her from the way he looked at her nowadays that Toby was not quite the complaisant companion of, say, a year ago. He wanted to touch her. She knew that. His eyes would rest on her lips and fleetingly on her bosom and it made her uncomfortable. At such times, with her own body indicating she did not know what, having no terms of reference, she thought more ardently than ever of a life away from Cullington Lodge, a job through which she would find out more about the mystery of her own growing self.

'Will you come out for a walk with me tonight?' Toby demanded.

'Can't. Too busy.'

'Then what about getting the train to Hamilton on Saturday? I can buy you tea and a French cake.'

That would put the cat among the pigeons, she knew. To be seen going on the train to Hamilton with Toby, like some old courting couple! He knew the unlikelihood of her accepting, but she turned away from the intensity of his face, bewildered by how complex feelings could be.

'Maybe some other time, Toby,' she offered. Something moved her to touch his arm and something else made her lightly kiss his cheek. They both started back from this, he as though stung and she as though she had just delivered the

22

sting. They parted in furious embarrassment, Algie yapping at her as he went, as though in reprimand.

The bustle on Saturday morning as Cullington Lodge prepared for the picnic reminded Wilfred irresistibly of his childhood days, when his mother had got them all ready for the hop-picking in Kent. (Kent had been in the news again, with a delegation to Asquith urging him to consider the building of a Channel Tunnel. What were they trying to do – make England and France one as Henry V had done?)

Normally because there was a lot of hurt and pain there he didn't look back but, as he dug out his weekend tweeds, he seemed to hear the imaginary voices of his brothers and sisters over the less strident tones of the Candlish girls urging each other about their tasks. Lily and Jane and Harry and Lisa and Philip and Connie and Flo and himself, not to mention the cousins who bunked up with them when times were hard. It had been the squash and squalor of the tiny house in Bow that had made a scholar out of him, because books had been the only refuge. He realised now how hard it had been for his mother, why she'd opted for drink and nights at the music-halls, but his father's violence, learned at the docks, had been another matter and something in him cringed still, in fear and loathing.

The family had scattered – some had emigrated after his parents' deaths, except for the eldest, Lil. Lil had been tougher than any of them. Together with her husband Alf she'd constructed this carapace of middle-class respectability that included Wilfred and his years at college. Lil's willing fingers had stitched gowns for duchesses and a secure future for her adored youngest brother. Wilfred was her proudest achievement. She didn't care about the rest. But just for this morning they all swarmed back, pushing, shoving, arguing, blaming, reminding Wilfred of the East End smells he'd thought he'd never miss; grubby clothes, old boots, the jellied-eel stalls, Ma Kerson's pies and the hurdy-gurdy playing at the street corner. Making his own way in life, living by his own aesthetic and moral standards, that was what he had wanted, but he knew his siblings, except for Lil, saw him as a prig and despised him for taking his wisdom from books and not from life. There was this sense of isolation. Being 'clever' marked you out, separated you. And there was always this kind of longing to belong, to be accepted, to justify yourself. You couldn't quantify loneliness but put it like this, he told himself: you need someone. Someone to smooth over all the hurts. Someone as young as Tallie? Was it possible?

There had been talk of taking the train to the Ayrshire coast for a day out but Donald wanted to go to the Ainsh river where he had played and learned to swim as a boy. It meant a walk of about three miles, laden with travelling rugs, picnic food, folding stools and the like and Kate had insisted it was too far for Mother to walk.

'I've walked all my life,' Janet had insisted. About halfway there a friend had a cottage and Janet and Kate rested a while in its cool recesses, plied with barley water, whilst the rest went on. It was not quite eleven when they arrived and children were already paddling or catching minnows at the shallow edges. The boulder-strewn river, not so impressive as the nearby Clyde, had its own devotees and where it gently curved was a favourite picnic spot in the warm weather and ready-made lido where boys taught themselves to dive and swim.

Just before the river altered course there was an old stone bridge and underneath it, extending for about a hundred yards, a natural pool. Huge boulders provided diving spots for the bigger boys, branches from overhanging trees were a partial screen for the nudity imposed by poverty and smaller rocks on the riverbed were stepping stones for those with penny fishing-nets. There were only a few swimmers as yet, though the big rolling sun was calling up a heat that would surely bring more.

On the side of the bridge away from the swimmers Belle and Tallie inspected the green river banks for the best place to settle. At length, screened by bramble bushes, they found the ideal spot and laid down the rugs and opened the stools. Donald settled to reading his *Glasgow Herald*, Russell wandered off to talk to a lone fisherman, the girls peeked in the hamper to make sure the sandwiches weren't spoiling and Wilfred put his hands behind his head and basked.

By the time Kate and Janet arrived Russell was restless and demanding action. He talked the men into a game of rounders which Tallie and Belle eventually joined. The midday sun turned up its intensity on this pastoral scene, making Janet put up her parasol and one by one the players declared the boiling conditions were sapping their strength and that they had need for some form of sustenance to replace the energy expended on merciless cheating.

Tallie had boiled a cow's tongue the day before, placed it in a basin with an iron on top, then sliced it to put between baps oozing with yellow butter. There were hard-boiled eggs to peel and eat with screws of salt and pepper, Paris buns, potato scones, apple and rhubarb tarts and Abernethy biscuits, the whole either washed down with still lemonade or some of the brackish tea Donald and Wilfred had laboured to produce over a fire of twigs. Appetites were huge but even so there was enough left over should anyone feel peckish later in the afternoon.

Other picnickers kept arriving, a mother with her brood of five, some little sisters playing with small pebbles from the river's edge, noisy boys who threw stones in the water and chased each other. They provided entertainment and food for comment. Seeing some children she taught, Kate disappeared behind her boater for a while, only reappearing once they'd gone out of earshot.

The golden warmth, the river's easy companionability and *divertissement*, made everybody feel languorous and well disposed. They played silly games like The Minister's Cat and I Spy and the girls jumped on Wilfred and Donald whenever they wanted to engage in anything contentious or serious.

'It's a day out,' Tallie insisted. She pulled at Wilfred's hand. 'Come and help me guddle for minnows.'

'What'll we keep them in?'

Kate profferred a jar that had held pickles. 'This?' The two went down to the water's edge and became as absorbed as children.

# Four

Halfway through the afternoon Tibby Robertson and her mother Maidie joined them. No one was very sure who had invited them, though Belle had let drop the intention of the family picnic and the banks of the Ainsh were available to everybody, after all.

Maidie opened a folding canvas stool and flopped down on it next to Janet, her plump bottom overflowing.

'Mrs Candlish,' she acknowledged. 'Tibby and I thought it was too nice a day for cheese-making and summer can't go on forever.'

Janet knew better than snub the farmer's wife. The Robertsons had farmed in Lanarkshire for over two hundred years and there were Robertsons in the banks and teaching in the schools, people of probity and standing all of them. They had their own pew in the church and the big farmer Alec Robertson sat on the local bench. Pity his and Maidie's branch had produced only female twigs, but as Tibby demonstrated they were strong and attractive ones and not likely to be overlooked.

So Janet shifted her parasol and gave Tibby's mother a civil enough nod.

'We've brought scones and cream,' said Tibby eagerly. 'Where's Donald?'

'Gone for a walk,' Kate offered from a supine position. Tibby was on her feet in an instant, casting around with her hand to eyes to see if she could spot where the eldest

Candlish had gone. Kate obligingly sat up and pointed upriver.

'Bring the laddie back for a nice scone and cream,' said Maidie indulgently. To Janet she said, 'My lassie made them herself. She has the light hand with the baking, though I say it myself.'

Janet made a non-committal sound in the back of her throat.

'She can knit, crochet and tambour,' added Maidie complacently. 'She'll make a good wife for some lucky lad, her father says.'

Janet said nothing. She didn't mind Donald enjoying himself with the girls, but if Maidie Robertson thought he had marriage in mind, she had another think coming to her. Janet wasn't prepared to let her eldest go just yet and Donald knew that. Her children would marry when they got the say-so from her and she wasn't ready to loosen the ties that held them. She wanted more furniture for the house, a moleskin coat for the kirk on Sunday, two silk bedspreads and money in the bank. Then maybe it would be time to matchmake, though something twanged resentfully and even with hurt at the thought of Donald going. It would be hard – it might be impossible – to share him with another woman.

Kate lay and basked, sardonically amused by the unconscious dramas going on around her. Now that Maidie and Tibby had arrived, she couldn't point out to her mother that Wilfred and Tallie had gradually forded the river while tiddling and then wandered off into the quiet unpeopled stretch of country beyond, where there were accommodating little hillocks, banks of trees and shrubs and certainly spots where one could be alone and unseen.

Nor could she decently say that Tibby would have to pass the bathers in the pool in her search for Donald, one of whom would be Russell in the altogether. Belle would be up there, too, probably paddling under the bridge out of sight of her mother and casting a sly gaze at the bigger lads as they threw their naked white bodies into the brown pool.

'Belle!' called Tibby relievedly. She ran to join her friend where she sat on a sun-warmed rock, dabbling her feet in the water.

'You're getting your skirts draggled,' she warned her.

'They'll soon dry,' said Belle easily.

'Some of the boys have nothing on,' said Tibby, looking past the cavernous shade of the bridge to the coveys of shouting, exultant youths.

'Including our Russell,' said Belle.

'Where?'

'There.' Belle pointed. Her younger brother stood poised almost arrow-straight, ready to take a dive, his hair already slicked back from previous immersions. He had been so preoccupied with jostling for the right spot, with impressing his peers, with enjoying the sun, the noise, the action, that he was unaware of the interested spectators.

Belle had seen that body grow up, from soft-boned infant through spindly adolescence to the narrow, sturdy grace presented now. His skin glittered with an almost opalescent whiteness in the sun. She hated to see him coming home from the pit nowadays, the coal eating into the whiteness and was glad for him, that he should enjoy the freedom and exultation of air and sun and water. His malehood did not embarrass her, but Tibby did not seem able to pull her gaze away and Belle began to feel it like an intrusion.

'Maybe we shouldn't sit here,' said Tibby at last. 'Come and help me look for Donald.' And she took Belle's hand and they ran quickly past the divers, looking the other way. For some reason once they were clear of the pool, they stopped and looked at each other, crimson-faced and interrogative and laughed immoderately.

Tibby saw the lone figure of Donald, far off, and cooeed and called till he heard her.

'Look,' said Belle, 'you go and meet him yourself.' Her face suddenly turned a little moody and almost truculent. She disengaged her hand from Tibby's and began to walk back towards the picnic. *She* hand't found anyone she

28

liked. Not *that* way. She was jealous and disgruntled, and obscurely upset that Tibby had seen Russell naked.

'When I get away like this,' said Tallie, 'I get time to think and I feel almost sure that one day I *will* run away.' She looked timidly at Wilfred, waiting for him to argue against such a course.

Instead, he said steadily, 'Well, if you did, you would have to lay your plans carefully beforehand. You would have to write to the matron of the fever hospital and get an interview and be told when you could start.'

'How could I get an interview?'

'You'd have to get some time off.'

'It isn't like that. I just fit it in when I can.'

'Tell your mother you want every second Wednesday afternoon.'

'I couldn't.'

'You'll have to make a start. Be brave. I'll back you up.'

She started pinkly. 'No, don't do that. You'll only make things worse if you interfere.' She thought deeply and then said decisively, 'All right. I will. I can offer to do some shopping in Perringhall for her. She sometimes needs things midweek.'

'Good girl. I'll miss you in the house but we can meet whenever you're free and do things we want to do. Go to the theatre—'

'Actually – go to the theatre?'

'You never been?'

'I've been to the penny geggy – you know, travelling shows.'

'Oh, you'll love it. We might even see Pavlova. We can go to Glasgow and have tea at the Corn Exchange.'

She stopped him with a hand on his knee. They were sitting on his jacket in a grassy hollow with buttercups all around them and brambles at their backs. 'Your time will be your own,' he pointed out.

'I've got to do it,' she said sombrely. 'You're the only one who knows it, Wilfred. I've got to do it.'

'I'm behind you, all the way,' he said intently. 'I want to see you blossom. I don't like to see you so frustrated and unhappy.'

She gazed down at her hands. 'I never used to be – scared, you know. When I was a little girl I ran away to the gypsies. I did, Wilf. I had tea in their caravan and an old woman read my hand. My father took me home and beat me with his pit belt. Another time they found me at the station, waiting for a train to Glasgow.'

'Don't.' He put his arms round her and said in her ear, 'I know what it's like, to be odd man out. You've just got to fight it.' His lips brushed her ears and he stroked her hair tenderly. It was she who looked at his lips and made it impossible for him not to kiss her. And the kiss was like a kind of flame that set them both alight so that their bodies did not seem to be able to get close enough to each other, to coalesce so that they would flame even more brightly and deeply. Though it had to be through their clothes. His fingers longed to undo buttons, uncover mysteries, but daylight was too unsparing.

When they walked back, self-consciously leaping across the stepping stones in the river, everybody seemed to be having a good time. Tallie looked and saw her mother with her head thrown back, laughing with a heartiness that brought the girl up short. She hadn't seen her mother so relaxed and happy in a long time and despite her recent conversation with Wilfred something in her was touched and softened. If only things could be like this all the time, instead of the constant whiplash of her mother's tongue. She knew now there were things she would miss about Cullington Lodge, the being part of a family with all its problems and drawbacks, but catching Wilfred's bracing look she knew now she was committed to breaking away. There was no going back.

Invigorated after his swim and some scones and lemonade, Russell was giving an impromptu performance of 'Everybody's Doing it, Doing it, Doing it', adding a scurrilous verse or two of his own that had everybody in stitches. Janet put her hand up to her mouth and giggled and Maidie shook so much she nearly fell off her stool. Even Kate, roused from her earlier assumed torpor, was on her feet, prepared to give her arch and funny version, when urged, of 'Hello, Hello, who's your lady friend?'

Nobody wanted to go home. As the shadows lengthened Kate and Donald revived the earlier picnic fire, piling bleached twigs and sticks on it till it gave off a commendable warmth. It was time for anecdotes and reminiscence, the coinage of country folk used to amusing themselves. Watching Tibby flirting with Donald, unable to stop herself from touching him, being near him, Maidie with unconscious empathy began to recollect her own courting days, when Big Eck Robertson had ridden over to her father's farm on his white horse to court her, even putting his ear to the ground to listen for her footsteps if she was late.

Tallie could not believe her ears when her mother joined in, with tales of an early suitor of her own who had been wont to peer longingly through the kitchen window at her and whom she'd discouraged by putting treacle all along the window sills. This merry mother, wiping her eyes and capping anecdote with anecdote, made Tallie feel discomfited. How had the girl who on her own admission had stolen her little brother's christening robe to masquerade as a showy white man-trapping petticoat turned into the carping old woman who made her life such a misery? Fearful, in case anyone should notice that her eyes were moist, Tallie lay back on one of the rugs and pretended to be asleep.

Kate went and sat beside a bemused Wilfred, a little apart from the boisterous story-telling.

'Is our bucolic ease all a bit much for you?' she teased him, her shrewd sullen gaze scanning his face.

'Not a bit.' He denied it.

'Has Tallie been bemoaning her lot to you?'

'Why do you ask?' he countered warily.

'You seem in close cahoots, the pair of you.'

31

'I try to encourage her to see herself as an individual with rights. Not just a cog in the family machine.'

Kate eased herself from sitting position to lying one, stomach downwards, and twirled a buttercup between her long fingers.

'My mother told me once, in a rare moment of confidence, that she had Tallie because my father came home drunk one night and forced himself on her. She had wanted to leave him but had nowhere to go.'

'They didn't get on? Your parents?'

'He took the pledge after Tallie and they must have come to some kind of – armistice, shall we say? She went on to have Belle and Russell, after all. I've sometimes pondered if the circumstance of a child's conception determines how a parent feels about it later.' She looked challengingly at Wilfred, daring him to run away from such advanced discussion.

'You could be right,' he said easily. 'But it's murky waters. Are you interested in psychology, then?'

'Oh yes,' admitted Kate, with a flash of real animation. 'We have to try and fathom the human mind. "The proper study of mankind is man", isn't it?'

'But you want women to go forward, I take it? Unlike Donald, you support the vote for women?'

'To a certain extent.' He saw that despite the sharpness of her mind, Kate was tarred with the same timidity and unsureness as Tallie and felt the first stirrings of some kind of affinity with this brusque, distant girl who held most of the world at bay.

To be mischievous, he postulated now, 'If women were given their real place, you could have gone to university instead of Donald. With your intellectual leanings.'

'You mean Donald was wasted on university – or vice versa?' She looked at him with genuine amusement. 'You'd better not let Ma hear you say that! No, there's a certain decisive quality about Donald that I don't have.'

'There's a lot of raw power to his thinking,' he admitted.

Wilfred gazed down at Kate almost fondly now. He felt

32

he was getting to know this enigmatic eldest daughter better and that he could show a brotherly sort of affection in his manner, as he did with Belle. (Affection was not what he felt for Tallie. Looking at her now, lying asleep or pretending to be, he was wrung with a hopeless tenderness for her.)

To distract himself he turned back to Kate.

'What will you do, do you think? Become headmistress of the village school?'

A reserve came down over her face. 'You mean I'm not good-looking enough to marry.' She said it half ruefully, half jokingly.

'But you are,' he stated. 'You have a handsome figure, Kate.'

'But it's a pity about the face.' She gave a glimmer of a smile.

Covertly he studied the face. Sometimes Kate's sallow skin seemed tinged with something darker, like the petals of a creamy rose before it fell, as though it reflected some dolour in her. High on one cheekbone there was a tick-shaped mark as though from some childhood misadventure. The chin was finely moulded, the mouth severe, but it was mainly the expression that took away any claim to beauty. There was no other word for it: it was forbidding. Touch-me-not. An idle note of compassion sounded in the orchestra of his thoughts.

'Once women get the vote,' he said, 'and they will – we can't keep from them what is theirs by moral right – they will forge ahead in all sorts of ways. They'll pour into Parliament, they'll surge into management and turn the tables on us men. We'll have to do the cooking and mending—'

'Some hope!'

'And women will have to ask for our hands in marriage. Eh, Kate?'

She sat straight and gave him a strangely hopeful look. 'I simply want to explore the capabilities of my own mind.'

'Knowing what you want is half the battle,' he said

sagely. 'You can make free of all my books. I've told Tallie the same thing.'

Tallie's eyelashes quivered betrayingly on her cheek as Kate gave one of her short, dismissive laughs at the mention of her name.

# Five

The matron's name was Jemima Macreadie but nobody ever dared call her anything but Matron. Tallie thought she had probably been Matron even when she had a rusk tied to her bib and sat up in a big perambulator. She had what appeared to be a single-breasted bosom as large and rounded as the dome of St Paul's and feet that thundered like farm carts down the cold hospital corridors, on their way to the office where Tallie sat petrified by fear.

She had a twitchy, rabbit-like mouth and steely pince-nez, which she adjusted now as she gazed across her desk at the girl.

'We normally have a waiting list. For some reason this year we do not, so you may be called quite soon. You will have to furnish a letter of recommendation from your minister and have your mother sign this form.'

She saw Tallie's lip quiver.

'Any problems?'

'No problem.'

'You will have to be punctual, reliable and hard-working; I do not tolerate any slackers on my wards. I hope you will not come here with any starry-eyed notions of going round with a lamp and a soothing word, like Florence Nightingale. Nursing is dedication and hard work. Do you understand me girl?'

Tallie gave her a clear-eyed look. 'I'm not afraid of hard work.'

Matron's gaze softened but by no more than a glimmer. 'Then you and I will get on. You may go.'

She wrestled with the idea of signing the necessary form herself or even getting Wilfred to sign it. But, emboldened by the memory of the hospital and its strange allure, the challenge she wanted to take up at whatever cost and steeled by some new courage that was seeping through her, she tackled her mother head on.

'You're not going into nursing, and that's flat.' Her mother put down her cup with a hand that showed no sign of trembling.

'I am, Mother. My mind is made up.'

'Who do I get to help me? Tell me that.'

'Tillie Mackerson from the village. Jean Cameron, if you like.'

'And where do I get their wages?'

'From the money you've never paid me.'

She waited for the roof to fall in, the grate to drop out of the fireplace and the windows to rattle as if in a storm. Even for her mother to strike her, so incandescent was her rage.

'It's that bottle-shouldered Englishman who's put this into your head.'

'I wanted to be a nurse long before Wilfred came.'

'Well, if you go, he goes. He can find some other soft mark. I'll not have him coming in here and not showing me the respect I deserve.'

There was more on the same lines. Her mother did not speak to her for three days but this time Tallie was not to be broken. The Reverend MacWhirter called in with his letter of recommendation and good wishes for Tallie's future, putting Janet in a cleft stick. Tallie came down one morning to find the form under a candlestick on the dresser. But signed. She gave a small whoop of joy and quickly put the form in her apron pocket before her mother changed her mind. The same day Janet indicated to Wilfred that he was no longer welcome at Cullington Lodge and had a week to find new accommodation.

It was Kate and Donald by letter who saved his skin. When he had difficulty finding anything comparably quiet and roomy, Kate pointed out how little trouble he was, how prompt in payment (she was also thinking of the books she could borrow) and Donald wrote: 'Don't cut off your nose to spite your face, Mother. I'll increase your allowance now that Tallie is going. I quite like the arguments I and Chappell have about politics and such.' With such intervention, especially from her own private oracle, her firstborn, Janet rescinded her decision and with little grace conceded Wilfred could stay on a bit longer. But she made it clear from the coldness of her manner and the scrappiness of the meat on his plate that he was being tolerated only.

Tallie thought that when she got the letter telling her to start that it was the best day of her life. She had to borrow from Wilfred to buy her uniform but promised to pay him back immediately she had any wages. He would have given up all he owned just to see the transformation in her. To celebrate, they went to Hamilton and had a high tea in one of the tea-rooms, with haddock and chips and a selection of dainty things on a cake-stand, with doilies. Tallie was sure her life was on an ever-upward curve and when they had a compartment to themselves on the train home, she kissed him and patted his face with her soft-palmed hands and even sat on his knee. He could take any amount of cold-shouldering from Janet for just a tenth of the fussing from Tallie.

The wards were huge, twelve iron beds and cots down each side, with a big coal fire in the centre of the left wall as you went in, protected from sick or delirious children by a solid brass fire-guard.

The children were from toddlers of two and three up to big boys and girls of twelve to fourteen, mostly suffering from scarlatina or diphtheria. Those who came from lousy homes had their heads shaved and others, unless their parents had intervened, had their heads shaved as a precautionary measure.

Tallie had thought she would be immediately involved in nursing the children, but the first day a great soft broom was pushed into her hands and she was instructed to first sweep the ward and then to mop and polish. She was shown how to move the beds, arranging them a specific distance from the wall and how to make them with neat 'hospital' corners.

When she had shown herself adept at such basic hygienic measures, she was allowed to 'pot' the smaller children and give them bed-baths. Soon she was feeding those too sickly or feverish to feed themselves and helping the convalescent to take their first shaky steps up and down the ward, going on from there to take temperatures and pulses.

In the meantime, she was getting to know the other nurses – MacCrindle, Armstrong, Jessup and others; the sisters, especially the terrifying, vinegary Sister Maclaren who could spot a dust mote at fifty paces; and the ward maids, Lizzie and Mina. She began to understand the hierarchy of power and just how low and unregarded a first-year nurse could be, no matter how willing.

One luxury was being able to take a bath or a shower, something which had been severely restricted at home. The food was miserable and rarely hot but the young nurses scoffed it up after their long shifts and it was sometimes supplemented by cakes and chocolates from grateful parents.

The harsh discipline her mother had imposed made hospital discipline easier for Tallie to bear than for some of her fellow trainees, who wept copiously in corners and were sorry they had ever even thought of the idea of nursing. Tallie in her first year was mainly happy. Not all the reprimands or hectoring or bullying – or sadness when a little patient died – could prevent that deep, solid feeling of satisfaction that came from her being her own woman at last.

When she went home it was clear her mother was managing without her perfectly well. Ellen Siddons from the village came in each day but being a solid garrulous matron in her thirties was not prepared to take much ordering around and Kate and Belle were obviously helping more than when Tallie was available. Janet listened to Tallie's tales from hospital with an avid interest but was no more supportive of Tallie's ambition than she had ever been, forecasting it wouldn't last and she'd be back home again one of these days, if she didn't go down with consumption in the meantime.

Tallie longed for a word of commendation but it was never forthcoming.

Tallie prinked her finger over the cup of tea, rejoicing in the delicacy of the tea-shop's cakes after the hospital dining-room offerings and watching Wilfred with proprietory pleasure as he returned from the men's room.

'So how are things at home?'

'Belle's had her hair bobbed.'

'I knew she had it in mind.'

'Your mother sent her to Coventry for three days.'

'Does she suit it?' Tallie demanded a little jealously.

'I like women with long hair.' He gave her a teasing little smile. 'I'm impervious to Belle's charms. You should know that.'

'But she tries them out on you. I've seen her.'

'She's only a child,' he said loftily. 'I can make allowances.'

'Toby Wilson sent some flowers up to the hospital for me. Pink carnations with gypsophila, with a poem,' she said. It was as well to let him know she had her admirers just as he had. She did her best to quiet the jealous churning inside her. Belle's fair and misty mass of curls had won indrawn breaths of approval since infancy and Tallie was only too aware that her own dark hair had little more than a kink to recommend it. She resolved to think about a bob. It would be easier to manage under her nurse's cap and putting long hair up as a sign of adulthood no longer carried the significance her mother attached to it.

She wondered what Wilfred would say if she admitted Toby's poem had touched her. 'Tallie like a candle flame,

Burning up my soul.' He'd always liked English at school, but she had not thought he had it in him to write poetry and she was intrigued in spite of herself.

Uncannily, as if he had answered what she was thinking, Wilfred demanded: 'What was the poem like? Any good?'

'It was actually. Quite good.'

'Repeat it.'

'Certainly not.' She blushed, looking uncomfortable.

They finished their tea in a strained silence but once out on the street, Wilfred pulled her hand through his arm and said, 'I hope Wilson doesn't have unreal expectations.'

'What do you mean?'

'You're my girl.'

'I'm nobody's girl. Yet.'

'After what happened at the picnic?'

'What do you mean?'

'Those kisses.' He pushed his face fiercely close to hers and said, 'Oh, God, Tallie, I've been thinking of you – of us – ever since. I want you all to myself.'

Relenting, she allowed her cheek to rub against his momentarily. 'It was nice that day,' she admitted. 'I have to say so.'

'And you think of me?'

'Sometimes,' she teased.

'And of us – touching? Being close in new ways? Darling—'

She saw one of the ward maids from the hospital coming down the street and pulled apart from him, looking intently into a shop window full of shortening skirts and pin-tucked blouses.

'What's the matter?' he demanded.

'Let Lizzie Porteous go past,' she muttered.

'What does it matter if she sees us arm-in-arm?'

'It might get back to Matron.'

'What you do in your time off is your affair.'

'That's what you think. She saw Annie MacCrindle kissing her fiancé goodnight at the hospital gates and read her the Riot Act.'

He shook his head, annoyed and mystified. 'I don't think you *want* to be seen with me.'

There was the suspicion of tears in her eyes. Somehow everything was going wrong with her precious afternoon off and there was a curious, undefined anger rising up in her against him. It baffled her. She'd done nothing but think about him in the days leading up to their meeting.

They took a turning off the main street into a quieter lane and walked, separately and without speaking, till they were in the country, surrounded by fields. He stopped by a five-barred gate, leaning on it. A lark rose from the field ahead and soared, trilling, into a blameless blue sky. As if reassured, they gazed at each other and permitted them-selves shamefaced smiles.

He took a grass stalk he'd plucked from the verge from his mouth and said abruptly, 'Would you marry me?'

She didn't look at him as she answered, staring almost trance-like into the middle distance.

'I would. But not yet.'

'Why not yet?'

'Because I've only just started nursing. I want my fever certificate.'

'Yes.' He noticed a light cloud, that had not been visible moments ago, veiling the sun. Just that morning he'd been thinking a modest house might just be possible, that he had enough books to furnish it along with a few sticks of furniture. He'd brought this image up in his mind deliberately, to shut out the darker thoughts that invaded whenever he read his newspaper.

But it was there, the threat he perceived despite the peace-keeping sounds made by Asquith, the Prime Minister. Something would set Europe off. In the staff room, the other day, the others had agreed it was there. For some reason he'd mentioned the Futurist paintings he'd seen in London before he came north, the fractured vision of the Cubists and others that Hillary the art teacher went on about, and Peter Walch the music teacher had instanced the broken protest in the music by the likes of Stravinsky and Schoenberg. Straws in the wind . . . 'For I hear the steady drummer, drumming like a noise in dreams.'

'What's in your mind?' she demanded on a note of anxiety.

'That I might join up straightaway if there is a war.'

'There won't be,' she said positively.

'The Germans may give us no alternative.'

'And why should it be so necessary for Wilfred Chappell Esquire to take up the cudgels?'

'I won't go into the philosophy of it.' They'd tossed the pros and cons about in the staff room, after all, till he was sick of it. 'The day is too lovely. I just have a wish to prove that might isn't necessarily right. I don't like bully-boys.'

She gave him a smile that lifted the sourness from the afternoon. She found his preoccupation with war something she could not take seriously. She was thinking of how supportive he had been in her struggle to get away from the domestic tyranny she hated. Certainly Matron was another kind of tyrant, but one she would suffer because nursing was what she wanted to do. That made the difference. She thought of the children, *her* children, *her* patients, who needed her, whom she could make better. She would tell Wilfred in a little what it was like to go into a ward when they were all asleep and the ward fire had burned low and there was this feeling of peace and tranquillity such as she had never known before.

But meantime, she had spotted a patch of flattened grass against the hedgerow on the other side of the five-barred gate, where she could sit with his head on her lap and they could talk and then she could lie back so that his lips would come down on hers and they could be lost in that hazy world of blissful sensation.

But even though she stroked his brow once they had settled a frown remained.

'You seem all wound up,' she protested. 'Don't think war.'

He caught her hand and kissed it.

'You wind me up,' he said, smiling.

'No, but there's something else. Isn't there? Tell me.'

He turned over on his back and said, 'It's my sister Lily. She's been out of sorts and now it looks like an operation.'

'People get over operations.'

'I just have this feeling.'

'It's because you're so far away. Can't you go and see her?'

'Not till term ends. Not with exams coming up.'

'Will she give up her sewing?'

'She may have to. *I* can send *her* money now, after all, if she needs it. But she'll miss the society gossip. Dressmakers pick up all the society secrets.'

'Such as?'

'The Prime Minister is mad for Venetia Stanley.'

'They say he's a terrible womaniser.'

He looked at her fondly. 'What would an innocent little provincial flower like you know about that?'

'I read things,' she protested.

It was clear his thoughts had reverted, sombrely, to Lily.

'You have to trust and pray,' said Tallie gently.

'I don't know if I can.' His tone was surprisingly bitter. 'I just keep thinking of how hard she worked. For me. She should be resting on her laurels now. Enjoying life.'

'Don't mope,' she pleaded.

'I want you to meet her,' he insisted. 'I want her to see you.'

She leaned across him and tickled his cheek with a blade of grass. 'Why?' she demanded teasingly. 'Why do you want her to see me?'

'Because.'

'Because I'm beautiful and irresistible, like Venetia Stanley?'

She watched his reluctant grin spread before he pulled her down to him. 'Because you're nice, sweet, lovely Tallie. Mine, mine, mine.'

They were lost in the mazy world after all. The shadows were lengthening from the trees in the lane before they eventually walked back to Perringhall in search of high tea.

# Six

Janet Candlish was polishing the leaves of the giant aspidistra by the parlour window of Cullington Lodge when she saw the stout figure of Maidie Robertson get off the new motor-bus and climb the stiff brae towards the house. Something about the set of her body and the fact that she was wearing her best hat, a massive thing festooned with silk flowers, made Janet put down her polishing cloth and remove her print pinny with hands that had started to tremble.

The look on her face as she answered the door, however, gave nothing away. 'Aye, Maidie,' she said, 'to what do we owe the honour at this time of day?'

Maidie gave her a look that would have demolished weaker flesh, but said nothing till they were seated like Gog and Magog either side of the parlour hearth.

Then Maidie touched an eye with a large, reddened hand and said, 'He'll have to marry her, Janet. The lassie is wi' bairn.'

The colour receded from Janet's face but her upright position did not waver. For a moment she was like someone turned to stone. Maidie Robertson cast her a quick look and for a brief second wondered if her statement had turned the woman opposite into something petrified and inhuman. An unexpected wave of pity hit her and she said hastily, 'Janet, it's worse for me. I've left her father raving like a lunatic.'

'I don't know what you're saying,' said Janet at last. 'Are you trying to tell me one of my laddies is responsible?' As though in a daze she had automatically poured two small glasses of the Madeira wine she kept for the minister's visits and handed one to Maidie, who took it almost as dazedly. 'I have to warn you, Maidie, to be careful what you say. We only have Tibby's word for it.'

'She's said nothing. Not a word. But you saw them,'

Maidie cried, pushing her hat up from her brow. 'You saw them, the day of the picnic. He was never away from her. And the night of the soirée, her father raised the roof because he kept her out so late.'

'I cannot say any more till I've seen Donald,' said Janet, through stiff lips. 'But he's not the only one your Tibby has fancied.'

'My daughter's a good lass,' Maidie countered.

'And it would suit your book fine if she made a catch like my Donald,' said Janet, her underlying fury breaking through at last. 'Let me tell you, he can take his pick of the young women in Glasgow. But he's in no hurry. She'll have to be a good one that catches my Donald.'

Maidie wailed. The big, fat tears ran down her cheeks. 'He can't leave my poor girl in the lurch. He'll have to marry her and the sooner the better, for she's thickening already.' Maidie crashed down her glass, careless of whether it marked Janet's polished table surface. 'You write to him. You get him down here. Or her father'll go up to Glasgow and let all his fine friends know what kind of a man he is.'

When she had gone, Janet poured herself another stringent glass of the wine and sat down before her legs gave way altogether. Funny how the minute she'd seen Maidie she'd known what the visit was about. Donald's face with its mass of thick, waved hair hovered before her like a mirage. The teachers at the school had all said from the start what a brainy boy he was. He picked everything up so easily, through exam after exam with top marks every time.

The shipping firm in Glasgow had such plans for him, too. They were talking of sending him out to New York for experience and then when he got back, the top job could be waiting him. What advantage could a wife like Tibby Robertson be to him? A big, sturdy, strong girl and not without looks, it had to be admitted, but as coarse as a wheaten loaf. No refinement. But then the girl didn't exist that Janet thought good enough for her first-born. If truth be told, she had not envisaged him marrying till middle age, if at all, and in the meantime he had sisters, hadn't he, and herself, to fuss him and keep his laundry fresh, his hand-knitted socks in good supply, his baths run on demand, whenever he came home? She was damned if she was going to share him, damned, damned, damned. But by evening she had written to him and told him it was best he came home at the first opportunity, and there was an urgent matter that needed sorting out.

When the family had problems, they tended to congregate in the kitchen with the door firmly shut against any importunings by the boarders. Wilfred and Ernest Waters ate alone in state that evening, with no Belle, no Kate or Janet to keep them company, wondering what was going on. At length, a shade disconsolately, because they enjoyed the evening chit-chat, they swallowed down their sago pudding and jam and made for their rooms, Ernest to read his evening paper and Wilfred to write to his sister Lily.

Kate had had a difficult day at school and was looking pale and bad-tempered. The news about Maidie's visit had not improved her mood.

'He would pick some fertile country girl who gets pregnant if he so much as looks at her,' she commented sourly.

'Mind your words,' Janet reprimanded her. Her daughter's bald way of putting things often offended her.

'She made a dead set for him at the soirée,' said Belle. 'And look at the way they came to the picnic, without so much as a by-your-leave. It was Tibby who made her mother take her, that day. I know Tibby,' she added darkly.

Russell said nothing. He had come in from the day shift at the pit and still sat in his filthy pit duds, his face like a sweep's and only his hands cursorily washed so that he could eat his meal. He never ate with due attention to formality or manners, using a knife and fork like the others, but the fork only, shovelling great mounds of food into his mouth. Janet had not noticed, but as he had grown into almost full young manhood he was almost as good-looking as her elder son. Where Donald's eyes were a light candy, his were a sharp, bright blue and his hair sandy fair where Donald's was darker. Now the bristles of his hair pushed up through the coal dirt like bright shoots and the eyes, startlingly clean and alert, went from face to face as the others discussed his brother's quandary and not very convincingly tried to build up a case for the defence.

At length Janet said, 'I'm deciding nothing till I hear what Donald's got to say.' They all noticed how the thin back seemed to have rounded and the wrinkles become more etched on her face as she stretched up tiredly to light the fragile gas mantle, a task she entrusted to no one else. 'Get the boarders' dishes in and get them washed,' she ordered Belle harshly. And turning to Kate with no less severity, 'Haven't you got a blouse to starch? Get on with it, then.'

Russell rose from the table and went out to squat, collier-fashion, outside the back door. He couldn't wash till the girls were finished in the kitchen. He watched swallows dive, swoop and soar in the encroaching twilight. Sometimes when he was dirty, encrusted with sweat and grit and carbon of the pit, he thought fleetingly of the pool at the Ainsh and diving into its clear, invigorating depths, to come up with the sun on his back.

At times like these he regretted having gone down the pit, except that it had proved something to him, something important, like how to be a man. He had known he couldn't follow Donald. It was no contest when it came to brains. But arguing with the older men down the pit had sharpened him up, so that he was beginning to know a little of his own worth. Politics, for example, was no longer just something for the other fellow.

Some of the men today had been talking about joining the army if there was a war. Russell could feel the possibility of volunteering grow inside him even now. He did not feel like going back into the kitchen where the recent unsettling conversations had taken place. He did not feel like washing. Or doing anything. He felt like fading into the dark like the disappearing day.

'What do you mean, you've been with her?'

It was Sunday and Russell had followed Belle down into the woods, where she had sauntered to get away from the house and its strained and enervating Sabbath atmosphere. Donald had come home on the Saturday as commanded and there had been rows, ructions and silences followed by the usual Sunday of church-going, no reading and hymns in the parlour. The long and the short of it was that Donald was insisting that the baby could not be his. And despite Tibby's mother's insistence that it was, it must be, it began to look, when you got down to the dates – the last time Donald and Tibby had seen each other, for example – that Donald was telling the truth.

Belle began to feel a strange sensation, as if life and breath were being slowly squeezed out of her body. Her mind refused to take in the import of what Russell was saying. If you put her up against a wall and asked her who meant most to her in all the world, who occupied a place of purest affection and joy in her heart, she would have to admit it was her younger brother. They had always played together as children, endless games of house and shops and school, with her always in her motherly role or as his teacher and mentor. When you were second from the bottom in the family hierarchy, it was nice when someone looked up to you and regarded you as a bit of an oracle. They had always had their private jokes and a kind of understanding that ran deeper than words or demonstration. What she felt now was a pain and desperation that threatened to swamp her totally.

Russell sat on the other end of the fallen tree trunk that served as bench and seat for local walkers and would not lift his head. Even when he was cleaned up for Sunday there were the marks of the pit round his fingernails and seamed in his knuckles, a fact, she realised, that always cut her to the quick because she could remember him as a little boy, the one bathed after her in the wooden bine on Friday nights.

The voice that came out from somewhere in the middle of his chest said, 'If you tell anyone, I'll kill you, Belle.'

'I won't,' she said swiftly, instantly. 'If she doesn't come out with it, I certainly won't.'

He looked up then. She saw tears sparkled on the end of his eyelashes. He wasn't going to tell her anything else and she didn't really want to know. What happened when people got close together was something she still kept at arm's length, because it frightened her. But despite her resolution not to quiz, she found herself asking, 'Where did you go, the pair of you?'

'Up the bankings,' he said hoarsely. 'If you must know.'

Oh, Russell, she addressed him silently, not there! The grassy bankings ran down from the little branch railway that carried the coal away from the pit and was a well-known wenching spot, though mostly for the more unruly of the population. As children they had all hopped along the railway sleepers, casting sly forbidden glances at the often irregular lovers trysting among the long grass and the pink saugh and once someone had found a pair of emerald green knickers there, lying among the buttercups.

What was bothering Belle most was the fact that Tibby was concealing her involvement with Russell. Was this because she was afraid of the dreadful consequences of going with two men or because she was still determined to snare Donald? Which one did she love? If you behaved in such a flighty immoral fashion did you in fact love anybody? Belle had always known Tibby had a wildness in her, one that made her run faster in school games, jump higher, laugh louder, dance longer than anybody else. She had so much sheer animal energy to her. She had a secretive side to her too. Not for nothing had Janet called her a hidden girl, meaning someone who wasn't straightforward, was a little bit sly. But you couldn't not like her. She looked again at Russell and suddenly knew with a dreadful clarity he had wanted to take what he saw as Donald's, just once. And Tibby – Tibby must have made it easy for him.

She thought briefly that perhaps she should persuade him to go in and tell her mother, Donald and Kate everything. Everything. Out in the open. But there was no telling how Donald would react. He thought little enough of Russell as it was, putting him down at every turn, as though he was some kind of worm to be stepped on. And she just knew with every pore of her skin what her mother's reaction would be. It would be of such a jealous ferocity and anger that Russell would never be able to live in the same house again. To have undermined Donald's province in such a manner would never be forgiven for a start. Belle's heart seemed to swell till it would burst and she said with such urgency that Russell began to cry, 'Tell them nothing, tell them nothing. Be like Dad, keep mum.' It was Russie and Bella, on the same side, as in childhood.

Once started, Russell's weeping went on and on. They had called it bubbling when they were children. 'Don't bubble,' he would say scornfully when she skinned a knee, and the unsettling thing was that she had never known anything up till now that made him cry.

'For Pete's sake,' she said in exasperation at last, 'you've got to go back in for your tea and they'll know from your face that something's up.'

He stood up, using his sleeve brusquely across his face to mop the tears. 'I don't want any tea. Tell them I've gone for a walk.'

'Russell.' She held him by the two front edges of his Sunday jacket and then could think of nothing to say to him. His face was like some desolate landscape that has been soaked and puddled by rain. 'Use your hankie,' she advised him, and then resolutely added, knowing nothing would break her determination, 'I'll tell them nothing. Damn all, Russell. Nothing. I promise.'

Belle was sure the secret was written all over her face

when she went back into the house, but everybody else was too preoccupied with their own thoughts to notice her.

Russell's absence was spotted, of course, at tea-time – always on Sunday, sandwiches, thin brown bread-and-butter and seed cake – but when she said airily that he'd gone for a long walk, fed up with all the confabulations in the house, her statement was readily accepted at face value. She thought, with a little secret thrill: I'm a better actress than I thought.

Donald, who had been like an uneasy ghost all weekend, decided he would go back to Glasgow without seeing the Robertsons again, as he had half-promised.

His mother went along with this decision. 'Don't let them hassle you into anything,' she advised. 'You stick to your guns and the truth about the wean's father will come out in the end.'

He went a bright red. He was finding it hard to meet anybody's eyes, especially his mother's. He wasn't letting on to any of them about the time Tibby had turned up at his rooms in Glasgow, and found him entertaining another girl. It would suit her to keep mum about it, too, whatever happened.

He wasn't used to having his mind and thoughts in chaos. He had a scholar's discipline. But Tibby's gold-flecked arms, her smiling eyes opening and shutting like a cat's, above all her warm, soft body lying next to his, invaded his senses with a proprietory longing.

Maybe, despite everything, he should claim her now. Yet the rational part of his mind that was still operating insisted he took a bit longer to make up his mind. Marriage was for life, after all, and a terrible commitment. Every argument his mother had used against it rose up again in his mind.

But the Robertsons, it seemed, were not prepared to wait. They had their pride, too, as Janet acknowledged when she got the long, rambling letter from Maidie. They were sending the girl away to her uncle's farm in Aberdeenshire, where she would give birth to the baby without scandal. After that, they would see what would happen.

The baby might be given out for adoption. In the mean-time, the family would appreciate it if Donald never had the gall to show his face again within a decent radius of the farm. If he did, the dogs would be set on him and failing that, there was always Eck Robertson's shotgun which he wouldn't hesitate to use.

# Seven

Ernest Waters sat with his knife and fork at the ready, looking down at the empty space in front of him.

Wilfred was forced to meet his eye.

'Where's our bloody dinner?' Ernest demanded. 'I've got to be changed and shaved and out of here for a council meeting in half an hour.'

'I'll see what's causing the delay.' Wilfred scraped back his chair and walked tentatively down the hall towards the kitchen. He could hear the sound of pots and implements being banged about and for once the door to forbidden territory was open.

Kate turned a hot face, stencilled with strands of hair, towards him as he knocked.

'Coming,' cried Kate irascibly. 'Your food's coming!'

'What's up?' Boldly, since there was no Janet in evidence, he advanced. There was a smell of burning cabbage and Kate was pounding potatoes with a ricer.

'Let me help,' he suggested.

'Plates,' she ordered. 'Cupboard.' With her lower lip extended, she puffed breath up over her sweating features. 'Sorry about this. Mother and Belle have gone to the cottage hospital. It's Russell.'

'What's happened?'

'I don't know the full story.' She pushed him out of the

way ladling stew, potato and the unfortunate cabbage on to two big willow-pattern plates. Wilfred had to wait till he and Ernest had digested this main course and some scrappy oatcakes and cheese to follow – and till Ernest had departed, still hungry and in a filthy mood, for the council chambers – before he could get any further information out of Kate.

There was a noisy wag-at-the-wa' clock in the kitchen and two high beds, no longer used, set into one wall. With a bright rag rug in front of the fire it seemed to him a warm and cheerful place. He pulled up a chair to the scrubbed table and interrogated Kate.

'Was it an accident at the pit?'

She nodded. 'He went to a miners' peace rally last night and there were fights all over the place.' Kate did not miss his slight grimace at the irony. 'I know. Half the time he doesn't know what he's fighting about. He's drinking with the older men. I try to keep it from Mother but she knows. At least she knows now.'

'I thought I heard him go out this morning as per usual.'

'He did. He must have been half-dead from the punching he had last night. He didn't see the truck coming. If it had been going faster it would have killed him. As it was, his mate got him out of the way but the push sent him sprawling and he got concussed. Knocked out.'

'Young sparks,' he suggested.

'Bad company,' countered Kate gloomily. 'He's in with the drinkers and gamblers now, the wasters.' She looked at him, her eyes bright and defiant, then was struck by a sudden thought. 'Couldn't you have a word with him, Wilfred? He and Donald have nothing to say to each other, it seems. Talk about brotherly love! He'll not even stay in the same room as Donald these days.'

Wilfred accepted this brief from Kate with many misgivings. Russell was allowed home from hospital after five days but was obviously pale and wobbly. Counselling schoolboys as to their behaviour was one thing and Wilfred had learned not to shy away from it, but entering the murky world of Candlish family politics was another.

The deciding factor was that he had always liked Russell, much preferring him to Donald with his off-putting pomposity, his cool assumption that because he had a first-rate intellect everybody should hang on his utterances as though they were Holy Writ, with no consideration for others' feelings. He could see as an outsider how intolerable it must have been for Russell to grow up with such partisanship and it was a tribute, he felt, to the boy's self control that his combative attitude had not shown itself more often.

He used all his skills, allusive, constructive and even flattering to bring Russell round to an objective look at the way he was behaving. The boy, it seemed, had the beginning of a political conscience, which manifested itself more in invective against the rich, the pit-owners and munitions-makers, than in any idea of how to improve the lot of the proletariat, a word he proudly brandished about like a new flag. 'See, what Lloyd George says is right. The build-up of arms all over Europe is organised insanity.' He loved getting into involved arguments about whether Scotland should have Home Rule – the idea of which the Commons threw out that very May of 1914 while he and Wilfred were weighing the pros and cons – but like most men was a bit ambivalent about the Suffragettes, with their burning of churches and slashing of pictures.

Coming to the end of a leisurely Sunday walk as Russell's convalescence was finishing Wilfred shook an uncomprehending head at him.

'You had the equipment to go on at school,' he admonished him. 'Why didn't you?'

Russell said nothing. He knew the reasons but they were too complex yet for utterance.

'I side with the have-nots,' he said obscurely. 'I want to stay with the mates I grew up with. I don't want to go away from here.'

Wilfred knew better than to make straightforward references to drinking and gambling. He felt instinctively that the accident had pulled Russell up short and that he and the boy had in fact established a proper friendship they were both beginning to enjoy. In all this he had to take proper cognisance of Janet, who was still barely civil to him over his encouragement of Tallie, but on the other hand there was Kate who thanked him gruffly for his sensitivity.

'I see you're lending him books too,' she commented. 'But you do know, don't you, they'll only tame him so far. You're dealing with one of Nature's rebels, a raw mass of feeling.'

'That's why I've given him poetry.'

'He'll only learn through his own experience.'

'Don't we all?'

'Poets and painters, mainly. He's got the kind of temperament that should properly belong to an artist.'

He looked at her with a keen kind of pleasure.

'You're sharp.'

She went red to the roots of her hair. She had come to his room to retrieve a tray after his Saturday lunch, provided upstairs because Belle had wanted the dining-room to entertain a few friends after a game of lacrosse. As always, she gravitated towards his bookshelves, pulling out one volume after another to sample their contents, like a connoisseur in a wine-cellar.

'Are you seeing Tallie tonight?' she asked casually.

'She's got a couple of hours off. I thought we might go to the moving pictures.'

'I wish I had someone to go with.' The words slipped out.

'Come with Tallie and me,' he offered magnanimously after a pause which did not go unnoticed.

Kate gave her short bark of a laugh.

'I've no notion to play gooseberry. That's not what I meant.'

'Why don't I introduce you to one or two of the chaps from Perringhall?' he offered. 'There's Hillary the art chap, a very decent bloke and Peter Walch the music teacher, neither of them hitched. And Martham, Latin and Greek, a widower.'

'Forget it,' she said shortly.

'No,' he protested. 'I would gladly do it for you.'

54

'What do you think this family is? Some sort of indigent charity for you to visit your largesse upon? First Tallie, then Russell and now me, the no-hoper who can't attract men on her own.'

He laughed at the disgraceful irrationality of it all.

'I've only been trying to help. You asked for my intervention with Russell.'

He thought she would see the funny side of her bad temper, as she normally did, but today there was no wry smirk, no lifting of those finely arched eyebrows which were almost the best feature of her face. She put her hands up and pushed at the thick mass of her hair, caught up in a loose knot on the crown of her head.

'Should I cut my hair too, Wilfred? Would I suit a bob?' she asked in a softer voice.

'I don't know,' he said helplessly.

'Tallie going away has complicated matters here, you know. Now Belle and I are stuck, helping Mother. Otherwise I might move to Glasgow. England, even.' She was pulling the steel pins out of her hair, loosening it distractingly and distractedly as she talked, holding out chunks of it to survey it as though the strands had already been chopped.

'You have to take responsibility for your own life,' he said sombrely. 'It's a choice we all have to make. The fact that your mother is such a strong personality has made it all so much harder for you girls. I can see that.'

She came and stood closer to him, looking younger, a great deal younger, with the mass of brown hair tumbled down about her back and shoulders.

'Security's here,' she postulated. 'Of a sort. But I get lonely. And bored.'

'I can understand that.' He thought that he was forever using these words these days. Did it make him a bit of a prig? What *did* he understand, after all, still held down in the staff room with his working-class Cockney vowels, still not sure of where he was going, what he was doing? Maybe he did use the Candlish family to prop up his own pitiful little ego? He shifted uncomfortably, aware that Kate had made him face something about himself.

'I'd really like to be like Trehawke Davies,' said Kate. 'Looping the loop at Hendon.'

'Because looping the loop in a monoplane is dashing and dangerous or because there's something special about a woman doing it?'

'Because it must be liberating. Whether you're man or woman.' The intelligent grey eyes perused his face and she lifted the strands of hair towards him once again. 'To cut or not to cut, that is the question.'

'Go ahead. Liberate yourself.'

'Scissors,' she demanded.

'No, not now!' he protested, horrified.

'No time like the present. You can finish it off.'

'No fear! Your mother would kill me.'

'Now you know what it's like for the rest of us.'

'Oh, Kate have some sense,' he pleaded. She was going through the left drawer of the desk, knowing that's where the paste scissors were kept. She found them and began hacking at her hair, which fell in loops and circles on to the faded Axminster. 'You suggested it!' she chanted ruthlessly. 'You said liberate myself. Now I do; now I am.' The hair fell relentlessly. After a bit she dashed over to the cheval mirror and looked at her image. The hair stuck out in jagged, uneven points. Wilfred looked on at this pantomime, transfixed with horror. Her hair was a mess, a most dreadful mess. He should have pinioned her arms to prevent her from doing such damage. Maybe, he thought, with an objective part of his mind, that's what she wanted.

Kate threw down the scissors with a shriek and collapsed on to the bed.

'Oh, God,' she implored, 'what have I done? Oh, Wilfred, help me, do something, please.'

Tight-lipped, he picked up the scissors as though they burned to the touch and tilting her head began to snip delicately at the ragged edges. After a few moments he became quite absorbed with his task. The main thing was to

56

even off the bob. The hair was soft and pleasant under his hands and he began to think he was making a reasonable job. But in the meanwhile, tears were coursing down Kate's cheeks and big sobs bade fair to escape from her heaving bosom.

'Oh come on,' he pleaded, wrapping his arms around her and hugging her. 'It's really not as bad as all that. After you've washed it, it will settle down. It'll look *très chic*. Green soap, that's what women use, isn't it? That's what Lily uses.'

The door to his room opened without a knock and Janet stood there. With a look like thunder she strode forward. 'What's going on here?' As she took in the devastating haircut and saw the swatches of brown curls on the floor, her gaze swerved towards Wilfred and Kate who had guiltily broken apart. 'Does Tallie know about this?' she asked with a dreadful sarcasm. 'You.' She turned to Kate. 'Downstairs, you. Whatever you've done to yourself, there's shopping to be done.'

Wilfred said in a hard, firm voice, 'Wait. Before you get any wrong ideas. Kate just decided to cut her hair and got upset when she didn't like the results.'

'Just so long as Tallie believes you,' said Janet scornfully. But she retreated without giving him his marching orders, as he expected. Was it because she didn't want the trouble of seeking a new boarder, or because he had recently agreed without demur to paying more or was she learning to accept he was part and parcel of the domestic set-up and instrumental in keeping Russell on an even keel?

Possibly the reson was that the old Tartar was even a little afraid of Kate, who had some of her own steel in her backbone. Uppermost in his mind was what Tallie might think. There would be nothing for it but for him to tell her about the whole incident. It wasn't as straightforward as it might seem, because there was something irked and less than accepting in Tallie's attitude whenever he mentioned Kate's name. She surely didn't think – well, things? It didn't help that she was at the hospital and Kate here, but she surely knew that all he and Kate had in common was a kind of greed for literature, for ideas, for argument. He could see how that might alarm Tallie with her less abrasive approach to life, but she must know that it was her gentleness, her sweetness of nature, that attracted him to her and that Kate was more of a chum, a mate, a kind of female fellow.

Suddenly he felt a strong physical pang in what he thought of as his loins. Kate in his arms had had no steel in her whatsoever. She had felt surprisingly soft and delicate and when she had bent her shorn head her nape where he had coaxed a V with the scissors had looked as frail and vulnerable as a fledgling's. If only she hadn't come to his room!

'She likes you,' said Tallie. The small box of chocolates lay unopened on her lap and she did not care whether the train approaching on the screen in front of her ran over the long-tressed heroine tied to the sleeper.

'Wheesht!' ordered an outraged picture-goer behind her.

'It's irrelevant,' said Wilfred softly into her ear. 'Tallie, can't we just enjoy being together? You're the only one who matters to me.' Eventually she allowed him to hold her hand, but hers remained cold and unresponsive.

He didn't see much of what was on the screen either and the piano accompaniment which he usually enjoyed tonight seemed to jangle his nerves. He kept seeing Kate's shorn head, set like a cameo atop that straight back, like a phoenix, he thought, feverishly; certainly the very stamp of the New Woman, fierce and proud with that unrelenting grey gaze. And provocative. Yes, provocative was the word.

# Eight

Tallie came dashing down the hospital steps towards the ambulance, her nursing cap askew as it always seemed to be since she had completed the family triumvirate and had her hair bobbed, too. But for once Matron had been too harassed to notice.

'Down to Moxon's Rows,' she had dictated. 'Two to be picked up there. Suspected diphtheria. Don't waste time, Nurse. Take the doctor's bag. He might have to do a tracheotomy on the spot.'

Tallie sat up front in the high sit-up-and-beg ambulance. It was the first time she had been on board and she was nervous but trying to give the appearance of calm. No driver had yet turned up and old Dr Hutchinson was certainly taking his time. Where was he?

She rubbed her eyes as no other person than Toby Wilson came towards the ambulance, importantly pulling on enormous gauntleted driving gloves.

'The doctor had a bad turn in our shop,' he explained patiently over Tallie's demands for explanation. 'Robbie the driver is taking him in the doctor's own motorcar to the infirmary in Glasgow, so it's me for ambulance duty.' The prospect clearly pleased him. 'I thought I might be lucky enough to have you for my buddy.'

'What did Matron say?' gasped Tallie at the irregularity.

'She said she was very grateful to me and that if nurses had any sense they'd learn to drive.'

It took one or two turns of the starting handle to get the great beast of an ambulance moving and Tallie hung on grimly as they bumped over uncertain roads towards the hamlet of miners' rows near the Moxon pit. The late July day was burnished and warm and the hedgerows starred with bramble flowers and wild roses.

'I didn't know you'd learned to drive,' said Tallie between stiffened lips.

'Might as well,' said Toby easily. 'Might be handy, if there's a war.'

'Don't talk war,' she pleaded. 'I'm tired of talk of war.'

'Time's coming,' said Toby decisively, 'when as the chap Sorley said in the paper, we'll have to act as of old, when men were men.'

'How can you say that?' she cried in some anguish. 'What goes on in the Balkans has surely nothing to do with us? What's Sarajevo to do with us? We have enough on our plate here.' She was thinking, hugging the doctor's abandoned Gladstone bag, that there would be nobody to perform the tracheotomy.

'If France is attacked, if they go for little Belgium, what option do we have?'

'It's up to Austria and Serbia to fight it out.'

'Come on. It's only a matter of time till Russia comes to Serbia's aid and the Kaiser's got to help Austria. We'll all be in it. The boil's been festering for a long time. Now it's got to be lanced.'

'We can still keep out of it. Lloyd George is against it. Churchill is against it – going in, I mean.'

'Doesn't matter what noises the politicians make. We're secretly committed to helping France, that's the long and short of it.'

'Secretly? How can they commit us *secretly* to a war?'

'Seems they can.'

Tallie had not put the question in hope of an answer. The whole argument had mounted to fever pitch over the past few weeks. All the young men she knew, including her two brothers, had this almost-mad, alienating gleam in their eyes – certainly it alienated her. It was almost as though they willed and anticipated war. Some bragged they would join up the minute the need became apparent. The rest, though more reticent, listened to them respectfully and repeated provcative newspaper headlines as though they heard some fairy horn blowing in the wind.

The sight of row after row of squat, miners' cottages, the doors wide open as the day was warm, children playing as their mothers hung out washing or shook rugs was almost hallucinatory after the tense, emotional exchange in the ambulance.

Tallie instructed Toby to drive to the far end of the third of the rows, where children were playing around the water pump. Jumping down she went to May Beattie's cottage. The door was wide open and Tallie went in. May Beattie lay in one of the 'set-in' beds, opening heavy eyes reluctantly.

'It's my time,' she announced. 'My man's gone for the midwife.'

'Where are the sick children?' Tallie looked around.

'Playing.' May waved a helpless hand. 'I cannae keep them in, Nurse.'

Playing in the wide, glazed 'sheugh' or gutter outside, Tallie identified the two little Beatties who were to be picked up. One was three, the other eighteen months. Both looked glittery-eyed and feverish and even as Tallie picked up Shona, the younger, the infant's face turned a fearsome purple as she coughed a dreadful, grating, impacted cough and went limp in her arms.

Tallie raced towards the ambulance. She thought afterwards what she did was not the result of *unthinking* but of a kind of concentrated, out-of-the-ordinary brilliant thinking of which she would not normally be capable.

Swiftly and capably she opened Dr Hutchinson's Gladstone bag and took out the instrument she had seen him use so often when diphtheria had closed up some unfortunate child's trachea. Swiftly she cleansed the baby's throat, made the cut, inserted the breathing tube. Almost instantly, miraculously, Shona's eyes opened then her dreadful colour turned back to the normal pink. Tallie flew back to the gutter, picked up Etta, the other child and shakily told Toby to get a move on and get them all to the hospital. He needed no second bidding. If anything, his skin displayed a greater degree of pallor than Tallie's own.

'You had not been instructed in the procedure,' scolded Matron. 'But, on the other hand, if you had not acted, there is no doubt the child would have died. So, well done, Candlish. You may have some free time this evening. And straighten that cap. I will not tell you again.'

There was no means of transport to take her home and no way of contacting Wilfred at such short notice. Tallie thought she would use the two hours accorded her walking in the gentle evening sun and then shampooing her recalcitrant bob. As she stepped outside the nurses' quarters she met Toby, coming from the ambulance garage and looking rather pleased with himself.

'Now I know what I'll do,' he said jauntily, 'if there's a war. I'll maybe drive ambulances.'

'I don't want to talk war,' she said summarily. 'I told you!'

'What do you want to do, then?'

'What do you mean, what do I want to do? I know what I want to do,' she said scratchily. 'Go for a nice walk.'

He fell into step beside her. 'We make a good team, you and me,' he offered chattily.

'I'm going this way,' said Tallie, taking a corner that did not lead to his way home. He did a little side-step but remained by her side.

'Might as well chum you for your walk,' he said easily.

It wasn't difficult to talk to Toby. He could be quite amusing, Tallie conceded, about the whimsies of the people who came into the shop. He knew the latest gossip, the latest musical comedy 'numbers', the tittle-tattle about who was courting or cutting whom. His conversation was a lot more small-town and parochial than Wilfred's but it rose out of their joint environment, it had a depth and resonance of its own and maybe it was what she needed after such a day.

He hadn't heard about Matron's famous 'death watch' on nurses parting from their sweethearts on the hospital steps and before Tallie could side-step he had pulled her into his arms for a goodnight kiss. Where was the harm, she thought confusedly. Maybe soon he would be driving an ambulance in France.

*

62

When war was formally declared on Germany on the fourth of August, what was strange at first, Tallie thought, was that nothing much changed.

The main street of Perringhall was, if anything, a little quieter, as though people had withdrawn into themselves to think about the Foreign Secretary's chilling words about the lamps going out all over Europe and, more to the point, Kitchener's plea for the 'first hundred thousand' volunteers for the army.

Then people began almost to deny it could have happened, they couldn't have got themselves into a war and anyhow, it would all be over by Christmas.

After that came the justifications: we couldn't just have stood by and watched while Germany crashed through a neutral country like Luxembourg and then entered what everybody thought of as brave little Belgium. Before we knew where we were, they would be invading Britain itself. That stiffened a lot of spines. Women got out their knitting needles to make comforts for the soldiers and the young swallowed their natural terrors and made for the recruiting office. A great uniting wave of patriotism swept the country and every amateur band found a jaunty, challenging march to play. Mothers still did their best to keep headstrong boys from volunteering, but the respect accorded those who did – and the uniform that was such a hit with impressionable girls – was a powerful propellant.

Janet Candlish was like almost every mother with eligible sons. She could not face the nightmare if they went and yet she knew there would be a wild sustaining pride in her if they did.

One or two village boys were already out in the trenches, out in the Ypres Salient in Flanders, where they were so well set-up their mothers' and sweethearts' letters reached them the very next day. The making of munitions to back up the troops was bringing money in to homes and trade, according to Toby Wilson, was so brisk he couldn't yet think of leaving his dad to cope alone while he carried out his still firm intention to join up.

The war did not come home to Tallie in a personal sense till part of the hospital was taken over for the reception of Belgian refugees. She would never forget looking out from a window in the nurses' quarters and seeing those forlorn, bewildered women and children straggle towards the entrance with all their worldly goods wrapped up in tattered shawls or pillow cases. One exhausted woman straddled her legs wide to pee and the water trickled thinly away down the drive. A baby emitted a long blood-curdling scream and an old woman fell on the steps and did not get up. Pity and terror entered Tallie's heart and a new emotion she did not immediately identify – hate, hatred for those who made such things happen.

She went home now whenever she had time off – home to the arguments about who should join up, and when. Wilfred, who seemed almost like one of the family now that he was allowed into the kitchen, was almost on the point of volunteering. Russell was still officially too young but didn't intend to let that put him off – plenty lied about their age and what's more the army knew they did. Donald was involved in Admiralty matters and it did not look as though he could be spared, certainly not yet. Maybe conscription would come, anyway, putting an end to all uncertainty.

At the end of the mouth of August, there was Amiens. The 'war correspondents' had not yet been muzzled so their sober, broken-backed prose told the whole truth, perhaps for the last time in the war. No panic, no throwing in of the sponge. Just the acknowledgement that in this instance the enemy had the edge. Nellie Brogan in the village went into mourning, her son Patrick killed by shrapnel. His brother was down at the recruitment office the next day.

Tallie knew it was the war that was making Wilfred moody. Not only that, but Lily, his sister, had died, just as it had begun to look as though she had come through her operation quite well and he could not forgive himself for not having seen her one last time.

Several of the young teachers at the Academy had already joined up and Kate and two other young women

64

had been offered teaching posts there in their place. It meant Kate saw a lot more of Wilfred and it seemed to Tallie they got on a lot better these days, with Kate being more even-tempered than she had ever been, though not always so with Tallie.

The papers had been instructed to be upbeat about the war news since Amiens, but the wounded coming back to Blighty brought the truth about Flanders. It was mud, entrenchment, bombardment, shrapnel, shell-shock and worse. After a singularly bitter letter from an ex-colleague who had joined up right at the start – 'the Old Men have landed us in it' – Wilfred greeted Tallie on her day off with the news that he had enlisted.

Despite the fact that it was in the kitchen of Cullington Lodge and that her mother and sisters were looking on, Tallie went into Wilfred's embrace and with her arms round his neck buried her head in his shoulder and wept. He lifted her face up with a bony forefinger and gave her a regretful little half-smile. 'Had to be done, Tallie girl,' he said, and sighed mightily as she wept some more.

They went down into the woods later after tea, and kissed with a desperate kind of fervency. 'I wish you could be all mine before I go,' he said in her ear.

'I want to be,' she whispered back. And she was. Because of that he said he was giving her name as his next of kin and they would be married on his first leave.


# Nine


Kate knocked on Wilfred's door and bore the tray with tea and scones across the room to lay it carefully on the bamboo table covered with the Darvel lace cloth. It was Saturday and he was due to leave on the Monday.

He thought her face looked even paler than usual, an almost papery white, the only colour the vivid blue eyes which were the attribute she shared with her younger brother. But her gaze was stormy and, for Kate, less than direct.

'You've set the cat among the pigeons.' The teacup rattled on its saucer as she positioned the tray.

'What do you mean?' He had been packing his books into two tea-chests which Janet had reluctantly agreed to store for him in the big landing press – she hoped to relet his room – and stood with à Kempis's *Imitation of Christ* between his hands, unable to decide whether to take it or his Housman with him as his sole reading material.

'Russell's done the deed.' He saw she had smudged her cheek with an inky finger. 'He's' listed too. Soon there'll be no men left.'

'I've done all I can do to discourage him. Didn't they spot he was lying about his age?'

'They couldn't turn down a spirit like his.' Despite everything, she could not hide her pride. 'And he's tough. They could see how tough he is. He says one Candlish has to go and if Donald wants a cushy war in Glasgow, then it's got to be him.'

'What can I say?' said Wilfred helplessly. 'I'd rather he'd waited. But it's every man for himself.'

She looked at him directly for the first time.

'I've something else to tell you. You won't like it.'

'What is it?'

'Tallie's sent a message to say she won't be able to see you off on Monday. She's confined to bed in the nurses' quarters, running a temperature. They're not sure yet what it is.'

'Hell's teeth. Can't I get in to see her?'

'Certainly not. It could be anything. She's quarantined.'

He pushed the Housman into his haversack and began to do up the straps. Kate's fingers landed on his, quelling all movement.

'It won't be so bad,' she said. 'There'll be leave. She says to say how sorry she is.' She looked away from him and said in a more muffled tone of voice, 'And to tell you how much she loves you.' Now her eyes met his. 'I suppose we'll all miss you.'

'Never thought to hear it from your lips,' he said, with an attempt at flippancy.

'Well it's true. We all think a lot of you. Belle and I both. Even Mother.'

'Who doesn't believe in doling out much in the way of affection.' He was only saying what Kate herself had indicated and certainly what Tallie had experienced.

'Who knows it better than me?' said Kate quietly. He felt overcome by a kind of curiosity which temporarily crowded out his concern for Tallie.

'Well, I have to say what the family feels for me – if true – is reciprocated. Tallie and the rest of you are what I've got now, now Lily's gone. I've been happy here.' Almost shyly he lifted Kate's hand and kissed the fingertips. 'So thank you.'

There was a little colour in Kate's cheeks at last, but her mouth was working and he knew she was close to tears. With what he felt to be brotherly tenderness he drew her into his arms. This harsh, brusque, defensive girl, it seemed to him, needed warmth and love more than anyone in the family, excluding Janet. There was a harshness there he had begun to think synonymous with the spare, unrelenting farmlands all around, with the starkness of the pit village, with Lowland life itself. But maybe now even Janet was allowing herself the luxury of feeling. Just recently he had detected an almost imperceptible softening, a vulnerability that perhaps the war had brought about but he felt might also have had something to do with the circumstances connected with Donald and Tibby. And now Russell. . . .

He squeezed Kate and said, 'Don't be afraid to show your emotions, Katie. Whether *she* shows it or not, your mother will feel Russell's going terribly. I hope you won't freeze each other out.'

She stood back from him, straightening her back and gave him her old sardonic, distancing stare.

'Is that how you see us? Incapable of feeling? What you don't understand, Wilfred, and how could you, being English, is that with Scots pride comes first.'

'But it's a sin,' he said gently. 'And there's no sin in sharing the grief, the terror, the sorrow that war brings. Is there?'

She went and stood by the sash window, her hands on the brass lifts and he thought her fingers trembled.

He was wondering what to do, what to say, when he saw one hand go up to her mouth. A harsh cry, broken and direct as a wild bird's, came from her and suddenly tears were rushing down her cheeks in what seemed to him a torrent.

'I wish you weren't going! I wish you weren't going!'

'You're upset,' he offered stupidly, 'because of Russell.'

'No. I mind about Russell, of course I do, but *you* being here has made my life bearable. I can't talk to anyone the way I can to you. What's going to happen to me now?'

She made no attempt to wipe the tears from her face, in fact she seemed to have reached an extremity where such things did not matter.

'Look,' he said, feeling all ability to cope seep away from him, down through his bones like the weakness of some virulent illness, 'look, I'm afraid, Kate, I have things to do –' He sat down on his favourite wicker chair, the one with a homely squeak he had grown used to, conscious of the fatness of the cushion, of the spidery art nouveau flowers on the wallpaper, of the thinness of the cup he had not yet drunk from, of the clouds scudding across the brazen blue sky outside. Suddenly he wanted to keep all this womb-like safeness, suddenly he did not want to think of Flanders and what he'd read about shrapnel thudding into skull and bones and muscle, mud and rain seeping everywhere.

'I'm scared,' he heard himself saying. 'God, I'm scared.'

She took two steps towards him and stopped.

'What of?' she asked, in a voice that was suddenly shocked back to normal.

'Dying. Getting wounded. Bleeding. Hurting. What I'll see.'

'You could never say this to Tallie,' she said, hungrily. 'Could you? It's what I mean about you and me —'

'Do you hear what I'm saying?' he demanded, on a rising note.

'I hear.' She was holding his head against her breast, touching his hair with ineffable gentleness. He looked up at her helplessly and she brought her mouth down on his, so lightly he wondered if it had been there yet imprinting him in a way no other caress had done in his life before.

'Katie,' he implored her, 'what am I going to do with you?'

She placed her hands on either side of his face, her thumbs caressing.

'I will come and see you off,' she promised. Everything about her seemed to have lightened, from her body to the expression on her face. 'Let me.'

'I don't know what to do about Tallie,' he said, equivocally.

'You can't do a thing.'

'You'll write and tell me how she is? Why did it have to happen now?' He grasped Kate's hand and said, 'You'll stand by her if anything happens to me, Katie? The telegram will come here, if there is one. I've given her as my next of kin.'

'The war'll be over be Christmas and nothing is going to happen to you. Not so much as a scratch.'

'You've sorted it out with Fate, have you?'

Her eyes ate him up. 'Of course.'

'You know,' he said, the mention of Tallie bringing him back to some kind of equilibrium, some determination to treat of ordinary matters, 'you'll find plenty to stimulate now you're teaching at the Academy. Hillary's deep, not easy to know, but a true artist, intuitive, worthy cultivating. And Martham —'

'Don't try to palm me off on half the staff room', she reprimanded him, almost jokily.

'I'll expect you to live like a nun till I get back, then,' he responded, on the same kind of bantering note. That's what it was, wasn't it? Banter?

She smoothed down the folds of her navy skirt. The waistband slid about her narrow waist in a way that it suddenly occurred to him must chafe the tender skin underneath. Mentally he unfastened the skirt and placed his hands where the tight band had been. Almost as though she had divined what he had been thinking, she looked into his face and gave a little half-embarrassed laugh.

'I'm coming to see you off.' She reiterated what she had said earlier and he did not persuade her otherwise. Suddenly it was very impoortant that somebody did. Tallie wouldn't mind. Poor Tallie! In the turmoil of his packing and leaving and the other turmoil which he was coming out of, please God, the turmoil over Kate, which was not a legitimate turmoil, he had not thought of what could be ailing her. Surely her immunity to the likes of diphtheria or scarlatina would be established by now. Perhaps the Belgians had brought some new germs with them. Maybe it would be nothing more than a dose of influenza, a chill, even.

What it had been like to make love to her came back to him, her miraculously neat and compact body, tight as a young bud at first. *We fit*, she had asserted triumphantly. *Wilfred, we fit.* He had hoped for one more time. It was not to be. He would send her flowers, a loving letter which would tell her she had to get better soon, to be ready for their wedding on his first leave, because she was his dearest, lovely Tallie.


'Oh God,' gasped Kate, 'I don't much like it here.'

The station seemed filled to the high-vaulting roof with sound, the clanking of engines and carriages and the high-pitched agonising scream of steam boilers emptying.

The train before had disgorged some wounded in their bright blue uniform and she had torn her gaze away from a youth with bandages across his eyes; from another, not

70

much older, missing the lower half of a leg. She had replaced both men in her mind with Russell and Wilfred and her thoughts seemed in the grip of something colder than ice.

Wilfred had fetched them both a cup of hot tea from a nearby wagon while she looked after his belongings. He scarcely touched his but she drank hers down in the hope of restoring sensation of some kind, banishing the ice-age, the ice-water in her veins. The soot-smell and disinfectant which seemed to characterise the platform where they stood drove out all memory of previous smells, as though the nostrils had been primed for this one function, to take in the rank station smells; just as the eye had a new acuity for minor detail, for the ground-down shoes of a mother seeing off her son, the blue shadows under a shawl-borne baby's stunned gaze, the wrong tawdry hat atop a girl's blaze of red curly hair.

The world's being torn apart, thought Kate, and we're letting it happen. These young men getting into carriages, carelessly banging doors, hanging out of windows, full of callow bravado, they should be driving new-fangled motor bread vans, delivering the post, cutting ham, driving furrows, doing up parcels in douce drapery shops. Not wearing the heavy, depersonalising khaki, their tender feet in those heavy boots. Suddenly she could visualise them all returning in the blue of the wounded, the halt and the lame. *What are we doing?* The question ran through her like a kind of madness, putting paid to any rational thought.

Wilfred moved his gear back towards an iron hoarding bearing the familiar black and yellow advertisement for Colman's Mustard, so that the two of them were an island apart from the continually shifting tide on the platform.

'How do you feel?' she asked, trying to force some kind of normality into her voice between lips that wouldn't stop trembling.

'Now the moment's come, better.'

'I wish they'd stop it. Just stop it. War is madness. Don't men see that?'

'They're not going to stop it, just for me.' He tried to get her to smile but it was impossible.

'Try not to worry about Tallie.' Her eyes skimmed off his face. 'Scarlet fever isn't as bad as diphtheria.'

'Didn't she have it as a child?'

'We all did, but her.'

'Poor love, stuck in a ward of children.'

'Yes.'

'Make her eat properly, when she comes home to convalesce.'

'I'll leave that to Belle. They get on.'

'Try to be less prickly.'

'I'm just me.'

'Nicer than you think, Katie.'

'No. Nice I'm not.'

'You are.'

'I don't get on with anybody. Anybody, but you.' Her cold hand was stealing into his and her blue eyes, desolate as a wintry landscape, would not allow his concerned gaze to escape.

'What makes you like this?' he demanded in exasperation. And then, he did not know why, he found himself touching the tic-like mark on her cheek, which had gone livid with the cold, asking curiously, 'How did you get this?'

She pushed his hand away, saying nothing.

'Tell me.'

'My father's pit belt. When my father drank, the belt came out. I was more defiant than the rest – then – and came in for more. My mother hit us, too. You see less of it now. Then it was known as knocking the spirit out of you. Discipline. You got locked in rooms, put on bread and water. The Calvinist way. Spare the rod and spoil the child.'

The statement was all the more shocking to him for being delivered in a calm, even conversational way. He gaped at her. That there had been beatings in his own family he didn't deny, but they had been rare, more out of exasperation than bad temper and often wide of the mark as they'd been a bunch of artful little dodgers.

72

'Then I can understand,' he said, thickly.

'Understand what?'

'Why you're perpetually on the defensive. But try to stand back from it now. Tell yourself you are lovable, worth something. Worth a great deal.'

'This is why I don't want you to go.'

'Don't,' he appealed.

'When I'm with you, I *am* different. I feel the way people are supposed to feel. I feel I'm in sight of something I should always have had by right. Does this make any sort of sense?' she added desperately.

'Katie,' he said urgently, 'I have to think of Tallie.'

'I know.'

'So you and I have to draw a line under certain feelings. Feelings that could get out of hand.'

'Yes.' Her hand curled up into its own coldness within his and removed itself. The old hostility which had been the first thing he had remarked about her came back to her features, so that he wondered about the impulses he had to stroke her hair, hold her by the waist, think about the delicate softness of her lips. Passing reactions. They had to be. He had Tallie.

A black monster of a train, its surface dulled by encounter with recent rain, fussed noisily along the platform and tipped the buffers with unexpected delicacy, like a rhinoceros toe-dancing. At once doors flew open, people got out, trolleys ate up luggage and passengers broke away from send-off groups to populate the carriages before the fust of previous occupants had had a chance to dissipate.

Wilfred got into a carriage and presently appeared at an open window.

'There's this,' said Kate, handing him up a carefully wrapped small object. 'It's a diary.'

'Well, thanks.'

'Write. Not just to Tallie.'

'I'll try.'

'And remember to duck. Russell says.'

After that, they said nothing. There was nothing to say.

Around them the ghastly cacophony of closing doors, moving rolling stock, engine whistles went on. Women sobbed. Couples clung in a desperate fervency, the men leaning perilously from carriage windows, the women's feet teetering. At last the guard's whistle went, the flag was down, the big iron beast with its war fodder moved with a terrible inexorable dignity from the station confines.

When it was almost too late she rushed up and kissed him. His own mouth was so taut the salutation scarcely registered. But he felt her breath.

'Love,' she said. 'Love you.'

At first he wondered if he had heard it. And then he was sure. There came a moment when he could not distinguish her slight, straight figure in blue topped with its perilous hat from any of the others waving from the disappearing station, and he sat back in his seat, staring unseeingly at fresh-faced sailors, rookies drawing out flasks and bottles, feeling a kind of exaltation wash over him that made him feel not quite real.

# Ten

Russell's regiment got to the Salient just before Christmas. In London, passing through, he'd seen Christmas trees for the first time, for most folk still worked on Christmas Day in his part of Scotland and trees were something he'd only read about.

He was getting used to the varied accents of the other Tommies – the end-of-sentence lilt of Geordies and the convolutions of Cockneys. The cheek-by-jowl existence in the trenches was something he quickly took on board – the pit had prepared him for that. His mates had quickly cottoned on to how young he was and their teasing was never too hard to take. Maybe they thought of younger brothers they had left behind and treated him accordingly. He was determined to show them what mettle he was made of and he grumbled less than most about the mud, the cold and the rats, joking except for when it got beyond the hasty quip. The bombardment was something else. That he thought he would never get used to, for there was no escape, the bloody rattle and noise went on and on, but he quickly adopted the philosophy of the more hardened campaigners: if it's for you, it won't go past you. There was a kind of harsh comfort in this. The more you thought it, the harder you got and the older. He was getting older by the minute.

'Mail.' The needling, mean little sergeant handed round the letters. There were three for him: one from his mother ('wear a square of flannel on your chest, it fairly keeps out the damp'); one from Tallie, bewailing the fact that Wilfred had been sent abroad without leave, but saying she was well over the fever and the third from Belle. As he opened it with mud and oil-grimed fingers, another folded letter sealed with red wax, fell away from the cream parchment notepaper that Belle affected. With a shift of heartbeat he opened the crackling page.

'Darling, what a shock to hear from me but you are a daddy. It is a girl and I'm calling her Catriona, after my auntie who's been good to me. We can get married when you come home on leave. I know it was you because I didn't go with Donald after the soirée. I saw him in Glasgow but there was nothing intimate. You know what I mean. You must believe me.

'When I heard you'd volunteered I felt very proud. Up here in Aberdeen they're volunteering like mad. We have to show the Hun. The baby was eight pounds. She has my hair and her chin is very like yours.

'It was wonderful with you, on the banking, especially the day when Catriona got started and the

75

thistledown blowing all over the place. Remember? I thought I loved Donald at first but now I know I love you. My brave soldier! I am crying as I write this. When will it end? I want to feel your arms around me and your loving lips. Remember the picnic? I saw you then and you did not know it. Diving. With the sun on you and you all bare.

'Did it mean the same to you as it did to me, darling? I have to know. I wrote to Belle and she said she thought it did. She said you were upset. She was prepared to send you this letter. I have forgotten all about Donald. It was my mother that wanted that match. I only think of you now and of the day I will see you again and hold you in my arms and show you how much I love you, as well as showing you *our* baby. I truly love you, truly I do, I truly, truly love you, my brave soldier. So don't get shot at or anything. Keep your head down. And write to me c/o Belle – she will keep our secret and when we get married that will be it. They can't keep us apart then. Yours ever and ever, Tibby.

Alfie Cheesman, twenty years of age, who had somehow acquired rosy cheeks and a steel-sharp gaze in a Battersea slum, edged along the trench with the tin mug of unspeakable tea and proffered it towards the chap he'd already decided would be his oppo for the duration.

When Russell had asked him why he'd joined a Scots regiment Alfie had replied, 'The Jocks can fight.' His own stocky frame looked permanently at the ready as though he'd put his fists up at the slightest provocation. But an instant kind of rapport had sprung up between him and the young Jock. No explaining it. Except Alfie hated whingers and he'd never heard a murmur of a whinge from the young 'un. Till now.

Russell was leaning against the black clay of the trench with tears running down his face. Come to think of it, he'd been a bit quiet since the mail came earlier in the week, but he wasn't one for confidences. He did not move his head but took the mug.

' 'ere,' Alfie volunteered, 'bloody Jerry's only putting out the white flag and asking for a Christmas truce, wot d'you think, Scottie? I know you're a bunch of heathens up there in Scottie Land but in case you hadn't noticed, it is Christmas Day. Makes a difference, don't it? Go on, cheer up, for Gawd's sake. You're a long time dead.'

Russell looked down at the item Alfie was carrying in his left hand, identifying it as a piece of Christmas pudding wrapped in clean muslin.

'What you doin' wi' that, Cheesie?'

'For the Krauts. Look!' He turned Russell round so that they both peered over the parapet into No Man's Land. A bunch of steel-helmeted German soldiers, white cloths tied to sticks, were advancing towards them about fifty yards away. They could not be said to look confident about this manoeuvre. But one put a loud-hailer to his lips and shouted: 'It is Christmas. No fighting. It is *heilige* day. Truce. Truce.'

Alfie scrambled up over the edge of the trench, slipping and sliding as he went and wordlessly Russell followed suit. All along the cruel wound in what had once been a pleasant field, British soldiers were scrambling up on to the beaten pock-marked grass and advancing towards the Germans warily advancing towards them.

'It is *Stollen. Sehr gut.*' The young German pushing something into Russell's hands was fair and freckled. 'I have it from my mother.' He indicated the obvious by lifting a hand to his mouth and going through the motions of chewing.

Russell felt in his trousers pocket and brought out the little mother-of-pearl penknife which Belle had given him. It was no use. He treasured it and would have gone spare if anyone had pinched it. But honour had to be satisfied. You couldn't take and not give.

'Here chum,' he said brusquely, pushing it into the German's grasp. 'Take it. It very good knife. Very sharp. Happy Christmas.'

77

'*Sehr gut!*' The German seemed overcome with pleasure. Now that Russell was close up against him, he could see the young man bore some virulent spots and that he had well-shaped, long-fingered, quite delicate hands. Violin fingers, they would have called them at home. He was the *same*. The same as the lads he fought with. Human. Not just Jerry. A man you could get to know.

'My name is Klaus,' said the German, smiling and showing good teeth.

'Mine Russell.'

'Bad war, Russell.'

'Very bad war.'

'I have girl friend, name Gisela. You have girl friend?'

'I have baby. Hair like mother. Hair colour corn. Chin like me.'

Alfie heard and turning, gave Russell a long, deliberating look before he began to smile.

'You young bastard,' he said, *sotto voce*.

But Russell was eating the stollen.

When the bombardment and fighting started up again after the Christmas truce, with what seemed like renewed ferocity on both sides, Russell was to look at dead or wounded Germans, some strung along the barbed wire like so many scarecrows, always thinking, even fearing, it might be Klaus with the mother-of-pearl penknife in his pocket and wondering if he'd know him. Once he thought it could have been him but whoever it was, was beyond identification. It was the only time in the war he was actively sick.

Belle alighted from the tram in Sauchiehall Street and ran towards Miss Cranston's Tearooms, knowing Donald would be sitting there fuming. The tearoom swarmed with business men and Kelvinside matrons treating themselves after shopping. What would happen if Zeppelins came over the North as they were doing over London? That would fairly empty the streets and the restaurants. Belle shuddered. These great, death-dealing airships haunted her dreams.

Donald's big, handsome head was half-turned in her direction as she raced in and before he saw her she caught a glimpse of desolation in him that touched her to the quick.

'Sorry,' she gasped, sitting down beside him. The cuffs of his well-laundered shirt glistened and the gold tiepin and cuff-links, the dark tweed suit spoke of quiet probity, a man to trust.

'You're *late*. I haven't got all day.' Donald summoned a waitress and ordered tea and cakes.

'Well I'm here.' She brought him to the point. 'What was it you wanted to talk about?'

'Tibby.'

Somehow she had divined as much. Carefully she said now, 'What about Tibby, then?'

'Has she had the child?'

'The baby? Well, she must have had. Else it would be the longest gestation in human history.' She could not keep the disapprobation from her voice. 'A girl, as it happens.'

'And they're both – all right?'

'Of course. What's it to you?'

'I'm asking as a matter of course. You know I've been in the States. Otherwise I'd have asked before.'

She leaned forward and said earnestly, 'Look, Donald, forget all about Tibby. The baby isn't yours; you've nothing to reproach yourself with.' Curiosity overcame her and she asked, 'You don't still love her, do you?'

He gave her a puzzled, bewildered look that touched her as much as the look of desolation had done earlier.

'I wouldn't like to go against Mother in this matter. She'd never get over the shame of it.'

'If you made an honest woman of Tibby?'

'Well, as the baby isn't mine —'

'You don't love the girl,' said Belle, angrily dismissive. 'You don't know the meaning of the word, Donald. You only like yourself, that's your trouble.'

'Not very much,' he said evenly, 'Not any more. And I did care for Tibby. I don't suppose I'll ever find another girl I'll feel the same about, if you want to know.'

'But you've been seeing someone else.' This much she knew. Her mother had wormed it out of Donald the last time he'd been home. Some young thing whose father was in shipping, with a big house in Bearsden.

'Not any more.'

What was discomfiting Belle was that her elder brother was beginning to behave more like her youngest one had always done, appealing to her to sort out his emotional problems and her stronger allegiance was – always had been – towards Russell. What if she disclosed to Donald what was happening now between Russell and Tibby, the well-laid plans to marry at the first opportunity? She was the only one privy to them apart from Russell and Tibby themselves. All kinds of trouble would break out when everything was revealed. Her mother would fight the notion of the marriage, as no doubt Tibby's parents would, too, because what had Russell to offer? And Donald was going to feel doubly betrayed. Belle found her heart was in no way hard enough to deal the blow.

'What's up?' demanded Donald. 'Don't you want another cake? You usually manage two.'

'Couldn't you have made a go of it with what was her name?'

'Fiona.'

'Fiona.'

'Well, she wasn't Tibby.'

'She couldn't help that.'

'No.'

'There'll be others.'

'Doubtless.'

'So cheer up.'

'If you ever see her —'

'I never see her!' Belle disclaimed vehemently. 'Why should I see Tibby?'

'Or write to her. Or she to you. Tell her I wish her well.'

'Well,' she conceded reluctantly, touched by his rare humility, 'I suppose I could do that.'

'I want to get things sorted out in my head before I join up.'

She dropped her teaspoon on to the floor and her face as she rose from picking it up was scarlet, her head suddenly swimming.

'Before you *what*? I thought your work was too specialised and important for that?'

'I'm a free man. I can volunteer.'

'No, Donald!' She was thinking, desperately, how she would tell their mother and decided she couldn't. He'd have to do it himself. 'Look. Wait at least till they start conscription. They say it will come. It's got to come. Go then. If you must.' She was babbling and she knew it.

'I wouldn't have to go, even then. Technically they can't have me. But morally – Russell's gone. Tallie's friend Wilfred's gone. And the other day I got my first white feather.'

She blanched. 'Who dared do that?'

For the first time that day, he smiled, but it was grimly. 'Fiona.'

She knew then he would go. The pressure was mounting, the papers talking about shirkers in ever-more derogatory terms. Part of her admired him, even wanted him to prove his manhood, but the more rational part of her shrank in terror from seeing yet another sibling subjected to the long attrition on the Western front. The papers kept the news cheerful, but all she needed was the letters home from Russell. She was adept at reading between the lines.

'I want you to break it to Mother,' Donald was saying. He summoned up what looked like a smile of relief. 'Tell her how good I'll look in my officer's uniform.'

'That'll be a great comfort. With two sons gone.'

'*Please* Belle.' Now he had unburdened himself he looked almost sportive. 'I'll bring you home some handsome rich subaltern.'

'Don't,' she said savagely.

'Unless you've found someone in the meantime? Have you?

'I've more to think about.'

'You're damn pretty. Prettier even than Tallie and certainly than poor old Kate.'

'Don't softsoap me,' she said. 'And don't *disparage*.' Somehow comparing her with her sisters seemed a mean-spirited thing to do, but Donald had always been adept at setting them against each other. She would show him. Grow out of all that. She began to regret her earlier softening towards him and her tacit acceptance that she would break the news of his enlisting to her mother.

But cross though he made her at times she was still resisting the thought of him going to war, superstitiously terrified that if she withdrew her affection from him the first bullet would have his name on it. She knew people looked at both of them admiringly as they walked out of the tearoom. Maybe they thought they were a couple. It was a bit like a rehearsal for the time when she would have a man she could call her own. She blushed when Donald kissed her goodbye, clinging till self-consciously he laughed and pushed her gently away.

Going down Renfield Street towards the station she encountered a marching pipe band, leading would-be volunteers towards the recruiting office. The kilts went with a fine swing, the music pulled something out from her breastbone like a fine, vibrating wire. The faces of on-lookers seemed set alight. No wonder Donald had decided in the end he had no option but to go. Your feet had no option but to skip to the music.

# *Eleven*

The letters had come. There were four from Tallie and two from Kate. Wilfred read them in the trench and they were soon almost indecipherable from the rain. Belle had given up teaching and was training as a VAD. Kate had put on a school pageant that included Henry V's speech before Agincourt ('I think of you and what it means to be English when I hear it') and Tallie was nursing a mixed bag at the hospital, including refugees from the Continent.

The harsh catarrh rode down his throat as he read, moved unbearably by the contrast of what they regarded as rigours at home – the shortage of potatoes, the way young people were losing all respect for their elders, the press going over the top and cheapening the deaths at the front with their base jingoism – with the actuality of the war as he and no doubt Russell and Donald were experiencing it.

*Agincourt*, Kate had written. They'd had mud there, too. He was remembering his Shakespeare, brave Harry's rhetoric about closing up the wall with our English dead. Well, they were here, the English, the Scots, the Welsh, the Irish and there were never enough of them to close up the wall.

He was tired, of course. It no doubt accounted for the emotionalism. But he'd been here on the Somme for what seemed like forever. Regretting often that he'd turned down the offer to train as an officer out of some kind of loyalty to his East End roots. Had he accepted he might have been miles away, within sight of the sea at Montreuil, where it was GHQ and the Commander-in-Chief, it was said, rode out each day with an escort of Lancers and two ADCs, all fluttering pennants, glittering lances and glossy horses. Agincourt again, without the mud. He'd heard a band played ragtime in the Officers' Club and WAACs waited on table with the red and blue GHQ colours in their hair.

He didn't want to believe, his feet in six inches of water here in Happy Valley, the last gathering point before the front line, that they could be so blasé. But it was probably true. His opinion of human nature and the officer class in particular, especially the ancient generals whose mistaken strategy had been paid for in young lives, had not gone off the graph in recent months.

But the tiredness was no doubt pulling everything out of focus so it was only the ever-present, subterranean anger that fuelled him, kept him going. Anger that the papers subverted the suffering into cheery patriotic prose. Anger that no one – no one – at home knew how bad it was, the men marching in their sleep, sometimes without boots, lousy, scabby, hungry and here, in the direly named Happy Valley, subjected to flies everywhere and everywhere the stench of dead horses and the very trees dying because the starving animals had gnawled the bark off.

No human dignity any more. Something unnameably evil crawling through the muster of armies. Everything crawling. Human, cattle, machinery. And relentlessly, with no relief given, the shelling that went on and on, that brought brave men to uncontrollable trembling and nervous collapse, shell-shock. Maybe what he was in sight of himself, for he had never wept with the arrival of letters before and now he did and it was the gap between the normality of home and the obscenity of his present circumstances that did it.

'Right there. You, Chappell? This ain't the public library. Calder, Smith, go with the professor here. Get that equipment painted.'

The little currant-eyed sergeant moved along the trench, his boots squelching. Smith said belligerently, 'What's the point, sarge? It'll be covered in mud anyhow.'

'The point,' said the sergeant, 'is that bright metal objects can give our position away by reflecting the sun. That's what they say at HQ. HQ's order is to paint. So get on with it.'

In No Man's Land the shells seemed to be landing ever nearer their trench. The men's eyes met those of their sergeant and for the first time in the campaign the crusty little NCO showed some empathy with his men.

'The guns are coming up. They'll get their answer.'

'If they don't get us first,' opined Smith.

'The stuff is coming, you got your mail, didn't you?' said the sergeant. 'You'll get your bombardment. The guns would've been up before but for the bloody rain.'

At that moment, a shell landed no more than a hundred yards away and blew up trees and a discarded lorry in spectacular display. Mud, shrapnel, wood, earth, spattered all around them as they crouched as low in the evil-smelling trench as they could, expletives pouring from the sergeant's lips. Wilfred felt his letters slip from his grasp and saw them disappear into the mud. He tried to regain them but they were beyond saving. David Calder, with whom he shared confidences between bombardments, gave him a rueful stare.

'There you go, mate,' he said fatalistically. 'Hope you'd read 'em.'

There was a lull after the last erupting shell. Even momentary relief from bombardment gave leave to a kind of euphoria. Orders came through that they were to stand firm, that reinforcements were coming up and far from retreating the big Somme offensive of July was starting and every inch of ground had to be fought over.

Up the line, they could see ranks of young rookies scrambling awkwardly from lorries and begin to dig fresh entrenchments. For a little, the rain had stopped, as well as the shelling and they caught brief snatches of mouth-organ music, even laughter.

Wilfred saw David Calder shared his ironic compassion for the newcomers.

'First bloody time we've ever had to conscript,' said Calder.

'Poor young buggers. At least *we* had the choice.'

' "Dear to friends and food for powder, Soldiers marching, all to die".' Wilfred spoke the lines almost to himself.

'Who's that?'

'Housman.'

'He wasn't wrong.' The mild studious Calder, who had another, rat-like, tenacious side to him in battle, Wilfred had discovered, passed him a cigarette from a soggy pack. They had learned to seize such moments of quietude with an almost mad intensity.

'What I'll miss,' said Calder, 'is climbing. You ever climbed?'

Wilfred shook his head. 'Not seriously. With proper boots.'

'I've climbed in the Cairngorms. Had a go at Ben Nevis. With snow on it. Like another world. Chaste. Clean. But you – what'll you miss?'

'Aside from holding a woman in my arms, things like buying books and looking at pictures.'

'You've had a woman?'

Wilfred smiled. 'That'd be telling.' The strange thing was that although it was Tallie's name in his head, the face he saw was Kate's.

'Anyhow,' he said reprovingly, 'what d'you mean, "what'll you miss"? You're not going anywhere.'

Calder said nothing. Eventually, his reflective mood passed and he threw his cigarette stub away. 'I want back to the mountains, mate,' he said. 'Chaste and clean, as I said. After what I've seen here, I don't much care for the human race. I reckon we've sold the pass.'

Wilfred smiled at him and waited. There was more.

'You reckon we'll ever be forgiven? For what we've done here? Doesn't matter whether you're French, or Scots, or English or German. We've let death in. Death reigns.' His blue eyes suddenly flamed and he said, 'And I've never been with a girl; I've not climbed the mountains I wanted. I've had to turn my back on what I was put here for. Sod it all, I don't bloody care any more, one way or another.'

As the light went, the shelling started up again. As the sergeant had promised, the British guns were up now but the sound of bombardment was doubled, the din hellish. Wilfred found himself in possession of his second Lewis gun, his first having gone in an earlier bombardment. Before the light went entirely, he brought out his pocket-book and brushed up on the instructions which he'd written himself in his neat, cramped hand.

The new machine lay reassuringly under his hands, the belt of bullets at the ready. A fine instrument of killing and how many Germans would it pick off if the Boche came out of their trenches and tried to take this sodden piece of earth where his feet were beginning to rot like old wood in his hopeless boots?

David's words reprised in his head. Would they ever be forgiven? Yet it had been about more than killing, hadn't it? He tried to recall the feelings that had swelled up in him so overwhelmingly before he volunteered, not just to be Jack the Lad, though that had applied. The need to crush down the awful assertive power of the German Empire, the desperation to prove might wasn't necessarily right, had become so powerfully apparent. Yet he was in the jaws of the terrible paradox: how could you change what was evil by using evil means? What was more evil than sending metal into human flesh, causing another sentient being unmentionable suffering, if you did not take away his life outright?

It wasn't Tallie he addressed in his muddled thinking at such times, it was Kate at her mordant best. Would he ever sort out his feelings about that particular problem, supposing he was spared to go back home again when it was all over? He had taken Tallie's virginity in exchange for the promise that he would marry her. He couldn't go back on that. And he still had very tender feelings for her; he didn't want strident uncomfortable Kate in his thoughts but she would not be kept out of them.

He had played the film of Kate seeing him off at the station over and over again in his mind – cold little hand, the giving of the diary, the final kiss. And sometimes he remembered the hazy pleasure of making love to Tallie with the sun on his back.

He remembered his mother too, though she had been dead many years. It was as though his very soul crept back into the womb as the only protection for the hell around. He wanted the things females gave, love, sex, sustenance, reassurance. Sometimes in the dead of night when he couldn't sleep he tried writing poetry, but the words came out broken-backed, jagged with anger. There would need to be a new lexicon after the war. So he got back to thinking about women – Tallie, Kate; Kate, Tallie . . . Sometimes it seemed they blurred into one.

Food was handed down the line. They fell on fresh oranges but apart from that there was nothing different, just the same old grey bread and bully beef. They had to put even that aside as their own bombardment started in earnest. Shell after shell soared over the disputed ground between the two armies. They saw a German arsenal go up in a thunder of noise and a welter of fire and fallout. It seemed to Wilfred when he put his head above the parapet that the Germans had retreated to their second line of defence. It was difficult to tell through the smoke and mist. In spite of the gut-wrenching fear something else rose up in him, a kind of vanquishing, deadly triumph that ran wildly through his veins like a scorching wine. The bastards! It was possible they were on the run! After weeks of stalemate, at last, at last!

He turned to go along the trench to urge the sergeant to rush fresh ammunition for his machine-gun and that of David Calder. There was nothing more goading or frustrating than having a new machine with nothing left to go in it.

But the little NCO was engaged in conversation with a very young-looking officer, the latter pale to the gills.

'Chappell, we're going over the top.' It was strange. It was almost like a plea from the sergeant that it shouldn't be so. But the young officer was trying to make some kind of address, talking about the necessity for courage and resolution while one hand whacked his gold-topped baton into the other, which was clad in a glove of finest new brown leather, and one knee trembled uncontrollably.

Where the rookies had dug in earlier Wilfred could just see an amorphous figure marching up and down, kilt and plaid flying, and could just hear a sobbing from the bagpipes that was unlike anything he'd ever heard before. A soul in torment.

He thought for the briefest flashing moment of Donald and Russell, where they might be, perhaps to the north where rumour had it things were even worse than here.

Then he was fixing his bayonet and praying wordlessly in a kind of muck-sweat and as he turned towards David

Calder he saw him fall to a bullet and knew he would not rise again, he was face down in the mud and although he tried to lift him he could not, could not, the blood came from his temple and ears and the sergeant screamed at him to move, move.

He ran along the trench and there were other bodies, his boots ran over them and from a dead pair of lungs there came a wailing screech like a banshee. At last where the trench ended there was no escape and he was on the ground above and advancing, he didn't know where, except there was killing to be done and he was a killing animal. He fell over something, a German soldier's leg and when he thought the body moved he ran his bayonet into it, thinking it was the best thing, it removed uncertainty. He ran on, thinking absurdly the rain would cleanse him, that shrapnel would miss him and then it did not, did not miss, something hot and needling struck his temple and had taken over his lower left leg and he looked down absently and saw blood.

He looked sideways and saw Smith, a Geordie, and a Glasgow boy called Pate, trotting beside him, Pate's mouth drawn back in a rictus that could have been mistaken for a smile.

'Where are we gaun?' he demanded.

'To finish the buggers.' The words had come from Wilfred, surprising him. Something was keeping him going. Something.

'They got Calder,' said Smith. That was it, thought Wilfred. Calder was gone.

'I'll keep goin' if you keep goin',' said Pate. There seemed to be a general movement of men, going in the same direction but there was nothing tidy about it, it was nothing like the plans the generals drew up.

They were on the German trench before they knew it and half a dozen dirty cold men engaged them in hand-to-hand combat, feet slipping everywhere. He knew he sent two men down and made sure they stayed down and Pate and Smith, those two runty underfed little shysters who always knew where the extra supplies were kept, were fighting and dodging like maniacs, like schoolboys playing at war, shouting and screaming, running away and coming back into the attack. One German ran away, his legs so leaded they could scarcely operate. They watched him go, too exhausted to go after him and then they were advancing again, knowing it was the crew of a machine-gun nest they had demolished, maybe the same gunners who had struck down Calder and there was relish in it.

The dark was coming down, big rolling clouds that blotted out the abused and skeletal trees, the gun carriages, the fallen men of both armies, the mud, the dying horses. Wilfred knew he was walking, but that soon because of his leg he would have to stop and now he did not know in which direction he went, whether he was going back towards his own regiment or towards the enemy. He seemed to have lost both Pate and Smith; he had a vague memory of Pate crying out and falling back and he thought he should have gone back to look for both of them but his brain wasn't working properly either, like his leg.

He came to a crossroads. He tried to draw himself back to normality by thinking of the peasants who would use these roads in ordinary times. Then he remembered a legend he'd once been told in the Peak district, about burying witches at crossroads so that they would not know which way to go, to Heaven or to hell and it seemed he was in the same position.

He struck off into a devastated wood, knowing it could not be long now and he was losing control over his own destiny. This was what did for you more than anything, he realised. You had free will up to a point then God took away the options. His leg did not feel as though it were there any more and his whole body experienced a curious floating sensation. Yet, he knew he was falling and it was into spongy moss he sank, the last image on his retina that of a tall tree, gaunter than any man.

# Twelve

Tallie came off the ward dropping with intense fatigue. She had worked almost round the clock and now she knew she had to have some sleep. She supposed she was hungry but sleep came before all else.

They were perpetually short-staffed, that was the trouble. Some of her friends had left to make money in munitions. The wounded shipped back to Blighty had need of nursing, she knew that and people like Belle insisted they had priority. But the war didn't stop children getting sick and civilian refugees also went down with typhoid and the like and a fever hospital was no soft option. Belle had gone into the VAD with a slightly romantic view of what she would be doing – succouring handsome officers who would all want to marry her. She would find out soon enough! Tallie supposed at base she was proud of her younger sister. There had been the usual battle with their mother about leaving home and now it was only Kate who lived there and she was doing the work of three at the Academy.

Bad though it was, her work demanding and sometimes harrowing, Tallie never forgot how much worse it might be for Wilfred at the front and for Russell and Donald. The newspapers could camouflage the truth as much as they liked, what was happening on the Somme wasn't something you could wrap up in pretty patriotic prose. An officer who had come in to see the refugees had told her July 1 had been the worst day in British history and that maybe a hundred thousand men had lost their lives that day, sixty thousand of them British. She tried to put the figure out of her mind; she couldn't visualise anyhow what it might mean and would not permit herself to think Wilfred could have been one of them. It was just that mail didn't get through now with the clockwork regularity it did when the war started. There would be a letter soon. Pray God! She was so tired she had scarcely the strength to send up her fervent plea to the Almighty.

Going out of the ward, she turned under the soft glow of the nightlight to look back at her sleeping charges, feeling despite everything, the bone-aching weariness, the invasive worry about Wilfred, a quiet satisfaction. Clean, fed, cared-for, warm, their little bodies given at least a chance to fight the infections that invaded them. She would never lose this charge of loyalty she felt, this need to protect the most vulnerable. A lot of her friends argued it was more rewarding nursing grown-ups, especially men, who were more appreciative, it seemed, and less demanding, than women. But to see a sick child restored to health was like no other shot in the arm Tallie knew and their readily given affection something she treasured after the harshness of her childhood.

'*Maman!*' The one word echoed from the far end of the ward where Jeannie Gray had taken over night duty. Tallie saw her head come up sharply from the report she was reading and watched while Jeannie walked over to the last cot and tried to get its occupant to lie down again.

Mons! It was Mons, the little Belgian who'd come in with no name and whom they'd called after the battle where British soldiers swore they had seen an angel ride the sky, an angel which for a time stopped the oncoming German cavalry. Right from the start Tallie had been *Maman* to her and now, desperately tired though she was, she could not keep her dragging feet from taking her back down the ward to see what ailed the child.

'*Maman! Maman!*' The little girl held out her arms to Tallie to be lifted and held. The tear-stained dramatic face was framed in dark curls. Jeannie Gray, new to the ward, drew in her breath at the sight of the sores which covered the infant's body, a sight revealed as Mons tried to tear her soaking wet nightgown off over her head.

'TB sores,' Tallie confirmed grimly. 'This poor little soul is suffering agony.'

'She'll wake the whole ward,' murmured Jeannie apprehensively.

Tallie took a blanket from the cot and wrapped the baby

in it, lifting her and cradling her in her arms, crooning to her, trying to soothe her.

'She thinks you're her mother,' said Jeannie, her freckled youthful face a map of compassion like Tallie's own.

'She's got nobody,' said Tallie. 'A family brought her with them but they can't look after her.'

'What'll happen to her?'

Tallie shrugged. 'Who's to say?' Mons was showing signs of quietening. Tallie walked up to the ward with her to the chair near the coal fire. 'Could you get her some boiled water?' she appealed to Jeannie. 'She's burning up. I'll just sing quietly to her for a little while. She likes that.'

'But you should be sleeping,' Jeannie protested.

'It won't take long.'

'Shall I get her a clean nightie?'

'Please.'

When the tiny girl had been made comfortable Tallie rocked her in her arms and softly sang *Jesus Bids Us Shine*. When she came to the words 'You in your small corner, and I in mine', she had to swallow before going on, for the tears were not far away, not just for Mons but for all of them, caught up in this terrible struggle, especially Wilfred.

The baby held out her hands towards the flames flickering in the big grate. The brass fireguard threw back winking sparkles of light and the seamed coal released bubbles of oily moisture that hissed with a quiet satisfaction. Eventually Mons slept and Tallie almost did so, too, but jerked awake as Jeannie gently took the infant from her and said, 'Go on, now. Your sister's waiting to speak to you in the corridor.'

'My sister?' Words were beginning to lose their meaning for Tallie in her fatigue and she repeated the question almost stupidly. 'My sister?' Pushing through the swing doors she saw Kate at the far end of the corridor, pacing back and forth.

'What is it?' Shocked into a kind of awareness, Tallie advanced on Kate.

'This came.' Kate held out a telegram in its familiar envelope. 'Last night. I got in too late to bring it over.' Kate's face was white and sleepless. 'Open it,' she said. 'I've got to get to school.'

'It'll be about Wilfred,' said Tallie. It seemed to her the world and time had stopped and she and Kate inhabited some kind of echoing space.

'You won't know till you look,' said Kate.

'You open it.'

'I can't. Mother wanted me to. But it's yours.'

'Please Kate.' Tallie extended a pitiable hand with the missive in it.

Kate tore the envelope open and read aloud. Tallie took in words like 'regret to inform' and 'missing, believed killed' before she tore the paper out of Kate's grip and raced out in the dull, misty morning. She stood at the top of the hospital steps not knowing which way to turn, the paper limply in her hand. Kate came out slowly behind her. Tallie thought dully: she could be our mother, she looks so old.

'Oh Kate, what shall I do?' she appealed. 'Not Wilfred. Tell me not Wilfred.'

Kate leaned against the railings and said in a hard, deep voice which Tallie scarcely recognised as that of her sister: 'This bloody war. This bloody, bloody madness. Why Wilfred? The best man that ever lived?' She moved down the last of the steps as though crippled, as though the pain inside her doubled her up and broke her.

At last Tallie's own grief found itself. She screamed and shouted though she didn't know at whom. Shocked and horrified figures ran towards her and Matron of all people held her in a firm clasp against that iron bosom till she was quiet.

'Don't you go and get yourself killed too,' said Tallie.

She had agreed to go out with Toby Wilson, not because everybody said she should. She should try, they urged, not to forget Wilfred, heaven forbid, just let his ghost rest, to be brave and rebuild her life for she was young, wasn't she, and it was what Wilfred would have wanted. She went because Toby had been at school with her and there was friendship between them and he kept asking.

How did they know what Wilfred would have wanted? When she thought of him now, her mind was full of questions as to what he had been really like. She remembered the kisses, his gentleness, his laughter, the physical closeness. But he had come up from London bringing a whole different way of being, bringing quickness of mind in place of the slow, deep pace and prejudices of a Lowland town. A lot of his book-received wisdom had been inaccessible to her, the poetry he liked to quote impenetrable. Given time, she would have been able to make sense of it all, but time was the one thing they had not been given.

'I'll try not to get killed,' said Toby Wilson perseveringly, 'if you'll try and think of yourself as my girl.'

She wasn't prepared to spare him. 'I went with him,' she said stonily. They were sitting in the tearoom and the waitresses were far enough away not to hear her urgent whispering. 'Do you know what I'm saying? I was – his, I went with him. I loved him.' Her brimming eyes refused to leave his face till she knew he had taken it in.

He would have looked forbiddingly handsome in his officer's uniform, except for the new, untrimmed moustache. Unlike Wilfred, he had accepted the offer to be one of those in command and had just got his first pips before he came home on leave.

'I know what you're saying. It doesn't matter. I love you.' He leaned forward confidentially. 'Do you know why I didn't volunteer, why I waited till I was conscripted? It was because of not being able to give you up.'

'Even when you saw I was with Wilfred?'

'Even then. I was prepared to wait.'

'Well, that was foolish of you,' she said with compunction. 'I've always thought of you as more of a friend.'

'That was all right then, but not now. I want you to think of yourself as my girl. We could even get married on my embarkation leave. What about that? Things get tele-scoped, Tallie. I haven't got the time to wait now.'

'What if he came back?' she said relentlessly.

He laughed harshly. 'After all this time? If he had been saved, rescued, captured even, you would have heard by now. Missing presumed killed means just that, Tallie. We know there was gas, that it got thousands. And exposure did the rest.'

'I don't want to think about it,' she said piteously.

'He won't come back.'

'No,' she admitted. 'I know that.'

'I'll try to help you get over him. I'll listen all you want. If only you'll raise your head and look to the future. We could have a family even. You want children, don't you?'

She gave him a quick look. If only he knew how much! She had always thought of herself with a family, maybe two of each, and working with children had only increased this desire to have some of her own. She had even thought wildly she could adopt little Mons. But there would have to be a husband first . . .

'You see!' Toby knew he had hit home and in his triumph he was prepared to be more than generous. 'All I'll say is: think about it. You know, you're looking better already. It was a good decision to come out with me. What shall we do now? Would you like to go to the theatre?'

Now that it was her time off, that for the first time in months she felt some spark of interest in living, she had a sudden impulse to grab at it all. She wanted new clothes; she wanted to hear music; she wanted to dance; she wanted male company. It wasn't something she could ever talk about, it was so sinful she felt Fate would punish her unrelentingly for it, but deep, deep down at some primeval level she wanted the things that had happened to her body, with Wilfred, to happen to her again. There, she had thought it, and not been sticken. She knew she would feel guilt, that after this outing there would be criticism from others, that they would say, those in the village who were never short of judgement, that she hadn't taken long to forget.

She never would. The place Wilfred had occupied in her life was sacrosanct. But it was hers and his only. Only she knew the truth of her life. Sometimes the cloak of sorrow would wrap itself around her, she knew that, and like faint grace notes of an old tune she would remember the wonder of those first days when he'd lifted her out of the drudgery of her days by his love and intuition.

But if you were in this life, you might as well live it, the good as well as the bad. And how could it be bad to give Toby something to smile about? She looked at him as they walked up the street towards the Theatre Royal with a rush of genuine affection and when he pulled her arm through his, she did not draw away.

When he was taking her back to the nurses' home after the show, they discussed their respective families. She knew their relationship had changed since his declaration, that they were working their way towards something new.

'My mother has always thought a lot of you,' he confided. 'She told me the other day she thought we were right for each other. Will you come to tea on Sunday? Just to please her?'

She agreed, though not till after a moment reflection.

'My mother saw your Kate the other day. Hasn't she got a chap? Mother thought she looked a shade haggard.'

'Well, there's always the worry for all of us about Russell and Donald.' She did not add how stricken Kate had been over Wilfred. It seemed dog-in-the-mangerish to want to keep grief to yourself and perhaps Kate had been fond, in her way, of Wilfred, though she had had no right to him. Tallie did not know how to sort out her feelings properly towards her sister. Perhaps she never would. They had always watched points, all through their lives and Kate's instinct had always been to squash her and Belle, keep them in their place. But at the same time, she did not care for the more frequent inferences that Kate was destined for dry-as-dust spinsterhood. Nor did she like to see her pulling the first premature grey hairs from her head or the burden of work she seemed to take on at the Academy.

She thought: if I knew how to get closer to her, I would. But how can I comfort her, when I can't acknowledge she has any right to grieve? And she has not been able to say a word to me, not a single word to show she knows what I'm suffering.

Sometimes, out of the blue, like a sharp dagger blow, she felt pure unmitigated hatred for her sister. Even while she experienced if she knew it was infantile; it came from that time in childhood when emotions were raw and uncategorised, when they flew at each other in unbridled anger, tearing hair, scratching, biting, rolling over and over in mortal combat till they were separated, each crying 'It's her fault' or 'She took the biggest bit' or 'Why should she go?'

When Kate had come home from school with all the prizes she could still remember the dull, unbeautiful ache of envy she had felt and then how hard it had been to follow on in class after Kate and have teachers say 'You're not the scholar your sister was'. It had been even worse to see the gleam of unarticulated pride in their mother's eyes and know it could not be hers no matter how hard she tried. But Wilfred was hers. Wilfred had been hers. Not for anything would she yield a fragment of what he had been to Kate's keeping.

Almost as though he had divined something of what she had been thinking, Toby said, 'You've always got on better with Belle, haven't you?'

'Well, Belle's younger,' she said defensively.

'I can just picture her in her VAD uniform. I'll bet all the officers give her the eye.'

'She wants to go to Flanders. She wants to be where Russell is, and Donald.'

'Thank God you don't,' he said. 'Thank God I'll be able to think of you here at home.'

'Somebody has to nurse the children,' she said, thinking not just of Mons but how it had felt to be at the receiving end of Kate's sharp fists and elbows, as though part of you never stopped being a child and in need of comforting.

# Thirteen

Donald Candlish drew in a juddering breath as he looked out over Happy Valley. Was ever name applied with more killing irony? The last gathering point before the front line crawled with humans, cattle, machinery against a landscape like the backside of the moon. He watched almost detachedly as stretcher-bearers brought in the casualities from the latest battle. Sometimes in view of the carnage he thought these men were the bravest and toughest of all. For him and his men this past month had not been so much about fighting as just surviving the constant shelling and aerial bombardment.

It was that that stretched nerves to breaking point, because there was no chance, no hope of escape. And he was glad that after he had sorted the present bottleneck of supplies, ensured that reinforcements were on their way, he was due a week's leave in Montreuil. Dysentery had left him weak and finding it harder to keep a rein on his emotions. The major had warned him he would not be able to credit there was a war on once he reached Montreuil. He was privileged, he knew that. There was no Montreuil for the poor bloody infantry. But he also knew that he was at breaking point, that he would be no use to anybody unless he had some respite.

'Lucky bastard,' said Costen, enviously. The young subaltern was all of twenty, with the lined face of a forty year old.

'Just as it's hotting up again, you're off to lay your head on some buxom WAAC's bosom.' But his gaze was more compassionate than his tone. He had seen Donald's efforts to control the trembling in the dugout they had shared and besides, with a bit of luck his turn for a special pass would come.

None of them had been the same since the court-martialling. One day when it seemed as though the whole

German battery had been turned on them, and mustard gas had started seeping again over the lines, the corporal had simply refused orders and run off into the green mist. The fact that he'd had a 'Dear John' letter from home had been mentioned afterwards: the corporal had been the quiet sort who kept things to himself.

It was the CO who had ordered a public shooting *pour encourager les autres*, but it had been Donald who had to pin the white cloth to the man's heart, as target for the ten men who made up the firing squad on that cold, ice-grey dawn. Afterwards, even the company buffoon had been silent and the men went about the stinking trenches like ghosts.

What Donald could say to no one, not even the padre, was how close he himself had come to deserting, technically at least. Maybe they all had. On the day his batman, Grieves, had been blown up, three months before, he had found himself climbing out of the dugout, and running, before something stronger than instinct had stopped his feet and he had slid back in, his head and heart thudding louder than all the guns. The corporal should not have died for what was in so many of their hearts. He had fought hard to save him from his fate, but the fact was that the authorities were terrified of mass desertion as protests at the prolongation of the war were being made increasingly on the home front as well as among the men who could see no end to it. In the days after the corporal's ignominious end, the only comfort he had was in young Costen's comment on the corpse: 'Did you see his face? Peaceful, wasn't it? He was glad to be out of it.'

As the lorry finally ground its way out of mud, Donald sniffed the air and thought from the green mist in the distance there had probably been another gas wave not far away. Gradually, though, as they neared Montreuil, the battlefield odours faded, the sharp smell of cordite and the stink of dead horses left his nostrils and the perpetual explosive barrage receded. As they drove through the narrow streets of the lovely old walled town he even caught a glimpse of the sea, like a memory from childhood. It was impossible to believe that only sixty miles away men were still dying in the mud and cacophony, as the major had said. It was also impossible not to cling to this mirage, this miracle, this vision, like a drowning man to a lifebelt. For so long, the living and the dead had been so inextricably mixed together for Donald, sometimes in the trenches so impossible to define, that to see order, beauty, even flowers, brought a rush of emotion so powerful he could only weep.

He was past caring whether the driver saw his tears, but turned his face towards the maze of streets anyhow. The generals who walked the streets all seemed to him to be venerable men, their hair as white as that of the Prime Minister, Lloyd George, back home. He felt a surge of unreasoning hatred for them. All the old men who made the decisions and sent the young to their graves. Flower of manhood was the phrase used, wasn't it? He thought of the underfed slum boys in his charge. Stunted flowers, most of them. Grieves had had 'bowly' legs from childhood rickets. Even the colonels and majors here were middle aged, portly, looking, with the eccentric set of their caps, the cut of their hair, the fancy red hatbands and tabs and red and blue GHQ armlets, as though they were playing at war.

'Jesus!' he burst out in protest.

Without changing his expression the driver, a hard man from Consett, replied, 'It's got nothing to do with Him.'

'How do you think the Yanks will take it?' Donald mused almost to himself.

'Did well,' said Consett from the side of his mouth, 'to keep out of it for as long as they did.'

Donald considered the bitter comment. It did nothing for his morale to think of fresh-faced Americans from Vermont, from Virginia, from the Catskills, being part of the massacre in the trenches, where it was becoming increasingly difficult to sort out the living from the dead. Death was in everybody's hearts. Death grinned back at you when you put your head above the sandbags, from the barbed wire where it had stuck its hostages, from the stinking mud where it obscenely half-buried its corpses. And all for stretches of shell-cratered ground that could not be held by either side, that looked like being fought over for infinity. He felt he was going to throw up again but took a breath of the Montreuil air deep into his lungs. Had to get a grip. Maybe the only way to survive was to pretend, like the generals, that it wasn't really happening. To take Montreuil for what it was, a last ticket to survival in a mad, mad world.

'We're here,' said Consett. The house that had been requisitioned for officers' recuperation was a handsome old mansion in a quiet street, with neglected, straggly geraniums in pots in the flagged yard and inside bourgeois furnishing that still spoke of loving, familial care. It still seemed to him a kind of sacrilege to take over somebody's home, but he felt happier in his bedroom which had a white-spread cot bed, bare floor and impersonal feel to it. He didn't want knick-knacks impinging on his need just to *be*; he wanted nothing to invade the luxury of privacy, the greatest luxury, he was now convinced, in the whole world, after clean water.

Downstairs he had had to report first to a harpy in VAD uniform, who had taken details of his recent dysentery and decided a course of chemical food was in order, to build him up.

'Take full advantage of the opportunity for rest and relaxation,' she advised, not unkindly. 'Try to put the front from your mind, difficult though it may be.' She smiled, a thin gentlewoman's smile and he had a sudden dislocating vision of her going with her basket to the butcher or baker in some Surrey town like Guildford. Reluctantly, he smiled back and felt the first trickle of battle-strain ebb away like muddy water.

In his room, he looked as dispassionately as he could at the trembling of his hands. He was learning that the harder you tried to stop it, the more difficult it was. In a little, lying back, he began to feel calmer, thinking of pleasant things. They did exist. He could hear in his mind shouts from childhood games and see himself running the length of a rugby pitch with the ball clutched to his chest. He conjugated a Latin verb, thinking how he had enjoyed exploring the capabilities of his brain at school and university. And presently, drifting into sleep, he thought of Tibby, the golden hairs on her freckled forearms, her easy acceptance of her own physicality, her corn-coloured hair lying on his face, the sensation so lifelike he put a hand up as though to remove the tickling wisp.

The next day, after breakfast, he walked through the town. There were few of the original inhabitants to be seen and those who were visible looked sullen and uncommunicative, as, he felt, they had every right to be.

Suddenly, coming towards him, he witnessed the most amazing sight. Riding down the street, as if straight from Agincourt, rode the Commander-in-Chief with his two aides-de-camp, accompanied by an escort of Lancers.

He thought for a moment that he might have been hallucinating, so little had the pageant to do with what he had just known up the line. The horses were groomed to perfection, their glossy hides catching the morning sunshine and pennants and lances gleaming as though they had just been freshly drawn in a child's picture book. It was a wondrous sight, at once magnificent and intimidating and ludicrous and obscene. The noise from the animals' hooves rattled around in the cavity of Donald's mind long after the cavalcade had passed and then he hung on to a nearby railing, feeling waves of nausea wash over him till precipitately he brought up all of his breakfast and presumably the chemical food.

Base show, he thought. Over and over he thought it. Base show. We are given minds to use and we permit not only the killing of young men whose seed has barely settled between their legs and then this vain panoply, this mockery of what is really happening.

His legs still feeling weak from the nausea, he pushed his way into the officers' club. A girl carrying a tray of drinks passed him, the red and blue GHQ colours in ribbons in her abundant golden hair and as she passed she tilted her mouth in a smile. That was ragtime they were playing, he thought. Scott Joplin, surely. He'd heard it in New York. He walked past the band and took a seat, waiting to order a whisky, thinking back to the landed gentry who were always up on a horse. He did not often remember his own father, or think about the farm labourers before him, but suddenly their plodding laborious lives seemed altogether more redeemable than those who maintained tradition at the expense of the hackled, the unshod, the unconsulted.

'First time here?' The young subaltern with his left arm in a sling sat down beside him and dextrously offered him a cigarette from a silver case. Donald took it and gratefully inhaled, nodding and saying with a rueful intensity, 'Beats Happy Valley, I'll say that.'

'Women,' said the officer, who introduced himself as Percy Barnett. 'There are *women*, old son. You forget what a woman smells like.' Two young WAACs strolled by and Percy beckoned them, offering to buy them a drink.

'Polly' – the girl pointed to herself – 'and this is Isa,' said the darker, more forward of the two. To Percy Barnett she said casually, 'Bought it, did you?' and equally casually he answered, 'Stopped one' and they turned enquiringly on Donald who answered with the same brevity 'Stomach' and after that the war wasn't mentioned. They talked about the tunes the band played; they talked about musicals they'd seen back home in Blighty; they talked about dance steps and soon they were even executing them and laughing as the Polly girl put her arm round Percy because he couldn't put his round her.

They weren't a patch on Tibby, Donald decided, but they were light relief; they could take a joke and holding a girl was better than holding a juddering machine-gun. He and Percy made a foursome with them for a day or two and gradually got to know a bit of each other's backgrounds, to put up with each other's eccentricities and idiosyncrasies, like Percy's execrable sense of humour, Polly's prudery over swear words and Isa's occasional moody silences. Unlike Percy, the girls came from humble artisan

104

backgrounds and were slowly feeling their way through the social levels and pot-holes that applied at GHQ.

After the fourth day, he began to think about getting back. There was no way of making the idea tolerable. He looked into the pit of his recollections and all he saw was horror. But he was also strangely fatalistic, as though the blood that flowed through his veins was a tired old blood and that if it had to be let there would not be much difference between it and the mud it seeped into.

Percy Barnett brought in a days-old copy of *The Times* and showed him a letter which the poet Siegfried Sassoon had sent out and which had been read out in the House of Commons back home.

'He says the war is being prolonged and that the sufferings are evil,' said Percy, his tone flat and without inflection. 'What chances are there they'll listen to him?' For once the look between the two men was free of cover-up or pretence.

'We could always mutiny, like the French at Aisne.'

'If you read Horatio Bottomley back home death in war ensures our salvation,' said the other. His mouth moved into a caricature of a grin. 'There can't be a bigger bastard left alive, than Horatio Bottomley. Yet it's him they listen to back home.'

They both swore then and confided their rage to each other.

'No one'll push me about when it's all over,' said Percy. 'And no mealy-mouthed so-called patriot will take me in. War is evil, period, full stop. There must never be another.'

'Amen to that,' said Donald wearily. Words were ineffective. Poets were no longer relevant, even if they were fighting poets. All he prayed for was the strength to climb on the lorry when it came to take him back.

He said so to the other and Percy put his good hand on his shoulder and squeezed it. 'Three more days, old boy,' he volunteered. 'Let me get you a gin. We've got to make the most of it.'

The girls joined them as usual when they came off duty,

but they had got wind they might be sent on admin to a field hospital and they were both a bit more restrained than usual.

'You're not listening,' Polly protested vexatiously at a point in the evening when the band had taken a break and the glasses were empty. She followed Donald's gaze and picked up a small knot of people just coming through the door. There were two officers, one with bandaged hands and another with bandages over his eyes and they were being ushered in by two nervous VADs, fussing like starchy sheep-dogs. Before the smaller of the two women turned around Donald said, 'Belle! It's Belle!' and started from his seat. He had known from the gestures and the hands, unlikely though it seemed. Perhaps he had known from something deeper in him. When the girl turned a startled face he saw it was indeed his sister and the officers and other VAD insisted the two should sit down together and celebrate the chance meeting.

'When did you get here?'

'Just today. And you?'

'I've been here four days. Getting over dysentery.'

'Are you all right?'

'Right as rain.'

'You don't look right as rain to me.'

At the end of the evening, he said desperately, 'Somehow we've got to see a bit of each other before I go back.'

'I'm working, Donald,' she protested. 'Is it Saturday you go? I'll try to get a couple of hours on Friday. I can't promise, you know how it is.'

'Will you be going to a field hospital?'

'Going *back*.'

'How was it?'

'As you might expect.'

He swallowed. Her jaunty restraint was something that touched him deeply.

The band was playing Joplin again when they met up on the Friday and she did a little jaunty two-step as she came towards him, still in her nurse's uniform with the bright fuzzy hair well tucked away under her cap. They sat down in a corner in a concentrated huddle, each determined to extract the last possible ounce of news from the other.

'Is Tallie getting over Wilfred?'

'She's going to marry Toby Wilson. You know, old Jug Ears. He's a major now, like yourself.'

He could not get over his surprise. 'I wouldn't have thought –'

'That she'd ever get over Wilfred? Seems she has.'

'But –' He didn't want Wilfred consigned to nothingness like that. It seemed like an affront to his own precarious being.

'Life still has to go on,' said Belle, with an extreme gentleness of tone and delivery.

'Any word of Russell?'

She looked away from him uncomfortably. 'Not really.'

'What does that mean? Tell me.'

'Well, the letters don't get through, any more than they have done from you, but so far, so good, fingers and everything else crossed.' The fresh young face gazing into his was serious, but not, he felt, wholly frank.

'There's something you're not telling me.'

'I have to warn you about Mother. She's suddenly quite an old woman, Donald.'

'Something. Something – something else. Is it about Russell?'

She twisted her fingers, fingers scrubbed to a hygienic pink.

'Well, you see—' She broke off distractedly. 'No. I can't tell you.'

'Go on.' Stonily.

'He and Tibby—'

'Go *on*. What about him and Tibby?'

'They got together, you know. For God's sake, Donald, I don't see why I have to be pig-in-the-middle, but he – took up where you left off. They had this – affair, he's mad about her and she saw him, the day of the picnic, in the altogether and that was it; she's always been a bit wild, Tibby, but why should I apologise for her, I'm just telling you how things are.' She stopped, ostensibly for breath and then came straight out with it. 'The baby – little Catriona – well, she's his and they are going to get married just as soon as ever they can; he's praying for leave—'

He didn't say anything at first. She thought it must have been like getting knocked in the solar plexus and she was distressed beyond measure that she had been forced to tell him the situation, but what way out had there been? He would have kept on and on at her till she revealed everything; he had always known when she was being secretive as a child: he was smarter than all of them. She looked at him now, her clever, bright, handsome brother, the one who had been destined to shine in a great career and she saw that he had steel after all, that where she had thought him scholar-soft the war had hardened him and that pale and ill though he looked, more *wounded* somehow than those with physical hurts, he had enough left of the Candlish pride for dissembling.

'Who would have said,' he wondered, 'that the little bugger had it in him?'

I would, Belle thought. He had it in him to be as clever and achieving as you, but because you were the first, the treasured one in Mother's eyes, he thought it was no contest, until it came to Tibby.

'You always sided with him,' said Donald now.

'I didn't!' she felt it necessary to deny it then found herself expostulating: 'Donald, you were always a law unto yourself. Mother built you up into a kind of god. There were times when we all hated you.' She smiled to take the sting out of this and covered his hand with one of hers. 'It's difficult now. I feel closer to you now, now that we're grown up. I don't take sides now, even when Kate and Tallie are having one of their brushes. Not even between you and Russell.'

She thought his eyes had moistened.

He said very deliberately, 'You look after yourself.

Don't let any officer johnnie like Percy Barnett soft-soap you after I've left here. Into doing anything you don't want to, I mean.'

'I don't know what you're getting at.'

'Yes, you do.' Suddenly he grinned. 'You must have noticed he's a bit smitten already.'

# Fourteen

She wished Donald hadn't said anything about Percy Barnett, because after her brother had gone back up the line, Belle was conscious of Barnett's presence at every turn, gazing at her, she began to think, beseechingly.

She had to dress his arm – the wound was taking longer than expected to heal and she was filled with silent admiration for the stoicism with which he took her not always very skilful ministrations. The arm was not ever going to be much good to him now, the shrapnel having destroyed a fair part of the upper section but at least the surgeons had managed to save it.

'What do you do in civilian life?' she asked him curiously one day, helping him to light a cigarette after a dressing.

'I was starting out as a journalist.' He smiled at the flicker of interest. 'Oh nothing notable; just an underling on a county rag.'

'Will you go back there?'

'Certainly. Can't wait.'

How will you manage to use a typewriter, she had been on the point of asking, then bit her tongue. Give him his due, he didn't look the sort who would give in. There would, she felt, always be a way round for someone like Percy Barnett. She felt a flustering begin inside her, because it seemed she was always seeing things about him to approve. His readiness with a joke, his light baritone singing snatches from popular songs to point up some slyly amusing situation, his determination to divert when gloom about the latest battle filtered into GHQ.

Sometimes it maddened her, made her want to shake him and insist; be serious. But then if you really were being serious about the war it became unbearable, so maybe his way was the right one. But then what about that beseeching look? He was adept at covering his insecurities, but they were surely there. Donald had told her the young officer was barely twenty-one yet had already seen nearly three years' service. Some of his work, mysterious and undefined, had been with Intelligence. That meant you had to have a secretive, careful nature and he never gave anything away that he shouldn't. Yet he looked so lonely that Belle was touched in a way she had never been before. She began to scold herself mentally for allowing someone who could be no more than a ship passing in the night to take up so much of her thinking. She was beginning to succeed because she had a disciplined nature – thanks to her mother – when Percy asked her to meet him one evening so that they could have a walk and a talk.

'You're very quiet.' They had strolled under an avenue of handsome trees and come to a point where a seat had thoughtfully been provided by a resident so that a splendid view of the town could be enjoyed. An angelus rang out in the quiet evening air and there was even the sound of a reaping machine in a nearby field, reminding Belle of Perringhall and home. Just that day she had had to treat an officer suffering from gangrene and she was still emotionally stirred up and upset. She tried to smile at Percy Barnett and instead found she was weeping. 'It's the quiet, the peacefulness,' she protested.

'You've tried,' said Percy sympathetically. 'How old are you, Belle?'

'Twenty.'

'Was it pretty bad, back at the hospital?'

'Dressings,' she said briefly. 'Sometimes we had to yank them off without steeping them. Dressings. And the smell.'

'But you'd rather not talk about it?'

'Not really. You have to get away. Sometimes.'

He gave her a look full of expressive sympathy and said, 'Do you have some fellow up to his armpits in love with you?'

She smiled slowly and a little tremulously. 'Not really.'

'Not really or not at all?'

'Not at all.'

'What's the matter with them, back home there in – where is it? Somewhere in wildest Scotia?'

'Not wildest anything. Just a nice place not far from Glasgow. I was thinking of it when I heard the farmer over there. Brings it all back.' And she sniffed, not altogether elegantly and balled her hankie to her eyes. He was looking at her a bit quizzically, something unfathomable in the treacle-dark gaze and she said defensively, 'What about you? Have you ever had a girl?'

'Depends what you mean by had.'

'Oh, no,' she said – and there it was, he was flustering her again – 'I don't mean . . . I just mean, have you fancied someone? In a nice way,' she added and then wished she hadn't.

He was laughing at her. 'What a hopeless little prig you are. But it's what I like about you.'

'You haven't answered my question,' she persisted.

He turned away from her and said in hard, angry tones, 'Not a million miles away there are places where the men go to – you know, relieve the strains of being away from their wives. I've seen a few with a ferocious dose of the clap as a result.' He gave her a glinting, half-haunted, half-humorous look. 'Haven't summoned up the courage myself.'

'So you've never been – involved?'

'Not really.' He turned to her almost as though control had given way to desperation and said. 'Would you let me kiss *you*? What would you think if I did?'

'I don't know.' Her head was whirling. It wasn't how she had envisaged this sort of thing at all. Surely it should just happen, not with a discussion beforehand. But he was looking at her with an almost comic urgency, twisting his cap in his hands and all of a sudden something in her surrendered. 'Go on then. I suppose you could.'

She kept her eyes open. Although she had flirted she had never been kissed by a man. His young lips were very tentative and a little cold. Maybe if she closed her eyes, then. . . . She was thinking of Russell and Tibby, how different it must have been for them, a tide that carried them off their feet: and even of Tallie and Wilfred, all that hand-holding and big-eyed gazing. This was just a little on the ludicrous side. Miss Touch Me Not with Mr No Experience. Laugher burbled up inexplicably from somewhere. She put her arms up and pulled his head down harder. He broke away momentarily to say, 'Oh Christ' and then came back to kiss her so hard and hungrily it felt like bruising.

Was this then how you got to know somebody? Really know them? She took from his embrace all the hard loneliness and desire of a soldier's life and gave back the timidity and fear which, despite an outward show of confidence, she had always felt towards men. The strange thing was how quickly what they both started out with, went, to be replaced immediately by a warm confluence of feeling, a kind of rapture that knocked both of them sideways.

They broke apart, embarrassed and almost afraid to look at each other and then laughing held each other close again, her being careful of his injured arm – oh, so careful – and him pulling her ever closer to him with his good one. This time the kiss was less frenetic, it went on a long time; they both wanted it to go on and on. And on. When they stopped, she grasped his good hand as though she would never let it go.

'You know I'm leaving tomorrow.' He didn't meet her gaze.

'I guessed.'

'I wish we'd had more time.'

'Yes.' The tears gushed to her eyes.

'You're the first girl I've ever kissed. Believe it or not. Not a lot of opportunity, you could say.'

She put a hand on his cheek, coquetting in a way she hadn't known she could do. 'How was it?'

'Wonderful. Look, could we go somewhere even quieter? I want to kiss you some more.'

They found a quiet spot behind a copse where they held and touched and kissed one another. She was not sure what was happening to him, but at one point his body convulsed and he fell against her, crying out savagely as his body weight fell on his injured arm. She could feel something sappy and wild rising up in her too but knew it was too soon; it was too indiscreet; it was sinful; it should wait and she calmed him, calmed them both, holding his head against her breast, teasing the thick hair with her fingers and filled with a love so outgoing and tender it seemed to her for a little while to embrace the whole world and the struggles in it.

At last he sat up, looked at his watch and said, with all the rue in the world, 'We've got to get back.' Compassionately his eyes raked her, the pretty nimbus of hair, the face changed and softened with desire and he said softly, 'Angel. My darling girl. Do you know how beautiful you are?'

'I wish you didn't have to go,' she said.

'Job to do.'

'Take care. Take enormous care.'

'Of course I will.' His old rakish look returned as he pushed the hair out of his eyes and donned his cap once more. 'I'll keep my head down, never fear. But so must you.'

He touched her hair and dress, almost shyly, as if to reassure himself of their existence. 'I just wish I had something to give you, some keepsake.' Impulsively he pulled a gold signet ring from his little finger. In the centre a

113

tiny but brilliant diamond winked. 'Would you wear this?' Artlessly she held out her right hand and he pushed it on to the third finger, lifting both finger and ring to his lips. 'To remember me by.'

'Will you write?' Her throat felt crushed.

'I'll try. But I don't know where I'll be – or you'll be – and it might be a bit useless. But write anyhow, we'll both write. And afterwards –'

'I've nothing to give you,' she intervened.

'I'd like your photo.'

'I'll have one taken.

When they parted he said urgently, 'Don't forget what I look like, will you?'

'Think of me every day. At one o'clock. And I'll think of you.' She looked at the ring, knowing what it had cost him to part with it. 'It's a beautiful ring, Percy. I'll treasure it forever.'

The next morning he had gone.

The third battle of Ypres, known as Passchendaele, began at the end of July, 1917, and instead of getting home to marry Tibby, as he had devoutly hoped after an injury to his foot, Russell Candlish moved up the line, taking the mud, the rain and the shelling once more for granted. The foot had mended quickly, too quickly, and every last man was needed for the assault. The indescribable had become worse. Aerial warfare added to the nightmare on the ground and tanks made the indescribable mud worse still. When the shelling allowed, he took out the sepia photograph Tibby had sent, of her and his daughter, and the bright-eyed, golden-haired child stared gravely out at him, pleading with him to come home and identify himself to her. 'She can say Daddy now,' Tibby wrote to him. 'She points to your picture and says your name.'

Also when he had time he thought of his brother Donald. A letter from Belle had informed him that Donald knew, that he had taken the information of his and Tibby's alliance rather well on the whole.

114

He did experience feelings of guilt now. Sometimes he looked back on the raw lad he had been in the Rows with something like appalled regret. Everything he had done in those days had been with a kind of blind ferocious instinct. He had resented and hated Donald for almost as long as he could remember but now he saw family wasn't just about that, about rivalries and grudges, it was also about loving someone whose blood was the same, who was subjected to the same dangers. It had taken the army to prove he could be as good as Donald, the army and Tibby, of course. That she could love him as well as being ready to submit to his clumsy, ardent fumblings was something that had gradually quietened and civilised him. For her sake and the baby's he was prepared to make a proper go of things after the war: get a decent education and go into something steady like teaching or even the Civil Service and there would be politics to take up the wild side of him, for there was still a part of him that wanted to fight and scrap for the underdog and there would be plenty of these when this dread calamity ended. But only since leaving home had he realised how ignorant he was.

He did not know what made him sit down one day and write to his brother, care of Belle. Partly it was seeking encouragement to go on with his education after the war. He remembered now how Donald, with all his faults, had tried to get him to stay on at school and had lost patience with him when he wouldn't hear of it. Their arguments had been more about the wild unstated rivalries that being brothers involved, with no logical sense to them on his part. Now he wanted Donald to see how he had changed – he had got his sergeant's stripes a month ago, so that proved something – and hoped that Donald would be able to suggest the practical steps he should take to achieve his ambitions after the war. He wanted Donald's approval, he supposed.

But more than that, he was groping for forgiveness. Although he and Tibby had fallen into a bit of passion one sunny afternoon, almost like a mantrap, and although what he felt for her and maybe she for him was the strongest emotion they had ever known, he had been aware, even when her golden flesh had been at its most seductive, her honeyed breath at its warmest, that he was taking something away from Donald that he shouldn't. It was the vain glorious triumph he still felt that was humbling, that made him think he was in need of grace. Belle's letter, reassuring him that Donald had 'got over everything', had been more than welcome, but now he wanted to go on and restore something that perhaps had never been right in the first place, some kind of relationship with his brother.

In the dugout with the flickering Davy lamp and the crunch of bombardment overhead, he laboured over his writing on the lined notepad:

You will be surprised to hear from me, but not half as surprised as I am to be writing to you. But it came to me the other day you and I know things now that the others at home don't know and even brave little Belle (ain't she?) doesn't. We know what battle means, bugs in your clothes, mud on your boots etc etc. Need I go on? So hullo from me to you and I hope and I am glad there are no hard feelings for I intend to be a reformed character when all this is over. You can believe me. And Donald, let me say I am sorry, and mean it.

He rambled on, knowing he was not expressing himself very well, but when you kept sliding off the mud you sat on and the feeble light in the trench flickered with every crunch of sound, was it surprising? He felt some kind of burden lifted from him when he had finished and given the letter over for posting. Somehow he felt then that Tibby and the child were more wholly his and he looked at the photo from home till the light faded entirely and it was almost pitch black, with the incessant rain still coming down.

There was no time or space for introspection in the days

ahead. At last Passchendaele was taken but proved impossible to hold. Inches of ground were fought over with a kind of insane insistence that went beyond bravery. Sometimes in the trenches it was difficult to tell the living from the dead and Russell began to think it was his own doppelganger that barked out orders, rallied weary men, fed the guns. He was totally efficient but in a sleep-walking kind of way, a way that did not allow for any human weakness, any time to mourn his fellows who were dying daily.

What they said to each other was that it couldn't go on. If all war was senseless, this was the most senseless war of all, for there was never any outcome except death in great numbers. It could not go on, but it did. It was as though a great kind of disembodied evil stalked the battlegrounds refusing to release its grip. Tired men marched in their sleep; some lost their boots in the mud; some had nothing but hard tack to eat; some died on the barbed wire, some with mustard gas filling their lungs, some with shrapnel tearing their limbs apart, some in No Man's Land; some shook, uncontrollably; a few ran, but most went on, knowing they would never forgive those who had done this to them, that some crime was being committed against humanity that would weigh heavy on the scales till doomsday itself.

Russell Candlish kept going in the Third Battle of Ypres, known as Passchendaele. In the rare times when the guns were quiet, he sometimes thought he heard a tiny voice singing, somewhere out in No Man's Land, and imagined that he saw the image of a little girl in a blue cotton dress, running and throwing a ball in the air. He knew it was his mind playing tricks and that of course it wasn't his child Catriona. But at the beginning of the war the soldiers in the British Army had sworn they saw an angel in the sky at the Battle of Mons. Men imagined that dead squaddies had come back to fight alongside them in the trenches. So who knew what was real and was not, any more?

The relentless torrential rain wrecked the streams and

dykes of Flanders drainage and the Passchendaele quagmire swallowed up everything that fell off the duck-boards.

# *Fifteen*

Tallie pushed the brass fender with her toe and the old-
fashioned rocking chair moved back and forward with the
motion that had quietened a legion of fretful babies. Had
she slept? She looked at her fob watch and judged that if
she had, it had been for no more than a few minutes. The
ward was beautifully, peacefully asleep. A little smile
played on her lips. It wouldn't be long till they sat up and
groped excitedly in the Christmas stockings they had been
promised. She and Jeannie Gray had made sure each child
had some little toy, a picture book, a few sweets. Even that
was more than most of them would ever have had before.

Her big family. That was how it seemed to her. 'A true
nurse,' old Dr Hutchison had taken to saying of her. 'The
true nurse has an instinct for her patient that takes her
beyond mere medical care.' His wise old marmoset face
had lit up with approbation. 'It's a gift. Nurse Candlish has
it.' Matron's face did not betray any emotion during such
commendations – she was never in favour of getting above
yourself – but even she was now prepared to trust Candlish
when she judged a crisis was over or a certain child well
enough to go back home.

While she had rested, Tallie had been half-thinking,
half-dreaming of the day when she might have a family of
her own. It was getting nearer. In the old days it would have
been unthinkable for a married woman to keep on nursing
but Matron had been forced by dire shortages to compro-
mise. Tallie could carry on till such times as Toby was
demobbed and they were actually setting up home

together. They had decided her home would be with his parents in the meantime.

And now the New Year's Day wedding was almost upon them. She had decided against white, not because she was no longer a virgin but because it seemed practical to choose a suit that would be useful afterwards. But Toby had insisted it should be rather special and it was – a beautiful ruby red with the lapels encrusted in jet beads and there was a matching hat to go with it. She would carry a small mixed bouquet, with a few holly sprigs in it – Jeannie's idea.

Strange, she reflected now, the circumstances that had made the wedding suddenly possible. A spurt of dire anxiety went through her. Toby was going to need careful handling in the days ahead. Not because, like some, he had returned from the front wounded or shell-shocked. But because a vicious bout of influenza followed by pneumonia had nearly put paid to him altogether and left him so weakened and frail there had been talk of his demob, never mind keep him away from the fighting as being more of a liability than anything else.

For someone else, this might have seemed like an intervention from on high, but Toby felt it keenly that he had never left Great Britain's shores. The commission of which he had been so proud had turned to dust and ashes. It was no good Tallie reassuring him that he did valuable and necessary work behind the scenes. He felt scaldingly vulnerable whenever he saw war returnees, men in blue uniform, men with sticks or crutches. 'You didn't ask to get ill,' she argued furiously, and nowadays he didn't even make any rejoinder. 'Your turn might still come,' she would persevere. But privately she knew it would not. There was a dread in her that Toby's lungs would not recover and she knew there were some who thought she was foolish to take on such an uncertain quantity.

It was difficult to explain to them. Toby diminished, gaunt and sickly was still Toby to her – the boy she had watched outstrip the others on school sports day, the class clown and rebel, the youth who'd carried home her books

119

and been there for her when Wilfred had gone missing. In some ways they were now so inextricably linked it was positively dangerous. If she withdrew her strength and support, she saw Toby withering away like an old branch on a tree.

When Jeannie went on about how romantic it was, her and Toby, all Tallie could think was that that wasn't the way it was at all. Wilfred had been romantic, what she and he had felt for each other, but Toby was the familiar, bred almost in her bones as she in his and she saw this as perhaps better, more sustainable. If anyone could restore Toby to health, she could. She could pour her strength into him, boundlessly. She was fiercely glad, without conscience, he did not have to go to the front. Hadn't they taken enough? Ever since Wilfred had gone she had loathed the war, hated those who still defended it, wanted it ended no matter how. When people complained that things had gone quiet on the Western Front all she had been able to think of was the lives saved. Long might the quiet go on. Surely the League of Nations had to come up with an answer, a formula for the peace?

Why should Jeannie's little comment about romance return to niggle at her now, in the soft-breathing semi-dark of the night ward? Why should she suddenly be able to 'see' Wilfred again, in her mind's eye, when for months she had not been able to fill in the features on his face with any clarity?

It was gone for ever, wasn't it, all that innocent joy she and Wilfred had known? Toby and she had something different, that was all. She felt like remonstrating with the guileless Jeannie, whose heard was filled with silly notions from penny novelettes, to make up for the romance she would probably never find herself, being shy and a bit plain and one of the growing numbers of women whose partners would have been the war dead. She shouldn't get angry with Jeannie, who was kind and endlessly willing. But the ache her words had started wouldn't go away, the ache for what might have been, the bittersweet ache to see Wilfred one more time, smiling and laughing as he came out with some silly anecdote from school or teased her about the solemn dedication to 'being awfu' good' which he detected as the central stratum of her nature.

She got up, quite precipitately, shaking out her dress skirt and apron, fearful of Matron's charge of looking crumpled. Softly she tiptoed up the ward, looking at each sleeping child, touching a hot cheek here, smoothing back a hair there. At the end cot she came to Mons, Mons who had been there longer than anybody, Mons who called to her still but by the Scottish 'mammy' rather than the earlier '*maman*'. To Tallie, the dark-eyed, darker-skinned little girl was more beautiful than any other child she had ever seen. She wasn't sturdy and red-cheeked like Scottish children, but had the bones of a fairy, Tallie had always thought, acknowledging the whimsicality.

They had shaved her head in the beginning but Tallie had resisted this and Mons now had soft dark curls that spilled around that perfect alabaster face, with its sweep of dark lashes, its quick mouth that looked as if any second it would break into smiles or protestation.

She felt the stocking at the end of Mons' bed. The doll in the pink dress was that bit more desirable than the toys in the other children's stockings. But then the others had parents, had brothers and sisters and a home to return to when they got better. With any luck they would see plenty more Christmases. Not little Mons.

Tallie looked down at the angelic sleeping child. Matron had always warned them not to get emotionally involved, but there had been this bond between herself and Mons right from the start, one the child recognised before she did. Matron's advice was good advice, but nurses were women, not automata. It would have taken a heart of stone to resist Mons' anguished cries of '*maman*', not to have given the desperately sick little girl the affection she needed. But of course all the love in the world was sometimes not enough. She had watched helplessly as the little body was laid waste by the TB germ, but she knew

121

Mons' unvanquishable spirit would rise with cries of joy to match those of the other children on Christmas morning and pictured her face as she held the doll in the pink dress to her.

Something rose in her throat that she could not swallow. Humbly she acknowledged that Mons had taught her all she knew about not giving in. She touched the child's coverlet, smoothing it with gentle fingers. 'Happy Christmas, little Mons,' she whispered and passed back up the ward towards her desk once more.


On the day of Tallie's wedding, Kate rose early and stirred the kitchen fire of Cullington Lodge into fresh life. Ellen Siddons would come in later but had imperiously indicated she did not know when, as she and her family would be celebrating Hogmanay, with all its customary first-footing, whisky and black bun, the night before. The war had given people like Ellen scarcity value, Kate thought, and made them a good deal more bolshie and difficult to dominate. Maybe the time would come when domestic service would die out altogether, except for the very rich.

Kate had everything set out anyhow, from the clothes she would wear to the table where she and her mother would partake of their usual breakfast of porridge and toast. She lifted the heavy iron pot in which the rich oatmeal had been gently cooking over the banked-up range all through the night and spooned generous portions into wide-lipped plates. Her mother came downstairs with a grey woollen crocheted shawl over her thick flannel nightie and sat down to join her. They did not speak till Kate had set the brown teapot on the table and the toast and marmalade at the ready. Then Janet Candlish said, 'A cold day for a wedding.' And she shivered.

'They'll not feel the cold,' said Kate, feeling some such qualification was necessary. She was curiously ambivalent about the whole thing, about Tallie appearing to put Wilfred behind her so easily, about the wisdom of them marrying anyhow, given Toby's precarious state of health, but you got caught up in the spurious sense of excitement, she'd found, whether you wanted to or not. The Wilsons had insisted on having the reception at their place, Toby being their only son and their position as shop-owners giving them access to fare other people couldn't provide. Mrs Wilson found the whole business of entertaining to her liking, while it was generally accepted that Janet Candlish was not one to go in much for socialising, beyond the occasional strategic cup of tea when she wanted to extract some goblet of news or gossip from her 'victim'. Janet had given in to Mrs Wilson's pleas to do the catering without too much of a formal struggle.

Kate looked concernedly at her mother now. No doubt about it, the war and its worries had taken its toll on her and she was looking frailer than ever. 'I'll boost up the fire for your bath,' she promised, giving the grate's cinders an unceremonious raking and piling dry sticks and small lumps of coal on top so that soon there was a hearty crackling and spitting and a forest of darting flames. She went into the scullery and lugged the zinc bath off the wall, placing it in front of the fire and pouring in water from two kettles and pots that had been warming overnight with the porridge. She put a large towel to warm and hung her mother's fresh undergarments to air on the chain above the fire. Finally she placed a screen beside the bath, for her mother insisted on her privacy. She herself had had her customary cold bath upstairs, part of her health regime along with an ever-open bedroom window as set out in *Women's Health and Beauty Magazine*. She was so hardy now she scarcely noticed the exigencies of a cold morning. Mind over matter was what she told herself, sternly.

She hadn't concerned herself very much about what to wear, but as she was to be Tallie's best maid a new winter's coat had seemed in order and she had chosen navy instead of the dark brown she normally favoured. It had bands of braiding round the hem and frogging down the front and she had picked a small hat, instead of the more usual deep-crowned and large-brimmed millinery, and had braiding put on it too. The effect was a bit Cossack, she thought, though she wasn't sure if Cossacks still existed in the new proletarian Russia. At any rate, the outfit would still be useful after the wedding and she supposed it lifted morale to have something smart to wear. Sometimes with her burden of work she was too tired to care very much about being female.

Her mother never wore anything but black but had purchased a sealskin coat to put the Wilson family in their place and a new toque hat with plumage, flowers and veiling sufficient to quell any Wilson upstart who might think themselves better than the Candlishes. Kate permitted herself a small smile as she checked out her mother's finery. She saw her mother's little vanities as forgivable. 'Your gloves aren't here, Mother,' she called over the screen. 'Where are they?'

Janet's voice came back at her, sharp and peremptory. 'I'll get them myself. I know where they are. Leave them, I said.'

'And so do I know where they are.' Kate was already half upstairs, to look in the top drawer of the tallboy where her mother kept her smaller items of finery, such as rings, gloves, parasols, umbrellas. Everything was carefully wrapped in tissue paper and put away each Sunday after kirk.

Kate found the gloves quickly, fine kid as befitted Sunday best. It was as she was closing the drawer that a scrap of colour caught her eye and from under the drawer lining she slowly drew forth what looked like a hastily opened envelope. She looked at the name on the front and saw with a start that it was Tallie's and then as her heart began to beat a slow warning tattoo she drew out the letter and saw it was from the War Office.

She read: 'We are pleased to inform you. . . .' The rest of the words jumbled themselves up in her mind so wildly that at first they were beyond comprehension. Then, as she made herself become calm, to breathe slowly and deeply, she could make sense of what she read. Wilfred was not dead. Wilfred had been brought back from Flanders and was in a hospital called Craiglockhart in Edinburgh.

She knew at once what had happened. The news had been sent to Tallie because Wilfred had named her as his next-of-kin, but Janet had taken it on herself to open the missive. And keep back the news. No wonder she had been apparently quiet and subdued these past few days. The enormity of her mother's action struck Kate like a heavy thump on the back. But why, why? Had it been to protect Tallie; had it been because Janet had never really liked Wilfred and preferred Tallie to have the security and comfort of marrying into well-off, well-doing trade? Had it been to save upset? From kindness or malice? Kate realised she did not know her parent well enough to prognosticate on her reasons. But she had no option now but to go down and confront Janet. This was a cruel and peremptory injustice towards Tallie and Janet could not be allowed to get away with it.

And yet . . . something stayed Kate's passage. Could she really upset the applecart on the day of Tallie's actual wedding? Tallie had made her choice and if she changed her mind now so many people would be devastated.

But Kate knew that wasn't all. Underneath the shock of what she had just read, something more atavistic, more powerful, more totally selfish was running its wild course. Wilfred was safe! Wilfred was home! It was true that perhaps she had had no right to love the man who was her sister's, but if Tallie had turned to someone else, then where did that leave Kate? Already she was on a train to Edinburgh, already she was walking down a ward full of the wounded, already she was picking him out and putting her arms around him and holding him, never to let him go.

Kate went slowly, almost dizzily, back downstairs and held the letter out towards her mother.

'Why did you do this, Mother?'

'You found it,' said Janet flatly.

'We should tell her,' Kate managed to get out. 'Even at this late date.'

'I'm telling her nothing,' Janet's face, though pale, was set and determined. 'If she marries Toby Wilson, she'll never want.'

'But she loved Wilfred.'

Janet laughed. 'What does that mean? You know what the old song says: "Love is bonnie, a little while, while it is new". That nonsense you're talking about, that never lasts.

'If you've any sense, you'll never mention that letter to anyone, either. Do you hear me?'

Kate pushed the missive into her handbag.

'Oh, God, I hope you know what we're doing.'

# *Sixteen*

They came out of Perringhall Parish Church into a brief, cold blink of winter sun and somebody threw rice. The photographs seemed to take for ever and Tallie was concerned that Toby would get chilled. Somebody commented then: 'It's a shame that Belle couldn't be here' and Tallie thought of the other two blanks there would be in the pictures: no Russell, no Donald. Maybe that was what made her mother look so – *alone* was perhaps the only word for it. If only she would smile, this once and let that harsh reserve go. Isn't she happy for me, just this once?

'Doesn't Tallie look lovely?' Jeannie Gray whispered in Kate's ear and Kate thought, yes, she does, she has something I can't put my finger on, some extra, soft, seductive quality I don't have, that brings men to her. All the old doubts about her own attractiveness flooded back: she had this confronting, upsetting manner, and then there was her sallow skin and the mark that showed up under her eye, especially in the cold. Only Wilfred had known what she was really like, someone desperate for warmth, like a

126

stray cat wanting to sneak into the hearth on a bitter night. *Wilfred!* She gave her tight-lipped mother a guilty stare, unable to believe what they had just done. The collusive evidence seemed almost to burn a hole in her handbag, yet the fact of it being there was a kind of strengthening, a terrible comfort.

The photographs over, everyone repaired to the Wilson household, a solid bastion of bourgeois tastes and comforts, where the goggle-eyed guests eyed a spread that was nothing short of a miracle considering wartime stringencies. Cold meats, a huge salmon in aspic, pickles, jellies, fruits and blancmanges with wines and cordials and Something Stronger for the males. Even a wedding cake topped with a cardboard cover that looked like icing. Jeannette Wilson was bursting with hospitable kindness and the knowledge that her only son had got the girl he wanted. Had always wanted. She tried not to notice how his shoulder blades seemed to stick out from the fine cloth of his uniform tunic, or the gaunt planes of his face. He was happy. All she wanted was to make this day as perfect for him as she could.

Toby's Aunt Mirren had come from Galashiels and when the feasting was over presided over the grand piano in the large front parlour, while relatives with vocal gifts rendered 'Dark Lochnagar' and 'Flow Gently Sweet Afton' at which point Toby's father, that stoic master grocer, was seen to wipe something that might have been a tear from his Bairnsfather moustache.

After this, there was some sedate dancing, much spilling of family anecdote and more wine and shortbread for anyone who felt in need of it.

Kate was standing beside Tallie, searching for words to say that would somehow convey how stunning she looked, yet finding them blocked in her throat by the knowledge of her own perfidy, when Jeannie Gray came up, pink-faced and over-excited and, smoothing the sleeve of Tallie's outfit with a half-envious hand, said, 'A day you'll never forget, Tallie, eh? I mean' – she looked round the lively

127

scene – 'what a spread! It's been perfect, like something out a story book, so it has. And you could never have thought it would happen, not after Wilfred.' She saw the consternation on both sisters' faces and realised too late how tactless she'd been, but got deeper in the mire. 'I mean,' she babbled on, 'after death there's life, is that not true? And I wish you every happiness—' She was near to tears now. Somehow she'd managed to upset Tallie, without ever meaning to, and not only that, Kate was glaring at her as though she'd seen a ghost, her face colourless, her eyes beginning to flicker. Next thing she was on the floor, in a dead faint.

'Oh, my God!' Jeannie appealed. 'Was it something I said? It never was, was it?'

Tallie was on her knees, slapping Kate's hand and asking people to stand back and give her some air. A Wilson cousin scooped Kate up and deposited her on the horsehair sofa. Someone fluttered off for sal volatile, someone else for water. Someone brought a fan. In a few minutes, Kate stirred. It was Tallie's face that hovered over her when she opened her eyes, so she closed them again.

'Should we get a doctor?' Jeannette Wilson asked. 'Is she bad, do you think?'

'No,' Tallie adjudged. 'I'm sure it's just the heat. And she's been overworking.' She met her mother's eye. 'Isn't that right, Mother?'

Janet nodded. In a little, Kate was able to sit up and it was suggested she retire to the small parlour to recover. Tallie took her arm and led her there, shooing everybody else away, even Toby for the moment. Even Janet.

'There,' she said, smiling relievedly. 'You're all right now, Kate, aren't you? It was just the excitement of losing a sister! I'll stay with you for a little while, then I must go and change. The cab's coming soon to take us to the station.'

Kate sat groggily but began after a moment or two to scrabble in her handbag. She took out a damaged-looking envelope and handed it to her sister. Her lips looked somehow swollen and the words themselves were stiff,

128

cardboardy words. 'Read that. Wilfred's alive. Read what it says.'

'Who got this? When did this come?'

'It came to the house. Mother opened it. I only found it this morning. By mistake.'

'But it was for *me*. It's addressed to me.'

'She wanted to save you.'

'You should have told me. The minute you knew. What were you thinking of? Now I've married Toby.' Kate had never heard Tallie sound the way she did now. Clipped. Merciless. Like a speaking doll.

'I know. But she wouldn't hear of it.'

'Do you know what you've done?'

'You love Toby. You couldn't go back on it all. He's been too good, too patient; he loves you. I really began to think you'd forgotten about Wilfred.'

Her face a sickly white, Tallie sat down as close to Kate as she could get and hissed at her. 'You want him, don't you? Well, don't worry. I'll tell him. I'll tell him what you did. He'll never look at you.'

'Tallie, it's your wedding night. Don't let this spoil things. Try to be glad he's alive. That's all that matters to me.'

'You liar!' Tallie summoned the word up from the depths of her fury and contempt. 'You've always been jealous of what I've had. Well, *you'll* not have him. I'll see to that. You're lower than the worms, lower than anything I can think of.'

'Please,' Kate pleaded. 'Go to your husband. He'll be waiting for you. Forgive me, if I've done wrong.'

'Never.' Tallie almost spat in her face. 'Never. You are not my sister any more and I will never forgive you.' She rose, backing away, her face streaked with tears, her hair wisping about her face. She made a brave effort at composure when she reached the door. As she went out a chorus of greeting and enquiry engulfed her and over the heads of everybody, she saw Toby looking at her, as if from a great distance, his eyebrows signalling distress, unease.

But in a moment he was at her side, holding her arm in an almost painful grip, saying, 'We've got to go soon. I've had enough of all this. Go and change.' She broke away from him but did as she was told.

They had decided to go to the small Ayrshire town of Girvan for a two-day honeymoon. It was where the senior Wilsons took their summer holidays and the landlady of the spotless small boarding-house, Mrs Gummer, knowing the family well, was prepared to open up her best double room out of season and give the young couple her best attention. Her cooking and baking were excellent but her small talk relentless. Even she, however, began after a time to realise there was some sense of strain between the young people and with a belated sensitivity decided to leave them to themselves.

Ghostly grey seas were visible from the visitor's parlour, though of course it had been dark when they arrived. Now a pale sickle moon presided over sands and sea. Tallie remembered the few occasions she'd been to the seaside previously. How different everything had looked in day-time and with a summer warmth presiding. She remembered Russell's rosy little face as he had whooped towards the sands with his red iron bucket and spade and Kate standing on the esplanade determined not to get sand on her shoes. Kate! Always difficult and thorny Kate. All the way to Girvan in the train, with Toby sitting as close to her as he could, holding her hand, she had been able to think of nothing but Kate and the fact that Wilfred was alive and whether she could talk about it to her new husband.

Toby had put her silence down to nerves and tiredness but now after supper his increasing perplexity made itself felt. He idled restlessly round the parlour picking up photographs to study here, knick-knacks there. Mrs Gummer had a forest of such items, from honey-coloured Mauchline-ware boxes to the brass and ivory trophies of her late husband's colonial past.

'Do you want to go up?' he demanded at last.

'We can't,' said Tallie. 'It's only eight o'clock.'

'We can suit outselves.'

'Let's enjoy the fire a little longer. Mrs Gummer built it up specially.'

He sat down disconsolately.

'Is something the matter?'

'What could possibly be the matter?'

'Something is.' He came and sat on the arm of her chair and rumpled her hair, leaving his hand on the nape of her neck. 'Tallie, darling, we're on our own at last. Man and wife. If something is worrying you, tell me. I want us to share everything. Come on, spill the beans. Is it a last-minute attack of shyness or something? I can wait, you know. I know you're tired—'

She turned her face with a cry into his chest. 'Wilfred's alive. He's come back,' she said. 'The message came for me but they opened it at home and never told me. Kate only blurted it out today. You know when she fainted? After that.'

His concern brought him to his knees in front of her, grabbing her hands, his face peering keenly into hers.

'Wilfred? Are you sure? What do you mean, Wilfred's come back? It can't be, after all this time.'

'It can be. It is.'

He sat back on his heels. 'Didn't they want you to know?'

'They didn't want to spoil things between us. I suppose.'

He got up onto his feet. 'Well, they were right, weren't they? It doesn't change anything between us, does it Tallie? We've got everything sorted out, haven't we?'

She knew she should be quite categorical then, that perhaps their whole future relationship depended on it. She knew anything else was the ultimate cruelty. And yet she could not get her tongue round any words. The only answer possible, the only answer accessible, was silence.

'You still love him?'

More silence.

'Tallie, answer me.'

'How do I know? How do I know what I feel? What will he think of me now, that I couldn't wait?'

'It doesn't matter how he feels. I mean, it isn't relevant. People have been let down before and got over it. All the time. You didn't do it deliberately. He was given up for dead.'

'What has he been through? They take in shell-shock patients at Craiglockhart, don't they?' She turned towards Toby, her pale face urgent. 'Toby, I want to go there and see him.'

'You can't,' he said, in wretchedness. 'I won't let you.'

'You can't stop me.'

'You mean you would leave me?'

'That's not what I mean.'

'But that's what it *would* mean. Go to him and I won't have you back.' His face was now as pale and haggard as her own.

There was a discreet tap at the door and Mrs Gummer came in.

'What about a nice cup of cocoa?' she volunteered. 'You'll no doubt want to get early to your beds.' Realising too late the innuendo behind her innocent words, the poor woman's ears burned red to their tips. 'I mean, you've had a long day,' she amended. If she had hoped for a pleasant five-minute chat before retiring, one glance at her guests' strained faces showed it was not to be. Oh well, all lovers had tiffs and they'd settle it soon enough when they got upstairs. They declined her offer of the cocoa and she bade them a civil goodnight.

Tallie had not had much of a bottom drawer, but the nightgown she drew from her small case was the most indulgent item in it. It was white lawn, tucked and tamboured and threaded with pale blue baby ribbons. She climbed into it while Toby took a long time in the bathroom. Glumly he got into bed beside her.

'Toby,' she said at last in a small voice, 'it isn't that I don't care for you.'

'I think it's best we leave it at that for tonight,' he answered bitterly. 'Some wedding night!'

'Please,' she said, into his back. 'Please, turn round and

132

kiss me.' After a moment or two, he did so, but they were both too upset for anything more than that. When he tried to draw her closer to him, he was convinced he felt her flinch and also that she was crying in the dark. With a growl of frustration he got up, dragging the eiderdown with him and settled himself in the wicker chair.

'You'll get your death,' she pleaded.

'What does it bloody matter?'

By morning he had got back in beside her. Despite everything they had eventually slept. They looked a bit more like the world, Mrs Gummer decided, plying them with bacon and eggs and morning rolls, but there was something not right, there was no shy exchange of glances, just a spoon-clattering, nervy exchange of civilities.

A mist lay over the sea but by ten o'clock there was sharp sunlight and they wrapped up well and went for a walk, stopping for a hot drink in a deserted café at eleven.

'Why did we come here?' said Toby bleakly. 'There's nothing happening here.'

'There's the shore and the birds and the waves. I love the solitude.' She led the way from the café on to the beach. Here the smells were different, stronger, salt water and seaweed. A gentle wind buffeted them, carrying occasional droplets of rain.

'I don't hold much hope for us,' he said.

'Why do you say that?'

'You can't put your hand on your heart and say you love me.'

'But I do.'

'Not the way you loved him.'

'Differently. Every love is different.'

'*You see.*' He broke away from her. 'On our wedding day, you tell me you want to go and see some other man. I don't see how we can go on from here. Do you want to make the break now?'

'I can't take your anger. What have I done to hurt you? I didn't know Wilfred was still alive. I still have to take it in.'

'He's between us now. So you might as well clear off. I'm not sure I want to make a go of it. A man has his pride.'

He strode off ahead of her, but when she climbed back up off the sand he was waiting for her, the same tortured expression on his face.

'I have to tell you,' he said. 'Something I was saving for last night. That I thought would please you. They're going to discharge me. Health grounds. My father wants to give me the main street shop. The idea was we would live above, make a go of it together. Now—' He spread his hands.

She jumped up over the last tussock of grass and met him eye to eye. 'I'm prepared to try and make a go of it,' she offered seriously. 'If you are.' His expression softened at the first note of concern in her voice. 'You'll get your health back. I'll look after you. I'm not somebody wicked, Toby. Don't make me out to be.'

'But you still want to see *him*.'

As the night before, when she had refused to answer him when he asked whether she still loved Wilfred, she was silent and as had happened previously a tide of furious anger and resentment washed over him, driving out all else.

So it was to be for the rest of the 'honeymoon', till they caught the train back to Perringhall.

Then he had to rejoin his regiment, until such time as his discharge came through. If his parents thought there was something not quite right between them, they solicitously held their peace. When his father talked of the arrangements for Toby taking over the main street shop, Toby made no demur.

Tallie saw him off at the station, her face still pale and enigmatic and his set in a kind of scowling mask. They seemed somehow to have lost sight of who the other was.

'You'll move into the house?' he forced himself to say at the last minute. 'My mother'll help you with the furniture.'

He knew that as soon as he was out of sight she would go to Edinburgh and that there was no way of stopping her.

# Seventeen

But first she was determined to have it out with her mother and Kate.

She had been unable to talk about it to Toby, but what had been boiling up in her ever since Kate's fainting fit and the disclosures of the opened letter had been anger of a most ungovernable kind against both of them. It had blotted out almost everything else. Even the wedding. All the old injustices had risen up in her – how her mother had opened out life for the others but kept her restrictively at home, a virtual slave. Without Wilfred she would never have broken out in the end and become a nurse. She remembered every careless blow struck when she was a child, every harsh, abusive word and Kate's near-collusion in all this, her ability to stand off from the rest of them, that detached look on her face that said it had nothing to do with her. She knew that deep down Kate too was afraid of their mother, but that was no excuse. Tallie was not prepared to let this state of affairs go on. Somehow or other old scores had to be redressed. It did not matter if all her family bridges were burned.

Somehow she managed to put on a semblance of normal interest when she and her mother-in-law paid a visit to the apartments above the main street shop, to talk about what was needed in the way of new lino, rugs and furniture. She felt the birth of a new sensation, a kind of flimsy security in knowing that she could have a place that was hers. Well, hers and Toby's. She offered to stay and scrub out the tiny kitchen but after her mother-in-law left, she threw down the scrubbing brush, emptied the pail of hot water, donned coat and hat and made for Cullington Lodge.

She went round the back of the house, pushing open the scullery door and calling out a flat 'Cooee' to indicate her presence. Her mother looked up from her rocking chair in the kitchen as she went, letting down the latch carefully.

135

'Where's Kate?' she asked immediately. Somehow with it being the school holidays she had thought Kate would be there, head bent over some book or work at the table.

'She's in her bed,' said her mother.

Tallie felt her legs tremble. 'What's up?'

Her mother did not answer immediately. She always did this – indicated she would not be interrogated but would offer information in her own time. But eventually she volunteered, 'She's not been the same since that fainting fit. I had the doctor in to her yesterday. He says it's neurasthenia. She's to take all the rest she can get.'

'Why did you do it, Mother?' Tallie burst out. She could not contain her misery any longer. 'Why did you and Kate keep the letter about Wilfred from me? You had no right to do that, you know. It was addressed to me. I was his next-of-kin.'

For the first time her mother engaged her eye.

'You should be grateful,' she said hardly. 'Kate's been by to see him in the hospital—'

'Kate has *what*?'

'And they've put a steel plate in his head. He's a sick man.'

'When did Kate go?'

'Day after the wedding.'

'She thinks he's *hers*. She does, doesn't she? Well let me tell you, Mother, I won't let her have him. I'll do to her what she did to me. I'll put a stop to it.'

She was wide-eyed, scarcely aware of what she was saying. 'If he's sick, it's me he needs. And I'm going to him: I don't care what anybody says.'

'You'll be the talk of the town if you do.'

'What do I care? It's all you care about though, isn't it? What people think. Not whether your children are happy.'

'What's happiness got to do with it? You have to do what's right in this world. And it's not right for you to leave your man. Toby's your man now.'

The words were like a cup of cold water thrown in Tallie's face. She drew in her breath on a hiccuping sob and sat down at the table, almost as though all life had been drawn from her.

'You should have given me the choice,' she said tonelessly. 'Even at the last minute, you should have given me the choice. What I felt for Wilfred – and he for me – isn't nothing, you know. You don't know what you did, Mother.' She broke down at last into sobbing. 'A steel plate in his head. Oh, is he dying?'

She saw her mother's eyes fly to a point behind her own head and turned to see Kate standing there, in bare feet and nightie, her hair not combed.

'He's not dying.' Kate came forward.

'You should be resting,' said Janet Candlish. 'The doctor said you were to have rest.'

Kate sat down opposite her sister, her eyes never leaving her face.

'He's not dying,' she repeated, 'but he's far away, Tallie. He doesn't know who anybody is. He lay out in a wood for God knows how long, after a battle and he was found eventually by some villagers and hidden till they could get him back to the lines. That's why he was given up for dead. He was wounded in the head and in the leg and he's shell-shocked; his memory is what the doctors call selective. You would be shocked if you saw him.'

It was as though their mother's presence was forgotten and there was only the two of them in the universe.

Tallie said, 'Oh my poor Wilfred.'

'Yes.'

'He'll remember me. It would be me he was expecting. Why should he remember you? What right had you to go?'

'Well, none, maybe,' said Kate humbly and unexpectedly. 'Except—'

'Except what?'

'You don't always know why you do things.'

'Ah, but you know very well,' said Tallie. 'Well, what did they say?' she demanded, almost callously. 'What did they tell you, the doctors?' She ignored Kate's deathly pallor and trembling lips. 'Tell me. It's you who went there.'

'That he's recovered well physically from his wounds. The steel plate is not even as bad as it sounds. There will be plenty going around with them in their heads, after the war, and they'll function well enough. He'll always limp – they can't do anything about that. But as to the rest, they don't know. Some days he's better than others.'

'But he didn't know you?'

Kate's blue gaze clouded. 'No.' The tip of one long finger almost touched Tallie's hand. 'I sat down at his bed. I said "Wilfred, it's Kate here". And he gave me a long look and I must have looked upset, for he said, "A woman moved is like a fountain troubled", and I know that, it's from *The Taming of the Shrew* so he must have made some kind of connection. You know, the heroine's called Kate.

'But when I said "Wilfred, do you know me?" he looked up the ward, and down again and then said, "Are you from the church come to save my soul?" I told him again who I was and then I thought maybe I'd better not persevere, I just poured him some barley water and saw to his pillows.

'There was a young lad down the ward making a bit of a din and it seemed to distract him. He asked me if it was Calder and then he said "No, no, Calder's dead, Calder's dead. I saw him and he's very dead". He drifted away into a kind of sleep then, because they'd sedated him. He opened his eyes later, gave me a kind of puzzled look – I thought that's what it was, anyhow – but then he went to sleep again and I just put some grapes on his plate and left.'

'He liked Calder. You wouldn't know that. Calder was his best friend.'

There was a kind of sigh from the rocking chair and both girls swivelled round to look at their mother. She was moving back and forwards at a furious rate and touching the little circular crocheted shawl she wore to her eyes. 'My poor boys! What's to happen to *them*? To Donald and to Russell. This war will take them all, one way or another.'

'You've upset her,' said Kate accusingly.

Tallie got up. She refused to show any concern, her mouth flinty and her stance hostile. 'Ah, well,' she said, 'I didn't come here for a picnic. The two of you will have to live with what you've done to me.'

'Has Toby gone back?' asked Kate with unwonted timidity.

'Yes,' said Tallie wearily. She did not tell them his news – that he was due to be discharged.

They were trying to draw her into a pool, some joint pool of suffering, as though the calamities of recent days had been inflicted on all of them, and they had had nothing to do with the grievous quandary of her feelings.

It was hard to draw herself away from them; they had lived so much of their joint lives in this little room and she did not know why she should suddenly remember the caraway sandwiches they'd had on innumerable Sunday teas and the church bells ringing across the fields while the sun shone with a clear sort of Sunday fervour and her mother presiding over discussions that had often ended in laughter and the perfervid gleam of something like happiness, like pleasure, in her mother's eyes. Did I love her then? she wondered. Were we happy? There had been jealousies, rivalries, fights. But something more. They had been a family and who but her mother had kept them together? She felt a strange, aching sense of loss for what had been and what could never be. She had no option but to abstract her own life and feelings from that of her family. But it was like being stripped and defenceless, with nothing between you and what was going to happen to you, which might be terrible.

Toby's mother was beginning to show signs of annoyance with her daughter-in-law. If the girl was going to stay with them till Toby came home, the least she could do was settle in and share the duties of house and shop, she felt.

But Tallie insisted she would return to hospital duties at the end of the week. It was a measure of how badly Matron needed her 'stalwarts' as she called them in that she was prepared to let Tallie sleep out. But wouldn't Toby need Tallie's care and attention? Jeannette Wilson pursued. She feared Tallie was going to be the mutinous sort, not at all how she, Jeannette, had been when she'd married into the old-established grocery firm. Girls were so different nowadays, with minds of their own.

'So why do you want to go to Edinburgh?' Jeannette wanted to know.

'Just to have a day out before I go back to work.'

'If you hadn't sprung it on me, I could have got someone to come into the shop for the day, and come with you.'

'Oh, I'll be seeing a friend.'

'What friend would that be?' Jeannette was nothing if not tenacious.

'An old nursing friend.' Tallie hastily recalled a name from the past. 'Mercy Anderson. She married a coal merchant.'

Jeannette would like to have pursued the matter a good deal more vigorously but there was something about Tallie's demeanour that stopped her. She could be very touch-me-not, like the whole Candlish family.

'Why are you wearing your wedding outfit?' It was Jeannette's last throw.

'Might as well. Mercy will want to see what it's like.'

So she was sitting in the train, still quaking a bit from the final interrogation, but wearing the ruby-red suit with its bead-encrusted front and the little hat that went with it. Something had been born in her as she thought about the Edinburgh trip, a determination to look her best, to be almost – bridal, was the word.

Going any distance by train was still a bit of a challenge. She was nervous about knowing when they got there and which side of the carriage to get out, but her determination to see Wilfred never wavered. Edinburgh seemed big and strange and a strong wind swept down Princes Street. Another day she might have admired the Castle and the Scott Monument but today the external world scarcely impinged on her consciousness. She could not get to the hospital fast enough and did not stop even for a cup of tea.

The hospital itself did not faze her. In fact, once there she

140

began to feel more at home. She went at once to the almoner's office, explained who she was and asked if it might be possible to see Wilfred's doctor.

Dr Fry was a small, grizzled man, probably in his late forties, with a goatee beard and shrewd, not unkind blue eyes behind ancient-looking steel spectacles. His coat was very white and stiffly starched.

'Mrs Wilson? I understand you are the patient's next-of-kin.' His gaze went immediately to the brand new gold of her wedding ring. 'His sister, perhaps?'

'No. We were engaged. Then he was presumed killed.' She looked at the doctor, but her gaze wavered. 'I met someone else. We were married, only a few days ago.'

He made a murmur of sympathy.

'What I wanted to ask you, Doctor, was should I see him? My sister has already been to see him but he doesn't know her.'

'What is your own feeling in the matter?'

'Of course I want to see him.'

'And your husband's?'

Tallie said nothing. She gazed at the tall, grey window, where a fly buzzed uselessly against the glass.

'I see,' said the doctor, dryly. 'A piquant situation, to say the least.'

'Where can be the harm?' she burst out at last.

'Perhaps,' said Dr Fry quietly, 'you could remove your wedding ring, then? Place it in your purse?'

'He has to know the truth.'

'But perhaps not yet,' Dr Fry suggested gently. He put the tips of his fingers together and appeared to go into a thoughtful trance. Tallie began to be afraid he would forbid her seeing Wilfred and she asked, as reasonably and quietly as she could, 'I must insist on seeing him, Doctor. I have not come all this way for nothing.'

His mind seemed to be made up. 'Then I will not insist otherwise.' But Tallie knew she had forced the issue.

Before she left the room, she asked, 'What are the prospects of recovery?'

141

He gave her an equivocal look over his spectacles. 'He has been through a testing time, no question of that. But I am constantly amazed at the ability of the human mind to heal itself, given peace, given time.' His empathetic gaze was on her restless, twisting fingers. 'The young man is up and about today. He was confined to bed when your sister came, as he was running a fever.'

She was shown into a large room where various figures in blue hospital uniform went about different tasks. Some wove baskets, some wrote, a few read and others simply sat about and smoked or talked. The atmosphere seemed cheerful and relaxed and there was even a shout of laughter from one corner. Tallie knew him at once. He was by himself and a book was open on his lap. She thought at first he was reading but then saw he was merely staring out of the window. She put a hand on his shoulder and said his name.

'Reading something good?'

'Not really reading. Not putting it together all that well. As yet.'

He gave her a smile, but it was without recognition.

'You don't know me, Wilfred?'

'Should I?' he enquired pleasantly.

'Well, only if you want to.' She sat down beside him. They had obviously been feeding him up because he was a little puffy, a little overweight, with hospital pallor and the kind of soft, spongy texture to his skin that came from lack of fresh air and exercise. He was in need of a haircut and the hand that shook hers, impersonally, was damp with sweat.

'Did they tell who I was?' she demanded.

'They may have done,' he said evasively.

'But you don't remember?'

'Sorry.'

A young nurse came over and held him by the shoulders, from behind. 'You all right, Wilf? Would you and your visitor like some coffee?' She seemed to Tallie to be giving her a kind of coded warning to go carefully. After a few minutes the coffee appeared and Tallie poured. He lit a cigarette and inhaled it deeply.

'Thing is,' he said at last, 'I lay out somewhere in Flanders for one hell of a long time. I was found by some French peasants and hidden by them, but just in time. I remember some of that. But vaguely. What went before, no. It's a bloody nuisance, but Dr Fry and co. seem to think it can be overcome. In time.'

She saw his hands were beginning to shake. He picked up the cup and saucer but the liquid spilled over and he put the objects down again quickly.

'Look,' he said, 'I don't know that I'm ready for visitors. Do you mind? It's my head, it's hurting.'

The little nurse who had offered coffee came swiftly to their sides. 'Had enough, Wilf?' she asked conversationally. 'Want to go back to the ward? You've done awfully well.'

Talie saw that he was no longer aware that she was there. He was fighting some kind of pain, whether physical or mental, she had no way of knowing. She felt a rush of gratitude for the nurse's professionalism combined with a feeling of her own total helplessness.

A young blond soldier shuffling a pack of cards gave her a compassionate smile.

'He's better than he was,' he offered.

'Yes.' She was touched by his instinct to comfort and smiled at him.

She did not follow Wildred to his ward. She did not go back to the doctor's office or the almoner. It wasn't that she didn't have questions to ask. She had questions aplenty.

But as she made her way back to the station, she knew there was nobody to answer them.

# *Eighteen*

Tallie's mother-in-law wanted to know all about the visit to Edinburgh.

'What did your friend Mercy think about your wedding outfit?'

'She thought it was lovely.'

'Has she a nice house? The one in Morningside?'

'Oh, yes. A very nice house.'

Jeannette Wilson clicked her tongue in irritation. She was getting so very little out of her daughter-in-law and her mind was brimming over with questions. 'I really do want to hear everything,' she said with a rapt anticipatory look, flopping down on the settee which had been delivered that very morning to the apartment above the shop, with a new bed and sundry other items. Paid for, Jeannette would dearly like to have reminded Tallie, by herself and her husband. They had done so much for the young couple, really set them up in style, the least Tallie owed her was a little consideration and a detailed daily report of what she was doing and thinking, especially till Toby was home again. She wanted to be close to this girl, close in the way of mothers and daughters. But Tallie could be remote and even chilly at times, positively monosyllabic in her replies.

Tallie turned on her now with a fierce little jerk of the head that pulled the unthinking little woman up short.

'I have a *lot* to do,' she said pointedly. 'I think I'll stop here now, if you don't mind.'

'But Toby wants you to stay with us till he's back,' Jeannette remonstrated. 'You and I can come over here every day and do a bit more. It's still so – so barren here.' And she indicated the pictureless walls and curtainless windows. 'Cheerless,' she added.

'I want time to think,' said Tallie. Jeannette thought she was distracted, somehow, her mind elsewhere. Well, maybe she was missing Toby more than she let on. She would like to have persisted further, got to the bottom of Tallie's unease, but there was something set and almost forbidding about her daughter-in-law's expression that made Jeannette realise persistence might lead to a flare-up of tempers. That was the last thing she wanted, being a conciliatory woman who liked to keep life on an even keel.

'This place is nearer the hospital,' Tallie defended her decision, seeing the need to be placatory at least. 'And I'm starting work again in a couple of days.' Aware of Jeannette's downcast mien she said in a generous rush. 'Oh, please don't think I'm not grateful for everything. You've been so good to us. But I've got to get used to being independent—'

'Till Toby comes back,' his mother amended. 'Oh well, if it's really what you want to do.' She realised Tallie was actually willing her out of the door and that no leisurely chit-chat about Edinburgh was forthcoming.

Tallie paid no attention to the many chores waiting to be done once Jeannette had gone. She sat on the new over-stuffed settee, feeling the strange sensation of silkiness and prickle that was horsehair, and allowed unalloyed pain to flow over her.

What had she expected to happen on the visit to Craiglockhart? That Wilfred would know her where he had not known Kate? That somehow, miraculously, the clock might have been put back and her wedding to Toby undone? She had been trying to prevent herself from facing up to the picture of Wilfred as it had been filed away in her mind since yesterday but now she could stave off the memory no longer. He had been like a stranger. No, the looks had not changed all that much, except that he looked paler, as you'd expect, his hair somehow darker by contrast; but the fine hands, the gestures, the turn of the head, these had all been the same. And the timbre of voice. She had always liked – no, correction, loved his voice. It was what Wilfred was all about, expressing his intellectual curiosity, his tilting at windmills, his ability to be amused by the vagaries of life while he listened also to what he had called 'the still sad music of humanity'. Wordsworth, that, he'd told her. If she turned to books now, more and more, for solace, for instruction, it was because he had taught her, where to look and how to look. All by the magic of his voice.

The other magic had been in his gaze and that had not been the same. She got up and rushed into the kitchenette, drinking water from a rough, chipped cup, not wanting to think about it, wishing she had not seen it, wishing strenuously she had not gone to Craiglockhart. The look had not really seen her, had denied her existence. It had filled her with a mad desire to shake him, to insist he acknowledge her, to take him away with her, anywhere, away from the hospital and its grim reminders of the war, to a place where things could be as they had been. Some good, quiet place. Somewhere.

She retched into the sink. Her emotions were running like wildfire through her, stretching her nerves, boiling over helplessly like jam in too small a pot. She gripped the cold hard edge of the sink and made herself take a deep breath, then another, praying for control.

In a little, something reached out and calmed her a little. She realised it was the silence of the house that was now hers and Toby's. The fact that she had been able to banish Jeannette, to claim territory that could not be invaded, began to pervade her consciousness like a starch stiffening fabric. Here she could think and not be gainsaid. Here she could face up to things in her own time.

On shaking legs she walked back into the room that would be the parlour, feeling a hard-won composure return bit by bit, like a tide lapping up the shore. The jobs that needed doing presented themselves in her mind, like children scrabbling at her skirts for attention. She must sew the brass rings on the dark crimson curtains and hang them on the bamboo pole. Once she had done that her privacy would be secure. Then she should make up the bed, with the crisp new linen sheets – wedding gifts – and heavy Ayrshire blankets. She even felt a little thrill of something like pleasure as she thought of the eiderdown that would go over everything, a dark glossy green satin with a ruched centre, surprised it should still matter to own it. After yesterday.

She hung on to her dangerous equanimity long enough to go out to the shops a little further up the street and buy bread, thread, a thimble, scones, fresh butter and tea. She was thankful that a close-mouth entrance meant she did not have to go through the shop downstairs that Toby would manage and which was staffed at the moment by relatives of Jeannette. When she got back in, she locked the massive door carefully. She made herself some tea but did not eat the scone she had buttered. She did not carry out any of the jobs she had categorised. She sat motionless in her new parlour while the light faded and the stuff of the curtains ran out from her fingers and fell in folds about her feet.

When the leerie came up the street, lighting only the occasional low jet necessary for public safety, she thought vaguely of her husband, Toby, hearing his voice in her head reciting the Stevenson poem 'O leerie, see a little child and nod to him tonight' to his cousin's small son at the wedding. Funny she should think of that and Toby's robust and playful empathy with those of tender years. Funny, because where he was really was a great distance off, as though on the far side of the shore at Girvan where they'd honeymooned, standing alone in pale moonlight where she could not put out a hand to touch him.

She liked the cold feeling that came with darkness. It lapped around her, anaesthetising her so that she slipped over the borders of consciousness into a kind of dazed sleep, from which she would start from time to time to draw the curtain stuff around her. Oh, that was better. Coldness. The flat and its shadows became known and familiar. Hers. Her fortress. The feeling of security and the cold became one, became bearable, allowed her to function, eventually to use the bathroom and lie down on the unmade-up bed.

She wouldn't go to Craiglockhart again. If Wilfred maintained by his look that he did not know her, she could not face that again. No, no, no. If he wanted her he would have to come looking for her. But he never could, because she had taken her marriage vows with Toby. It was Kate who had done this to them, Kate and her mother. It was good about the cold because it froze her anger. She did not feel strong enough for anger any more. Anger would overwhelm her totally. But if she had the flat for security and the list of jobs to do entrenched in her mind, she could cut herself off from anger. She would never speak to her mother or to Kate ever again. She would be hard, cold and hard. Encrusted with frost and ice as in the coldest December. She would not go to Craiglockhart again, because Wilfred had come back, yet not come back, and it was more than she could bear.

Back at work, it was easier to forget the notion that she had somehow let him down. If she had not accepted Toby's offer of marriage, not been so keen to get on with her life after the first telegram, she would be free to go to Wilfred as often as she liked and help him in his fight back to health.

But bit by bit she was beginning to see she could not have the luxuries of guilt and remorse because if she gave in to them she would not be able to function. And the children needed her. Those who had not been sent home in her absence greeted her with cries of delight, remembering the stories she had told them, the little indulgences she allowed from ward rule. Even Mons turned in her cot with a smile that seemed to say, It's all right. You're back. Tallie threw herself into her duties with a determination and relief that surprised her.

The house above the shop was more or less straight when she had an evening visitor. It was Kate, her hair pushed uncompromisingly up inside a schoolmistressy hat, her face taut and pale.

'Are you going to let me in?'

It had been in Tallie's mind to keep her at the door but in the event she found herself widening the aperture involuntarily to let her sister pass.

'We need to have things out,' said Kate, with a sharp peremptoriness. She looked round the room that already spoke of home, a new home, with its aura of bright freshness. Flowers in a lustre jug on the table. A clock ticking companionably on the wall. A little overcome by the recognition of Tallie's autonomy, she sat down on a hard chair.

'There's nothing to have out,' said Tallie.

'Why have you not been up to see us?'

'After what you did?' Tallie let the words hang in the air. She went on with her task of smoothing clothes off the Pirie pulley, ready for ironing. 'I have my own place here,' she said into the lengthening silence. 'I have no need of any of you at Cullington.'

'You can't cut off your own mother. You know what worry she has had. Two sons at the front. Even Belle out there, caught up in it all.'

'I don't propose to upset myself by going over it all again. But what you and she did was unforgivable—'

'It was from the best of motives. It was to save you further turmoil.'

Tallie deliberately laid aside the last of the garments she had been smoothing and walked over to her sister's chair, bending so that her clear hazel eyes looked straight into her sister's blue ones.

'You cannot have the gall to tell me that. Not face to face.' Kate's gaze dropped and Tallie said triumphantly, 'You want him for yourself. Poor Wilfred! You think he'll ever be well enough to start anything with you?'

Kate's gaze fluttered upwards again and Tallie went on, unable to stop herself, wishing to inflict maximum hurt, 'I've been to see him, too. You didn't know that, did you? He's in a bad way. He'll never be back at teaching. At anything.'

'Are you going back to see him again?' demanded Kate desperately.

Tallie turned her back on her, refusing to answer.

'I thought not,' said Kate softly. 'You've begun to see

sense. We should probably have told you about the telegram—'

'*Probably*?'

'Yes. Probably. But it was your wedding day. To Toby. What would it have done to him if you'd called off at the last moment?'

'Leave Toby out of it,' Tallie commanded furiously.

'But he can't be left out.'

'Yes, he can. You and my mother will stir no more pots, let me tell you. Keep out of Toby's life and mine. Leave me alone, from now on.'

'Then you won't come up and see her? Your own mother?'

'I'll see the others. You and her – never.'

'That's your last word?' Kate did not sound argumentative or challenging, but broken and sad. 'I hoped by coming here we could mend some fences, but I see it's not to be. Maybe in time you'll feel differently.'

'I said never.'

'Very well.'

'And leave Wilfred alone. Let him mend in his own time. When he's well enough he will know what service you did him.'

'Don't blame me for a situation of your own making.'

'Keep away from him.'

Tallie could hear her voice rising dangerously. She caught that glimmering look on Kate's face that meant defiance. She flew at her sister and would have shaken or struck her had Kate not stepped hastily backwards. She fled up the hall and out of the front door and Tallie banged it with all her might behind her.

When she had gone she did not cry. Her breath came rapidly, her breast heaved but she did not cry. She wanted this to be a victory. She ran to the front window and watched Kate's thin, dark-clad figure disappear up the street, then when it had finally gone she twitched the dark red curtains close. She was alone in her castle, her fortress. And what would Kate have that would ever match that?

*

'Have you seen your mother recently?' asked Jeannette Wilson timidly. She had to be timid in all her dealings with her daughter-in-law these days, for Tallie had become quieter and moodier than ever. But surely the fact that Toby would be home at last, tomorrow, should be enough to cheer her up and made her a bit more sociable? Jeannette had come up to the new apartments bearing extra tea and butter and a pound of seed cake to welcome the returning hero.

'No, I haven't seen her,' said Tallie, with a studied indifference. She didn't bother to explain – that was another thing that perplexed Jeannette. Soon there would be no verbal currency left between them at all. Jeannette sighed to herself. Toby deserved better. Charitably she told herself things would improve once her son was back. They had better, or even she would have to brace herself for some kind of confrontation with Tallie.

'Daddy and I will leave you to yourselves tomorrow.' Jeannette tried ingratiation.

'Right.' Tallie was dismissing her again. 'Thanks for the cake and stuff.' And *stuff*, thought Jeannette angrily. The offhand and uncaring manner wounded her but she struggled for normality.

'Try and get to bed early,' she offered. 'You'll be tired after your long shift.' She was hinting as best she could that Tallie should be fresh and better-tempered for Toby's homecoming. She went, as she often did these days, because she could feel an explosive situation coming up and she could see no earthly reason why it should be so. But for Toby's sake, so that he should get well and have a decent life, she persevered, sighing mightily as she went down the tile-walled stairs.

Tallie had a free day to welcome Toby home but did not go to the station to meet him. Instead, his first glimpse of his wife was of her standing in front of a cheerful coal fire in the bright newly furnished parlour, with what looked like two spots of rouge on her cheeks and her figure thinner than a scarecrow's under a dress of printed cotton.

151

'Tallie.' Despite everything he went over and held her.

'Welcome home,' she said.

'Everything looks wonderful.'

'You don't look so bad yourself. How's your chest?'

'Better.' But he coughed.

The kettle had been at the ready and she made tea. The table was set formally with the wedding china and delicacies laid out on a three-tiered cakestand. She offered him a daintily-cut ham sandwich.

'The war looks to be going better at last.'

'I thought we'd never stop the Germans after St Quentin.'

'They had all these extra battalions after the peace terms with Russia.'

'Foch'll do it. But we'll never know the cost.'

'No,' she agreed soberly. 'But it could just be the beginning of the end. At long last.'

He raised his cup. 'Here's to those who're still out there.'

'I'm glad you're home.'

'Are you?' he asked ironically.

'Of course.' But she did not meet his eyes.


# Nineteen


Kate Candlish ran downstairs to answer the jangle of the doorbell, tidying hair back from her face into a clasp as she went. She had spent the morning making jam with rasps and gooseberries from the garden, with the small amount of sugar she had been able to scrounge.

It was one of the jobs she had promised to get down to now that the school holidays were here, as well as a major cleaning of the lodgers' rooms – Ernest Waters was still with them and a quiet and harmless junior clerk from the pit. She really wanted to burrow into her books, longing to explore new territory as she had always done when she had time to spare. But although Ellen Siddons still came to help every day, she had been bolshie this year when it came to spring-cleaning, arguing she had enough to do with her normal schedule.

Kate tried not to let thoughts of Tallie intrude too much but she had to acknowledge that in the past, before she had gone nursing, they had all taken her contribution to the running of Cullington Lodge too much for granted. No point in going back over the past. Nothing could be changed and she, Kate, did more than her share nowadays. Elements of guilt had to be lived with.

A young woman with a biscuit-coloured straw hat threaded with blue ribbon atop a mass of red-gold hair stood smiling at her on the doorstep and Kate's gaze travelled swiftly down to the woman's right hand, which clasped a toddler in button boots with a mass of ringleted curls exactly the colour of her mother's. So familiar was the infant's trusting face, so like Russell's at the same age, it took Kate all her time not to scoop it up and cuddle it. This maternal side had surfaced in her, she had observed, over recent months.

But Tibby Robertson had cut herself off from them when she had been expecting this baby and Kate felt some explanation for the visit was in order before she smiled back. Before – despite the upturned baby face above a well-starched broderie anglaise pinny – she opened the door any wider and permitted entry for either Tibby or her offspring.

'Have you heard anything from Russell?' Suddenly the tentative social smile on Tibby's face had fled and been replaced by a look of acute anxiety. 'I just wondered, I've written and written but I don't think anything's getting to him and I haven't had a letter for months.'

The door opened wider and Kate's defences collapsed. 'Come in,' she commanded. 'No, we've heard nothing either. My mother's going out of her mind with worry.' She looked down at the little girl and said as delicately as she knew how, 'We didn't even know about what plans you and Russell had, not till Belle met up with Donald and put him in the picture. She felt he should know first before it became common knowledge, as it were. Have you come back to stay with your parents?'

'They can't resist *her*.' Tibby indicated her daughter. 'Even my father's come round.' Sweat lay in a fine film over her freckled, high cheekbones as she asked, 'Do you think your mother might like to see her?'

Kate did not quite know what to say, but was prepared to test out the situation. 'Wait here,' she said, leaving the twosome in the tessellated hall and diving unceremoniously into the morning-room where her mother was reading the weekly paper.

She came out looking red-faced after what seemed like rather a longer interval and said to Tibby, 'Come through. She'll see you.'

Janet Candlish ignored Tibby completely but addressed herself after a moment or two's scrutiny to the child. 'Do you go to the Sunday school? Are you a good girl?'

Catriona buried her face in her mother's skirts.

'Would she like a biscuit?' Kate asked, delving into the biscuit barrel.

'I had to know if you'd heard anything,' Tibby appealed to Kate. 'To be honest, I think the worst. I don't think I'll ever hear from him again.'

Janet Candlish spoke at last. 'Do you ever think now of what you did to Donald?' Her voice was hard, lacking all forgiveness and Tibby gave her one appalled look then burst into uncontrollable weeping, collapsing into one of the hard chairs by the door.

Kate demurred no longer but swept the bewildered little girl up into her arms, taking her to the window to point out the birds in the kitchen garden.

But Catriona's eyes were on the sepia photographs in their silver frames on the window sill – one of Belle, in her VAD uniform, one of Donald, the major, looking devastatingly handsome and one of Russell, his cap at a jaunty angle and that defiant half-smile that was so much the essence of him.

The child pointed excitedly to Russell. 'My daddy!' she proclaimed. 'That's my daddy!' She struggled strenuously down from Kate's arms and before she could be stopped had snatched up the precious photograph and pressed it to her lips. 'My daddy come back.' Beaming, she handed the picture back to Kate, who replaced it on the window sill without a word.

There was a muffled sound from Janet. She brought a lace-edged hankie from the cuff of her blouse and plied it to her eyes. For a moment Kate did not know what to do, whether to take the baby into the garden until the two weeping women composed themselves. But then she heard her mother speaking.

'Dry your tears, Tibby. You heard what the bairn said. Her daddy will come back.'

With a strangely dignified gesture Tibby pushed the bright hair back from her face. 'No,' she said, quietly composed at last. 'In my heart I know he won't. When things were bad, really bad, in the spring, I could understand why we heard nothing. But we're supposed to be pushing them back now and if he was alive, Russell would have written.' She looked at the older woman directly, for the first time. 'I think we should prepare ourselves for the worst.'

By September – still with no news of Russell – the inexorable tide of war seemed to be turning in the Allies' favour. The forces in Salonika actually began to advance after years of inactivity. In the Middle East, the British captured Damascus. It looked as though Turkey was about to collapse.

Back teaching at Perringhall Academy, Kate blessed the *rapprochement* that had taken place between her mother and Tibby which enabled her on the Saturday to go and visit Wilfred. Catriona had the freedom of Cullington Lodge these days and Tibby rolled up her sleeves to help with the chores and ingratiate herself with Janet.

On the train to Craiglockhart Kate pondered on the strange quirk that had admitted Tibby to the domestic scene at Cullington yet still kept Tallie from it.

Tibby reported that everyone was remarking how different Tallie looked since her marriage. On her occasional days off from the hospital she served in her husband's shop and people had reported that you could cut the atmosphere between them with a knife. Toby was poker-faced and bad-tempered and Tallie uncommunicative. The Wilson family had always been bonhomous and outgoing and this new, bleak attitude from the junior shopkeepers was driving customers away. Tibby thought Tallie looked sallow and unwell, as though all the life and light had gone out of her. It was Tibby's opinion that even allowing for worries over Toby's health, Tallie should buck up and thank her stars: her man was home and safe, unlike those of so many others.

Despite Tibby's admission to – almost – family rank, Kate had not enlightened her over the estrangement with Tallie, saying only that she was too busy to visit very often these days. No point in filling village mouths with gossip, though she suspected the trained ranks of curtain-twitchers knew something was afoot. Let them speculate all they liked. Despite everything, her heart was lifting at the prospect of seeing Wilfred again. It was a fortnight since she had been and on the last occasion there had been something, something she could not quite analyse that had made her think improvement was at last on its way. Like a blind wayward steed her mind careered ahead into the future, to the time when he might be well enough to leave hospital and she might be able to be with him. She would give up everything, she would settle anywhere, no matter how humble, if marriage was a feasibility. She had to cut Tallie quite ruthlessly out of all these speculative thoughts. She had to tell herself that Tallie had had her chance and that when she had elected to marry Toby, that was an end to

156

it. Tallie would have to accept and lie on her chosen marital bed.

Sister approached Kate on arrival at the hospital and informed her that Dr Fry wished to see her.

'Sit down,' the little man commanded sharply. He was looking closely at his notes, a procedure he did not hurry, before looking up at Kate in his unsettling, appraising way. At her anxious stare he became more reassuring.

'I thought you should know there has been a change since your last visit. A catharsis, if you like. A lot of material coming out since we eased off on medication and the retrieval of a good deal that was deeply painful. He has been talking about you, Miss Candlish—'

'He remembers me?' A deep, dark flush spread over Kate's face.

'Yes, and the sister he calls Tallie, I have told him of Tallie's marriage and my own feeling is that he has begun to accept that.'

'Does he want to see me?' she demanded urgently.

'I have no reason to believe he does not. But take things slowly. He has come a long way, but he will need a lot of support during his recovery. With luck, however, that might not be too long delayed.'

She did not know which band played the music for her steps down the hall towards the open room where Wilfred was waiting, with others, to receive their visitors. It might have been a Salvation Army band playing 'Onward Christian Soldiers' or an orchestra in the theatre pit playing the overture to 'The Maid of the Mountains'. Or it might be Chopin or the improvisation of the little man who played in Perringhall for the silent pictures. Music there was, though tumbling madly through her head, because she had been right in her divination last time, improvement was on its way and today, *today* he would look at her and really know her. Wouldn't he?

Involuntarily, her hand went up and touched first the livid scar on her face and then the hair escaping from her navy straw hat. She wore a new cream tussore blouse with a brooch at the neck of gold and tiny seed pearls, new button shoes with a stylish heel. She had taken pains with her appearance but she was never sure it was enough. All the old reservations about her looks swept over her, denuding her of confidence. When she saw him looking at her from across the big room, she was not sure at first whether recognition was there but as she got closer she saw he was smiling and leaning forward. Then he got up, a shade clumsily because of his leg, and held out his hand. He was no longer just a patient.

'Wilfred.' She did not let go of his hand as they sat down close to each other. 'I hear you are feeling so much better.'

'I remembered you. Last time after you'd gone.'

'You did?'

'They tell me Tallie's married.'

'Oh yes.' She did not know what else to say.

'If you see her, give her my best.'

She could not look at him. Her transgression on the day of Tallie's wedding caught her chest in a stricture and bound her tongue, but she managed to stumble out, 'Shall we try and get a cup of tea?' and offered her arm so that they could approach the tea trolley on the other side of the room.

'Why are *you* here?' he demanded, when all this had been accomplished. 'Why are you bothering about an old crock like me?'

She could not answer him. Suddenly the recent positions had been reversed and it was she who looked away while he pursued her with gentle enquiry.

'Have you got yourself embroiled with anyone while I've been away?'

'Embroiled?' She laughed. 'No. I haven't.'

'Do you remember me joking about you living like a nun? While I was away?'

She said slowly, 'You remember that?'

'I remember all our conversations. They were important to me.'

She spoke as though she were a lost traveller asking for directions in a strange land. 'What does this mean?'

'It means I don't seem to mind about Tallie because I wanted you.'

'Are you just saying that?'

'I'll be able to put it to you properly one day. I'm still sorting it out. It's a feeling of – completion – when you're around. Kate, have *you* got the guts to stick with me?'

He looked at her radiant face and put his arms out to enfold. her. She was murmuring things into his shoulder but it didn't matter that he couldn't make out what they were, it was the feeling of her, as it had been the day he'd cut her hair, the day he'd left for the army; the feeling and smell and taste of her, coming back to him like waves of honeysuckle eddying over a summer field, that was all that mattered.

'Do you want to wait, Kate?' he asked her on her next visit. 'The padre here will marry us if I ask him.'

She had been restless and solemn faced since the start and now she came away from the window, where she had been studying the patients on the lawn and sat down close to him with a look of resolution.

'I've something to explain.' This said, she fell silent till he urged her to go on.

'When word came that you were not missing, presumed killed after all, it was my mother who opened the telegram. Because it was Tallie's wedding, she decided not to tell her.'

His face suffused with an angry red. 'Your mother did that?' She nodded. 'And you?' he said, with a dawning look. 'What about you, Kate?'

'I only discovered the telegram on the day of the actual wedding. I think now I should have told Tallie. She'll never forgive me that I did not. But I genuinely thought it was too late by then. Do you believe me?'

'I don't,' he said, stonily.

'You don't?'

'I want the truth. Only the truth is any good between you and me, Kate. Did you do it deliberately?'

'I wanted you for myself,' she said bleakly. She had turned her back on him.

159

'But you know you should have told Tallie.'

'Would it have made any difference?'

He shook his head. And after a pause said, 'No. I know now it was you I wanted.'

'Supposing she'd held you to your promises?'

'Then I don't know.'

'I wouldn't have let you go through with it.' Her look was stricken.

They were angry and ashamed.

'You should not have done what you did,' he reproached her, with no warmth in his voice, only judgement, cold and hard.

'And you are saying it was me you cared for and yet you might still have gone ahead and married her, if that had been what she wanted?'

'Is she happy with Wilson?'

'How can I say? I couldn't keep it to myself; I told her after the ceremony and she feels bitter, very bitter towards me and towards our mother.'

'Who behaved, I have to say, totally in character.'

'She wanted security for Tallie.'

'She wanted to run Tallie's life for her. Always did.'

There was a sourness and a bitter chagrin in the room now that made it impossible for them to speak to each other. 'I'm going for a walk,' she said, and got up and went out, pulling on her coat. From the window he watched her march round the chilly grounds twice and then come back in again. They drank tea somebody brought for them and still did not speak. At last she said pitiably, 'This isn't doing you any good.'

In a subdued voice he said, 'But you had to tell me. And it couldn't have been easy.' His hand went out and stroked the back of hers, still blue-grey with cold and fear. 'I'll try and I'll try,' she offered in a low voice, 'to make you glad you picked me.'

It was there between them, this distortion of the happiness which had been so palpable on her last visit, but they knew they would have to live with it and hope it would straighten itself out. On her next visit, he said he had got things more into proportion. They had missed each other and clung like burrs. He brought up again the padre's willingness to marry them immediately. When she agreed, he initiated arrangements that day. The hospital agreed to lay on a tea and two of the nurses to be witnesses. Kate informed her mother, refusing to listen to her pleas to be married at home, about wanting to be present.

It was only Wilfred's wishes that mattered to her now. Every moment away from him and in anyone else's company seemed wasted to her. He was now well enough to be discharged as soon as they had made practical arrangements for a life together.

'I don't feel ready to teach again,' he said. 'Maybe I'll never be ready.' She acknowledged this. He was well and happy in her company, but slower in some of his responses and physically awkward and the Outside World, as he called it, still held daunting terrors for him. He had his disability pension, of course and his savings would almost cover a home of their own, but with nothing over for emergencies.

She persuaded him that it might work if he came back to live at Cullington Lodge. Her mother went along with the proposal, reluctantly, but knowing she would be on her own otherwise. It was she who, somewhat surprisingly, suggested Wilfred might even start up a hen farm on the plot of land adjacent to the house, which had never held anything more than a few fowl and the old cow Daisy who had kept them supplied with milk and butter throughout wartime exigencies. It appealed to both Kate and Wilfred as good useful work, in the open-air, not too demanding as they could enlarge at their own pace and offering nourishing food to the war-weary populace. So their new life together began. Kate gave up her teaching. It all happened quickly in the end and she had to keep pinching herself mentally to be certain it had really taken place.

# Twenty

'That was quick,' said gossip Jessie Farquhar, leaning on the mahogany shop counter with the air of someone who hoped to be there for some time. 'One minute, teaching at the Academy – I always thought myself she had the makings of an old maid – then the next, married to the Englishman. And me, I always thought' – she directed a broad look at Tallie – 'that it was yourself he fancied.'

She got all this out while Tallie stonily measured flour and tapioca, determined not to be outdone in the sport at which she excelled, baiting those who thought they were a cut above her like the snotty Candlishes. Like her cousin Ellen Siddons who worked for them, Jessie cleaned kitchens and rubbing-stoned doorsteps, in her case to keep a good-for-nothing husband in drink. Her shawl was threadbare, her boots turned up at the toes, but her tongue could still 'clip clouts' as they said in the village.

'You're no' looking all that well yourself', she went on consideringly, aware of the shadowy figure of Tallie's husband, Toby, loitering in the back shop. They would have to put up with the likes of her, because she knew very well customers were falling away. Maliciously she looked at Tallie's slender, even stringy, figure. 'You wouldn't be expecting another wee Wilson the grocer, would you? Time auld Janet Candlish had some grandbairns, is it no'?'

'That'll be one and six, Mrs Farquhar,' said Tallie without expression. Jessie looked at her downcast, washed-out face and cried contemptuously to the figure in the back shop, 'Canny take a joke, can youse? I'm saying to your wife, Toby, it's time you filled the cradle, is it no'?'

She got no response out of either of them and gathering up her shopping reluctantly she shuffled out of the shop, giving the door such a slam behind her the bell jangled for a furious few seconds.

Toby came through from the back shop. 'That's it,' he

said. He strode to the door and turned the card to 'Closed'. 'I've had enough of it for one day. When are you going to give up the hospital and be a proper help in the shop? The window needs dressing, the whole jing-bang needs freshening up—'

They had been through this argument several times in the last few days. The doctor had backed up Toby's case by saying Tallie needed to take things easier. Married women had enough to contend with, without taking jobs outside the home.

Still, Tallie said nothing, her eyes filling up with tears. Toby said with a hint of contrition, 'What is it that's really upsetting you? What she said about babies? Ignore the ignorant old bitch. Her man needs to tie a knot in it—'

Tallie shook her head. 'It's not that.'

'What she said about you and Kate, then? Ach, they'll soon put that out of their stupid heads and be on to something else. You're going to have to do it, Tallie, or you're going to destroy the pair of us.'

'Maybe I will give up the hospital,' Tallie owned, her breathing shallow. She could not talk about the death of little Mons a few weeks before, it was too painful, but nursing was not the same somehow and she was very tired. The war had gone on a long time and taken it out of everybody. The doctor had warned her she was anaemic and would have to try and eat better.

As they climbed the stairs to the rooms above, Tallie knew that although all these things applied, the state of the marriage between herself and Toby was what really had to be resolved. In her cruel, instinctive way, Jessie Farquhar had gone to the heart of the matter. There could be no new little Wilson the grocer because there was no true marriage. There could be no true marriage because she had no feelings of any sort for her husband. It was not that she did not love him. It was that she had no feeling whatsoever. She could not respond to his kindness, his patience, his anger. And Kate had done that to her, Kate who was installed now at Cullington Lodge, with Wilfred, and from all accounts so

163

blissfully happy she was being nice to people she had previously snubbed with an icy disdain.

Toby gave her a compassionate look as they took off their shop overalls. He saw that at least Jessie Farquhar in her uncouth way had pierced what he had begun to regard as a frightening apathy. Tallie clattered the cups down on the saucers as she prepared some tea.

'I suppose it's what they're all saying,' she burst out, 'that our Kate's got the better of me. She certainly thinks she has.' She turned with a new look of resolution in her eyes that lifted Toby's spirits even as it alarmed him. 'Well, I'll show them, Toby. We'll show them. I'll give up the hospital and we'll get the shop going again.'

'You mean it?' After so many dejected arguments he could scarcely believe his ears.

'I mean it.' There was a bit of colour in her cheeks as she stabbed biscuits from the biscuit barrel on to a plate with jagged gestures. 'Toby, I think we should get the lettering done above the shop – gold lettering on a dark green background. I don't think we need the sawdust on the floor any more – they're doing away with that in the bigger shops.'

'Wait,' he said cautiously. 'Wait. If you're coming out of whatever you've been in,' – he did not know how better to put it – 'what about us?' He moved closer to her, where she stood by the sink. 'What about us, Tallie? You have to admit I've had the patience of Job.'

'I don't want babies. Yet.'

'I'll take care of that.'

'But when we've got the shop on its feet—' she volunteered.

She watched a slow red warmth climb up his cheeks and felt as little surge of female – what? Triumph? Pleasure? Power? At least it was feeling. Very young and green and untried, but feeling.

'It's not that I don't want children. Eventually. But I want them to have a better chance than I had. Especially if we have girls.'

He sat down, putting his head in his hands. 'Christ,' he appealed. 'I hope we can pull out of this.' He was thinking that it was the one shot in his armour he had not used – Tallie's sense of pride. It had taken a shrew, a targe from the Rows, to activate that and he thanked the woman profoundly now, from the depths of his unspoken soul. There was nothing they could not attain – they could have the best shop in Perringhall, the best-educated children, if that was what Tallie wanted. All it needed was for them to pull together, for her not necessarily to love him, not outright, not yet, but just for her to let him love her, as he had always done, always would do, right reason or none. He looked up at her at last with his love naked in his eyes and she said in her new, quick, half-bossy way, 'What would you like for supper? Will I get some best ham up from the shop?'

'If you'll eat it,' he answered unequivocally, 'and stop eating like a sparrow from now on.'

'Can I come to you?' he asked in bed.

She had taken a bath in the big, peeling bathtub and had been putting on the cambric honeymoon nightie when he had stopped her. 'No,' he had said. 'No nightgown. Tonight, just skin.'

It felt like they were sharing the big new bed for the first time. In a febrile kind of way she kept getting flashing images in her mind of Kate and Wilfred at Cullington, sharing the big brass bedstead in the largest room, which she presumed would now be theirs. Perversely as Toby's hands touched her, gently and almost reverently at first, she made herself remember lying in the fields with Wilfred and the time he had taken her virginity. She had wanted it so much but it was only now, in her new savage determination to make a go of her marriage, that she remembered it might not have been all she had expected it to be.

'Don't think of him,' said Toby grindingly. He turned her to face him, forcing her mouth open to his kiss. 'I ken, I ken,' he said, lapsing into the vernacular. 'I ken what they did to you, but you're my lass now and I'm going to take care of you.' He looked at her small young breasts and brought his mouth down worshippingly on either nipple before kissing her stomach and the little curly patch of pubic hair. With a swooping, triumphant possessiveness, he picked her up and rolled her over and then over again, so that they almost fell out of the bed.

He hoped for her laughter – how he hoped for that! – but it did not come. He looked down instead at her tense, impassive face and his impulse was to throw himself away from her, to rage and shout or throw something. But he knew also if he gave in to her terror it was the end of anything between them. He could not give up now, when she had made the first moves that afternoon, asking him what he wanted for his tea, then having the bath, not stopping him when he had thrown her nightgown to one side. Besides, he was going to take care of her, as he had promised.

He felt rather than saw the rush of relief on her face as he moved imperceptibly away from her. This was why they had stopped even trying to make love, because she tightened and closed up against him. Now it was pity for her that kept him going and a desperation to save what could be saved, some kind of integrity of feeling between them, that they would lose at their peril.

He tried again, patiently, slowly, judging the slightest response in her and answering it with a skill he didn't know he possessed and at last he had his reward. Her body began to rise and fall like a gentle tide, she put her mouth to his voluntarily and grabbed the hair at the side of his head. He felt her part slippily and he came to her, still by some miracle gentle but that was only the start; soon they were like horses riding the waves, far our, far out, then crashing, moaning, in her case crying out, as they were thrown on the farther shores of passion.

'You're beautiful,' he said. In his poetry and in his wooing he had known how beautiful she would be and now, lying against her bare breast, tired as a swimmer, he could have wept from the release the knowledge gave him.

166

He thought again how pride had saved them – her pride and his passion. That was how it was going to be. He did not care how he paid for what had just happened or what cold winds of reservation might blow through his mind in the morning. Falling asleep, he remembered her declining verbs and identifying the capital of Sweden in the classroom and then the sun glinting on her hair when he and his dog had met up with her in the woods. He remembered the whole sum of her and in some mysterious way it was added to him. You waited and it all came to pass.

Matron was not pleased when she handed in her notice, but Tallie had pointed out that things were bound to change: peace was coming – the central powers were talking peace, weren't they? – and things would start getting back to normal, which meant women staying home and looking after their men properly. Everyone wanted to rush peace along; they suddenly could not wait any longer for it. Unmarried women could do as they liked, but surely the married ones had no option. Fleetingly, Tallie knew Kate would have argued this point with her till the cows came home, but then Kate always went too far and besides, who was she to talk, who had given up everything to look after Wilfred? And what was she doing thinking about Kate anyhow, for it was Tallie's intention their lives would never meet up again. Cullington Lodge, her mother and Kate and even Wilfred, were now behind a barrier in her mind a lot less breachable than the Maginot Line. A thick, heavy, concrete, barbed-wire wall that she didn't even want to see over. While she and Toby were busy making a life together that would show everyone just what they were made of.

Toby's health became one of her paramount challenges. She fed him three good meals a day, kept him from fishing or going out in the wet, nagged sneezing children to use their hankies when they came into the shop, found out the best way to treat colds when they did get into his chest, rubbing his chest with camphorated oil, dosing him with Scott's Emulsion, warming his coat and gloves, none of which ministrations he seemed to mind in the least.

When Tallie became pregnant – they realised it must have happened That Night, when Toby had not taken care of things, at all – all reservations about her daughter-in-law's recent behaviour deserted Jeannette Wilson and even Hector 'Daddy' Wilson forgot the harsh words he had been preparing for his son about letting the shop go down and substituted instead a reasoned discussion of the accounts.

'Something'll have to be done,' the older man rumbled nevertheless, 'though I don't know what.' Tallie wheedled the money for the new shop lettering from him and got down on her hands and knees to scrub the last of the hated sawdust off the floors.

'You mustn't overdo things,' Jeannette protested, horrified. 'You should be putting your feet up.'

'No need for that,' Tallie retorted briskly. She went on arranging shelves, edging them with lace paper borders, polishing up the brass scales, spending long minutes on the pavement outside deciding whether to dress the window with just a few selected items, or a bit of everything, or one central dramatic theme.

Seeing things were going on, customers began to trickle back and Tallie would entice them to come again by flicking an extra flake of butter on to a modest pat, or holding out a scrap of cheese for sampling, or finding a broken biscuit for a good child. The more cynical came in to marvel at the change and could not quite decide what had brought it about. Puzzling about it brought them in again. Even so, supplies were variable because of the war. People wanted change and because of shortage change was the last thing they could have.

'Jam,' said Tallie, one evening. A late harvest had brought a glut a blackberries and golden Victoria plums. Her thoughts went back to the jam-making rituals back home, when every year her mother had made jam and jelly of every variety. The memory of the ritual of warming pots, sifting in sugar and watching that the seething jellypan did not boil over, tugged at her demandingly. With protestations about being careful Jeannette loaned her brass jellypan and using up, guiltily, a small horde of sugar from the same source, Tallie turned out pot after pot of rich-tasting jam and jelly. Pleased and astonished at the profit it brought, she began also to make scones and pancakes on the griddle in the upstairs kitchen, using the recipes she had learned by heart from her mother's instructions and once a week, a huge clootie dumpling, eked out with grated carrot, which she sold cold by the slice, to be eaten like cake or warmed up with the bacon in the frying pan.

Her in-laws shook their heads in delighted admiration but Jeannette once again entered her caveat about Tallie doing too much.

'But the Candlishes have always rolled up their sleeves and got on with things,' she admitted. 'I saw Kate when I went past this hen farm they've set up the other day and she was working like a navvy, hammering in big heavy staves to make a fence. I hear things aren't going too well for them – their first batch of hens had some disease or other. Fell off their perches, one by one.'

Tallie did not deceive her. Despite the closed expression she was taking in every word.

'Let her be,' said Toby, grinning at his wife. 'You know you can't stop her. She's talking about getting another shop already.'

When Sunday came, Tallie said to Toby in a casual way, 'When we've had our dinner, we'll have a bit of a walk.'

'Where had you in mind?'

The pink rose up in her face. 'Up past Cullington.'

'Do you want to go in?' he queried, half-teasingly.

'You know I do not. I just want a look at this hen farm.'

'Whatever you say.'

He thought she had never looked prettier, in her new boater with the bronze grosgrain ribbon matching her skirt and the cornelian filigree brooch at the neck of her cream blouse. He drew her arm possessively through his as they stepped out together in the measured way that became a married couple.

He was thinking of the baby, of the time when they would be pushing it out together in its perambulator and the later time when there might be another one inside and a toddler at the handle, when he heard her begin to breathe short, shallow gasps.

'What is it?' he demanded in alarm.

She was looking ahead to Cullington Lodge where it sat as always on the prow of the brae, its grey stones somehow reminiscent of battlements; of a keep of some kind.

'The blinds!' Tallie grasped out. 'The blinds, Toby. They're drawn. Every one.'

He looked at his wife's grey face and put out a hand to steady her.

She gave a cry that made him think of some wild bird. 'It can only mean one thing. Russell's dead.'

He thought: *or Donald*. But she was shaking her head as though she had heard the words in his head. 'No, I've had this feeling all week. It's not Donald. It's Russell.'

'Then we'll go in,' he urged her.

He could not look at the pain on her face. 'No, no, we'll not. Not even today.'

She turned back on her tracks, leaning on him as though she were an old, broken woman, her face crumpled with distress and tears.

'I want to go home,' she said. 'Our home. I want to go home.'

# Twenty-One

Belle Candish sat in a crowded train coming up from London, gazing without seeing from the window, ignoring the cheeky attempts of three young sailors to start a conversation with her.

There was a certain war-nearing-its-end hysteria detectable in the air. Posters in the capital had blazoned Horatio Bottomley's demand that they should hang the Kaiser, others had announced a mass meeting in the Albert Hall calling for nothing less than unconditional surrender. Back in the Flanders she had just left, the tanks had still rolled and the guns rumbled but even there, the feeling was abroad that whatever madness, whatever evil had stalked that broken and desecrated countryside had at last retired to its lair, gasping its expiry.

And in these last days had occurred the most poignant deaths of all, of those who had soldiered through the heat of battle only to fall at the final post. She could not believe it had happened to Russell. Missing. Believed killed. Not her little brother whose shining nine-year-old face had somehow been superimposed on his battledress whenever she had thought of him all during the war. Not Russell who had not been able to wait to get back to his Tibby and his little girl Catriona. His pride in the baby had invaded all his letters, though he had never seen her.

'Would you like a square of chocolate?' one of the young sailors asked her, the silver-paper wrapped morsel in his outstretched hand. Seeing the tears stand up in her eyes before she hastily wiped them away, he said roughly, 'Dinna greet, hen' and sat back nonplussed and embarrassed in his seat.

She took the chocolate to spare his feelings, half-choking on it as it went down. The others in the compartment fell silent and presently sank against each other in sleep.

She was able then as she had not done since she got the

news to remember Russell properly. They'd been in-separable practically since he was born, she his half-mother who lugged him around wet-rusked on her hip, picking him up when he fell, nursing him when he cried, sticking up for him in battle and protecting him when in trouble. And in return he'd chased off wild boys who threatened her with puddocks or stones, brought her hard green apples from dog-guarded orchards, assured her safe conduct when they went guising at Hallowe'en, even against the ghoulies and ghosties which had franticked her vivid imagination. Was there ever such a stout little boy, so ready to face the giants of retribution or to stand up against a heavy-handed older brother such as Donald had been? And how would Donald feel now, and all those who had never known what Russell was really like, as maybe only she did? She could grudge even Tibby for loving him, for in her grief, she wanted to keep Russell all to herself. We were pals, she repeated over in her mind. True pals. And in the crowded, redolent, overheated railway carriage she carried out her own requiem for the man she would always see as her little brother, observing his bright presence in her mind as it had been in so many childish games, running wild over pit bing and field, paddling in cold burns; but always turning towards her, laughing and daring, wanting her there.

She had written to tell Percy Barnett immediately she'd got the news, but she thought now: what had been the use? She'd heard nothing from him for months and even allowing for hold-ups in the mail she was becoming convinced he had not been as committed to her as he had sworn to be. When you thought of it, they'd both been caught up in a totally artificial situation, the spell of a sunny afternoon, away from the mud and guns; when they had snatched at a little passing human contact as a thirsty rifleman might snatch at a drink of water. No more than that, maybe, despite all the constructs in her mind about the day they might meet up again, even about marrying him after the war was over. He'd given her the ring and it had put other men off, possibly, but it could have been the action of a young cad or a soppy romanticist who'd regretted it as soon as he was away from her. The other VADs, harder than she, had insisted she should take on board this possibility, for her own good.

She wasn't very sure why anyone should love her, anyhow. Despite what Tallie always alleged, that she was her mother's favourite, demonstrations of affection had not abounded as she grew up. And when she was younger she had suffered, as they all had, from her father's reputation as a heavy drinker, a brawler, a wife and child beater and from the barefoot poverty and deprivation he had imposed on them. Though she stubbornly remembered, selectively she knew, the times he was sober, and not unkind, and gave them ha'pennies for Lucky Bags and sherbets. In the way of those as badly off as oneself, other children in the Rows where they had once lived had not been slow to mock her lack of boots, the Friday night rows when her father came home from the pub or her tears when she had not been able to go to the Co-op Gala. These things stuck and took away a basic confidence, which a later improvement in the family fortunes had not been able to restore, though her own capabilities did, except when she was low and longing for love and reassurance.

Percy had gone to public school and spoke with what Donald would probably call in derisory fashion a cut-glass English accent. But then Donald had affected a Glasgow Kelvinside way of talking and Belle, like her sister, watched her diction now that she was grown up and seldom spoke in the broad Lowland accent she had had as a child. Only Russell had remained defiantly 'broad' and unaffected, refusing to dissemble in this as in any other area of his life. She was back to Russell again and the pain seemed it would never go away. It was all tied up up with the fear that she would never see Percy again either, and the suspicion that the sweetness of that interlude at Montreuil had been nothing more than a brave hallucination.

She looked at her watch. It was one o'clock. And she had promised to think of him every day at this time.

'You can't stay away from your own mother forever.'

Belle sat in the harshly new parlour above the shop and gazed disbelievingly at Tallie.

'Let them come to me,' said Tallie, her mouth a hard line.

'Your mother's your mother. You have to honour your parents. It says so in the Bible.'

'Well, I don't go to church any more. And how can you, after what's happened to our Russell?' Both young women were fighting for composure, determined that the so-frequently shed tears over their brother would not flow again, or they might flow forever.

'That's your decision,' Belle conceded. 'But make it up with Ma and Katie. You must see what a terrible position I'm in, with a foot in both camps. It's not the way a family should be. It just adds to the sadness and it fills the gossips' mouths in Perringhall.'

Impulsively, Tallie came over and put her arm round her younger sister's shoulders.

'Don't get involved, Belle,' she insisted. 'None of this has anything to do with you. Or with Donald, for that matter. You and Donald are welcome in this house any time you care to call.'

Belle looked down at the cup of tea and Abernethy biscuit she was balancing on her lap, letting her breath out on a long, dispirited sigh. She'd told Tallie what it was like now at the Lodge – her mother locked in uncommunicative silence, her Bible open unread on her knee, Kate railing against the generals and all war and Wilfred retiring to his room, strained and taut. She, Belle, was doing her best to keep some kind of domestic heart beating, to knit things together somehow, but how could she, when so much had fallen apart?

She had never thought Tallie could be so hard, not about Russell's death, but about the effect on those at home. It was a time for pulling together, for mutual comforting, but Tallie would not be budged. The only time she had shown

174

any emotion was when Wilfred's name had been mentioned and then there had been a trembling of the mouth, a quick rush of emotion over her features like a ripple of wind over a lake.

Belle gave up. Toby was looking at her as much as to suggest she shouldn't upset Tallie in her present delicate condition, nor did she wish to. She picked up her things and went.

Kate Chappell entered the morning-room at Cullington Lodge, the morning paper hanging limply from her hand and said to her mother, bent over her breakfast, 'It's all over. They've signed the Armistice. The fifteenth is to be Victory Day. Donald will be coming home.'

Wilfred limped in, his face shadowed by the beard he was starting to grow and ate his food without a word. Presently Kate heeled her eyes with her right hand and walked over to the window. 'I can see flags,' she said tonelessly. 'Down in the village, I can see flags.'

They had signed the peace papers in a railway carriage in the forest of Compièigne and at the eleventh hour of the eleventh day of the eleventh month, the guns had fallen silent all over Europe. Four days later the Boy Scouts and Boys' Brigaders of Perringhall cycled down the main street sounding the 'all clear' on their bugles and the bells of Perringhall's three churches rang in a clamorous din.

Kate took Wilfred's arm and they walked slowly down to the small town square to share hesitantly in the celebrations. They had not been able to get Janet to join them; she said she wanted to get things ready in case Donald got home soon. Getting things ready meant dusting aimlessly over surfaces already without spot or speck, but at least she had got out of her chair and was joining in the general conversation once again.

Belle had gone to sing in the church choir and then help put the long trestle tables out on the cobbles so that members of the women's guild could lay out sandwiches, buns, cakes and jellies for the celebrations. Someone in the town had dragged out an old piano and the choirmaster came from the church to play tunes people could dance to, while further up the street he had competition from someone else on melodeon. They were building a bonfire to light later on Castle Hill and a maroon was to be fired at eleven o'clock, on the instant.

Although Cullington Lodge had not succumbed, everybody else, it seemed, had hung out flags and bunting of some sort, home-made or otherwise. Little girls were resplendent in their best dresses and small boys with money to spend bought fireworks and frightened the cats and dogs into hiding.

Kate and Wilfred walked past the shop run by Toby and Tallie. It was closed, like all the rest. Kate kept an eye open for her sister. She thought on this day above all they might meet and exchange a word. But though Toby and Tallie had joined the throng on the street, as soon as Tallie caught Kate's eyes across the street, she turned her head sharply away. After a few moments Kate saw, from the corner of her eye, her sister and her husband leave the festivities and return to their apartments above the shop. Later she could see their faces behind glass and then those of the in-laws, Jeannette and 'Daddy' Wilson, peering out when a regimental band marched down the street and cheering broke out and that seemed as though it would go on forever.

So they were not there at that moment when Kate looked past the sticky-faced children tucking into their tea and the minister trying to get enough hush to make some kind of speech and the old man lying drunkenly under the Mercat Cross and saw, under all the flags and bunting waving about in the fresh wind, her brother Donald coming towards her like some brave image in a dream.

She flew out of Wilfred's grasp and into his arms, hugging and patting him, laughing and crying. 'When did you get back? Are you really all right? How long will you be home for?' He was laughing too, his big, handsome head thrown back, well aware, thought Kate, with a brief flash of her old acuity, of how well he fitted the picture of the Return of the

Hero. And then she banished the thought, for there was no reason to believe he had not been as heroic, or not, as the rest and he was precious and solid and *there* and she was not the only one who wanted to pat and cheer and hug him.

'Welcome home, old chap,' said Wilfred, diffidently.

Donald thumped him on the back. 'Remember the arguments we used to have?' he demanded, cheerily. 'Do you think we sorted everything out, then? Was it worth it, Wilf?' There was a deep irony making his voice gruff, and the pain behind his eyes was unmistakeable. Wilfred grasped him then and held him, convulsively, while Kate looked at the ground.

Then she got in between both men and held on to their arms. 'This is all getting a bit too much,' she adjudged. 'Let's go home.' It wasn't easy to make progress, for people wanted to stop them, to express their delight at seeing Donald, to shake his hand, tease him about his medals, invite him to join them in a dram, tell him their own war dramas.

But when they were ascending the brae towards Cullington Lodge, he slowed them down deliberately anyhow, to ask for further details on how his mother was taking things.

'Badly,' said Kate briefly.

'And Tibby and the child?'

'Tibby knew,' Wilfred interjected. 'She came up to make things up with your mother and told us all Russell would never come back. She knew.'

They looked at each other with grim faces and Kate said with an unwonted gentleness, 'But Tibby is young and strong and can start again.'

'I want to see her.' His sister looked at him quickly but he was inscrutable and did not volunteer more.

'If our mother knew how he went, I think it might help her,' said Kate. 'She can't come to terms with the fact that he went more or less unscratched for so long and then, just in sight of home, as it were, the bastards took him. But how?'

Donald's face had gone a strange putty colour under its weatherbeaten tan.

'I made it my business to find out,' he said. 'Before I left. How he went.'

They were stopped in their slow tracks once again. Kate had a sensation of fading, of not wanting to hear what might be coming next. Wilfred put out a hand and caught hers.

'All right,' she conceded. 'Tell us.'

'If you weren't there,' he began, 'you couldn't begin to comprehend. The sewers and dykes were shot to pieces by the bombardment. The rain was ceaseless and the tanks turned the mud over and over. Passchendaele was a quagmire, from start to finish. You had to keep to the duckboards—'

He stopped, lifting up his head as if for air.

'I don't know if we'll ever get over it. Any of us. Who were there. But they went missing. It was as simple as that. If you slipped off the duckboards, the mud just swallowed you up. Sometimes nobody saw it. Sometimes somebody might manage to get you out. But in Russell's case, that's what happened. You slipped off the duckboards and that was it. Missing. You went missing. He got through without a scratch and the mud had him.' He turned away from them and leaned against a fence, turning towards them at last with a ghastly sort of grin. 'But I don't think we can tell Mother. Or Tibby. Do you hear what I am saying? We'll say a bullet got him. Quick and clean and merciful.'

Wilfred nodded because Kate could say nothing. 'Yes,' he agreed, without irony. 'A better way to die.'

# Twenty-Two

'So this is Catriona?' said Donald. He was sitting in the kitchen, finishing a late breakfast, his khaki sleeves rolled up, when Tibby entered the kitchen door, her little girl by the hand, and in the other hand a basket of shopping for the day's dinner. He rose and kissed Tibby in a stiff gesture, not allowing their eyes to meet, then returned his attention to the child. She had picked some flowers on the way and held them out now towards him. He took them and sniffed them extravagantly. 'Lovely,' he enthused. She took them away from him and handed them towards her grandmother. 'Nice flowers,' said Janet. 'Wuvly,' said Catriona, parrotting her uncle and they all laughed, the ice partially broken.

It wasn't till later in the day that he was able to have Tibby to himself. Catriona and her grandmother were napping and Belle had gone off to meet a friend for shopping. They walked into the lightly wooded area near the house where Tallie had once gathered firewood. The leaves were beginning to fall and the non-deciduous trees had a dry autumnal rustle. He suddenly didn't know what to say, words he had rehearsed in his head deserting him.

'About Russell,' he began.

'Don't talk about him,' she ordered curtly. 'I still can't bear it, so just don't.'

'I just wanted to say I understand what happened. He wrote to me and explained—'

'It was between me and him,' she said, only marginally more conciliatory. 'And there was no explaining to do.' Hers was not a face that bore pain prettily. There were lumps under her eyes and her mouth looked distorted, as though with an effort to keep invective from spewing forth. 'I have his bairn,' she said at last, 'and that is something.'

'She won't want,' he said quickly. 'I will make her my personal concern.'

'No need,' said Tibby, 'My father provides. He dotes on Catriona.'

'I'll pay for schooling. Clothes. Music lessons. She'll want for nothing.'

'You'll marry, Donald,' she said. 'You'll have your own commitments.'

It wasn't how he had meant it to happen. Perhaps the question had always been there, but he had certainly not seen the present time as propitious.

'*You* wouldn't marry me? Would you?' he said.

There was that same almost-ugly look. Suffering, he thought swiftly, didn't necessarily ennoble. Did it make people mean, breed the need for retribution?

'Not if you were the last man alive,' said Tibby.

'I don't think you can mean that,' he said carefully.

'Ah, but I do.'

'I thought once you quite liked me,' he said, hating himself for the stupid banality of the words.

Her gaze flew guiltily towards his face and away again.

'You're like one of the family now,' he pointed out. 'You and my mother seem to get on—'

'There was no place else to go when I lost Russell,' she said. 'They went through the motions of sympathising at home, but I couldn't talk about him there.'

'That's good, good.'

'Belle especially. I can talk to Belle. It brings him back. One of the hardest things of all—' She stopped.

'Yes, go on.'

'Is coming to terms with him being cut off, before he'd done all the things he'd wanted to do. Before he was the man he could have been.'

He said reluctantly, 'People say this about him. They felt this promise in him.'

'*You* couldn't see it for believing in your own cleverness, Donald.' Although the words were harsh her tone was gentle and even joshing.

'I wish you wouldn't say things like that.'

'I'm only saying what your sisters say. That you were

treated like a little tin god. "Run Donald's bath for him." "Darn Donald's socks." Your mother did it, I know that. No wonder there's a cloud on her face now when she talks about Russell. It's as though she wants to make up to him, through me and Catriona. But she never will. She never can. There's no second chances.'

They had come to a fallen tree trunk and he motioned to her to sit down. 'Or do you want to go back?' he temporised humbly, anxious to show he would defer to her wishes. She gave the matter some thought and then shook her head briefly. The sun had come out, belatedly, and warmed the crumbling bark.

There was an expression of bewilderment on his face.

'Is it the fact that he's gone that makes everybody talk like this? I don't begrudge Russell any of it, God knows. If he'd been spared, we might have mended a lot of bridges. I was going to do all I could for him. What I don't understand—' He swallowed and looked away.

'What don't you understand?'

'The difference. That you perceive between him and me. Am I so different?'

'Well, since you ask, the difference was he cared about other folk. He was always ready to stick up for the underdog. I know it got him into trouble at times. But the thing was, he had a heart this big.' And she spread her hands.

'And mine isn't?'

'You were always too full of being Donald.' She thought she had probably gone too far and qualified her words. 'You asked. So I'm telling you.'

He leant forward, his elbows on his knees, watching the efforts of an ant to shift a tiny piece of twig. It was suddenly of great importance that it should be able to tug it under the leaf nearby as it intended. Half a mile away, a lark was singing before the inevitable steep plunge earthwards. A steam train heading south let out a long, mournful-sounding whistle that carried him back, somewhere, into the dim recesses of his childhood. Had he always been King of the Castle, Cock o' the North? When what he was glimpsing now was the shadow of an upraised hand, a sense of violence that had to be staved off, withstood? A protest broke from his lips, a wordless expostulation.

He said, his words tenacious and slow, 'Well, the war's sent all that out of the window. I'm changed. You don't go through hell and out the other side, without changing.'

'In what way?' She was looking at him closely, observing him minutely, almost ruthlessly.

'If you had seen me,' he said in a low, angry tone. 'If you had seen me, the great Donald, up the line, shaking and trembling, unable to issue orders, you wouldn't think me the superman you make me out to be.'

'You? Shaking?' She sounded cold and disbelieving.

'Oh, aye, even me. I am only mortal. I had this young batman. Came from Govan. Grieves was his name. Alexander Grieves, known as Sanny. You couldn't keep the little bugger down. I can see him still, running a match up the pleats of his kilt and swearing – he had the foulest mouth of any man I've ever heard – as the lice crackled. It didn't matter how rough it got – and it got rough, I tell you – he was there, with this filthy tin mug full of the most repulsive tea you've ever seen in your life and a dog-end or a gasper he'd scrounged for you, from God knows where. He went up in the air before my eyes, bits of him everywhere.'

She looked at him quickly, her alarm real now. He was holding his right wrist with his left hand and was shaking all over, with a fine tremor. He said, 'It's all right. It'll pass. Give it twenty minutes.'

'Donald,' she said anxiously. 'I'll walk you back.'

'No,' he said dismissively. 'Ignore it. I'm a helluva lot better than I was. We have to talk about things. Don't let's go back just yet.'

'What things?' she demanded, a little wearily.

'Like us getting married.' He overrode her rising protest. 'No, no, *listen*. I'm making sense. You and Catriona would both have security. A woman needs a man at her back. Not

182

one like my own father. Maybe it was his lack that made me
– well, over-ambitious. But I would be a good husband to
you, Tibby. I thought of you often out there.'

She tried a different tack. 'What sort of catch do you
think I would be? Someone with an illegitimate bairn?'

'You're not the only one whose lover never returned.
Nobody'll judge you harshly—'

'You haven't been in my place.'

'Just let them say anything about you in my presence.'

She looked at him quickly, grateful despite her
resistance. Taking advantage of what he saw as her slight
softening, he grabbed her hand, prised the fingers back and
kissed her palm. Looking directly into her eyes, he
pleaded: 'Could you bear to hug me? Let me put my arms
around you? Forget what I said about marrying. Just be
here for me. Just for a minute?' She thought she heard his
teeth chattering slightly. She allowed him to pull her closer.
She could feel the fresh soap he had used and the touch of
lavender oil on his springy hair. Her lips rubbed by accident
against his cheek and he turned hungrily towards her
mouth. She had been going to break away but then found
she did not. He held her in an increasingly masterful grip
and said insistently, 'Don't you want to settle down?
Please, Tibby. It's this one thing I want.'

'I don't know what *I* want.' She found the strength to
push him back slightly and drew in air, like stiffening. 'I
want a life, certainly. For the baby and myself. I want to
start enjoying things again, simple things like buying
dresses and going to dances—'

'I'll buy you dresses—'

'Maybe' – softly – 'I want to buy my own. Kate says I
should train to be a typist and be self-supporting. She says
with the start of the vote for women it'll be easier—'

'You're not a New Woman, Tibby.' He sounded very
positive.

'How do you know that? I might be.'

'You're made to love a man and have babies and spread
your lovely golden warmth.' He took hold of her hair, none

too gently, and buried his face in it. 'I thought of the golden hairs on your arms and the freckles on your bosom.' He was fumbling at the buttons on her dress and her fingers would not obey her command to do them up again.

'Tib,' he said, triumphantly. 'Golden girl Tib. Come and lie down on my jacket.' The leaves rustled under their joint weights and he pulled her over on top of him. There was nothing pitiable about him now; no trembling. Looking up, he said, 'You are my Beatrice, my Isolde, my radiant, strong woman. You are the woman I need: I can't do what I want to do without you.' With a deft, complex movement he reversed their positions so that she was under him and he was urgently pushing up her skirts. She tried a half-hearted protest but he laughed and her own mouth softened in a kind of smile, her limbs seemed to flop away from her, her hair drifted and she sighed. He was fumbling and pushing as he said, 'I can't be a minister without a strong wife and that's you, Tib.'

He watched the expression on her face and it was so astounded, almost comically so, that he laughed and having failed as yet to grapple with total success with her under-things, fell down against her, kissing her frantically and saying, 'I haven't told anyone else, not even those at home. I'm going to be a minister of the church and dedicate my life to something worthwhile.'

He fell away from her, to one side, but their faces were still so close their racing breath mingled. 'What do you think of that?' he demanded.

She stared at him for what seemed to him like an eternity, then, said, disappointingly, prosaically, 'I don't know what to think.'

He was over her again, kissing her frantically.

'Don't think!' he commanded. 'Just marry me. Just let me love you.'

She said against his shoulder, like an incantation that would not be suppressed: 'The baby sings to her daddy. How can I marry you, when the baby still sings to her daddy? Out in the field behind the house. You know how they make up the words? She was singing about a little girl and a dog and a ball and a butterfly. And I said, 'What's that song you're singing?' and she said, 'It's a song for my daddy'. And I said 'Where is he, pet?' and she pointed up to the sky.'

All the while she spoke she was weeping and at the same time touching him and lifting her strong body upwards to meet him, her breath expunged in soft little cries of protest and desire. He found what his urgent, aroused malehood was seeking and entered her powerfully, with a cry of conquest and ecstasy and her limbs closed around him while their mouths met in a raging insistence that they should be one. Long abstinence had tried them so that they both wept briefly when it was done, but she rose first and quickly to shake out her skirts and tidy her hair into its bandeau, while he tried to pull her back down to him to come into his arms again.

Her lips felt bruised and sore and she brushed them with the back of her hand, sitting down beside him because her legs were suddenly quite weak.

'Are you all right?' he asked, almost humbly. 'Was it good for you? It was for me.'

'We shouldn't have done it.' She said the words sadly. He had hoped to see her face transformed, but the ugly, livid look was still there, under her eyes. And something else. Shame, maybe. Regret. He felt a twinge of guilt.

'But you liked it.' He tried to tease her.

'It takes you out of yourself.'

'Is that the best you can manage?'

'It's something.'

'You might get to love me,' he offered hopefully.

She had fixed her hair and straightened her clothes to her satisfaction and now she deliberately changed the subject. 'I can't believe what you just said. Did you mean it? About becoming a minister?'

'I mean it, all right.'

'I can't see it,' she said candidly. 'Not you.'

'Nevertheless.'

'How is that going to help anyone? You'd be better going into politics.'

'Politics skims the surface. Change has to begin at a much more radical level. In the spirit of man.'

'You're not going to become another God-man?' she demanded. She was referring to a long-haired, Messianic figure who had haunted their mutual childhood, half-feared and half-pitied, ranting in the twilight at the end of the pit rows or under the Mercat Cross in the main street.

His smile was constrained. 'No, no street-corner preaching. I'll go back to university, take a Divinity degree.'

There was a long silence, while each was privy to their own thoughts. Then her protests broke out again. 'Don't decide things like that while you're still – well, you know, coming to terms with things. Talk it over with Kate and Wilfred. Even your mother.'

'You know me,' he said briefly. 'It's not how I do things. I'm my own man. I only know I have to try and do something or it will be the same all over again, in twenty years' time. It's as though I have some pact, some covenant, if you like, with the likes of Grieves. And Russell. I've told you first, Tibby. I want you along on this great adventure.'

'I'm not much of a religious person.'

'You go to church.'

She sighed, plucking at the grass in front of her as if it might reveal something, some insight. 'I don't see people getting better. People don't change.'

'What else is there? If we don't turn away from war, love our enemy, do good to those who wrong us, what future is there? Quite simply, we have to open our hearts up to one another. To love one another. Or we die. The human race is on its way out.'

She caught a gleam in his eye that dried up the saliva in her mouth.

'Maybe what you should be doing, Donald,' she stated, keeping her voice very flat and ordinary, because of the quaking she felt inside her, 'is just be having a bon time.

186

Isn't that what they called it in the army? Maybe Russell and Grieves and the rest of them would rather you just went out and danced and enjoyed yourself, the way they would have done.'

He smiled a private little smile. 'No. My crusade is already under way. *In here.*' He tapped his temple. Then seeing how deep her perturbation went, he leaned over and pulled something from the pocket of his jacket. It was a very tattered, leather-bound copy of the Gospels. 'Look. Someone gave me this in Central Station once. I took it and thought nothing of it. Everybody got one. I carried it about with me more out of superstition than anything else. Then . . . look at this.' He handed over the battered volume, pointing at a pitted hole near the middle. 'If it hadn't been for this, shrapnel would have entered my heart and almost certainly have killed me. The Bible saved me. I think it was a sign. After that, I read it every day, no matter what.' He tapped it. 'The beginning of wisdom.'

She said nothing. He knew he could only explain so much to Tibby. Part of her attraction for him was that she was straightforward, practical, non-intellectual. A kind of earth-mother, though she would not understand the term. He meant rooted, solid, inimitable. Timeless mystical woman. Her bigness made him think of billowing clouds, soft fields, harvest moons. He did not want some slip of a thing with no bosom.

Neither did he crave to unburden himself any further to anyone. What happened to him in Flanders had been a process so complex and mysterious and agonising – what the church called 'the dark night of the soul', he supposed – that he no longer wanted part of it. He knew he carried his experiences about with him still – they were like a dark sack dragging behind him – but one day, soon, he hoped, he would sever the ragged rope between them forever and rise, like a phoenix, into the certainty of his faith.

He had sorted out so much in his mind, since Montreuil. Sorted out about his own stupidities when he went into the war, caring as much about being officer-class as the reasons for fighting, when it was the poor bloody squaddies who were to die on the barbed wire and in the pitiless craters in their massive numbers. Men who had been too young and green to figure it all out and who were just beginning to suspect it might have been for nothing. Braver men than he. All his education had done for him had made him more vulnerable. More aware and maybe more cowardly. He had not evaded his duty. But he had done it with raw terror and full comprehension in his heart, knowing steel killed a man, shells took him apart, gas petrified and mud buried.

Tibby stood up. Her face was still a picture of bewilderment and he felt a sudden compassion for her, for the matters he had sprung on her so precipitately. Getting up and putting his arm around her, he said, remorsefully, 'I'm rushing you, I know. But we've got grown-up things to do now, Tibby. Things like giving Catriona security.'

She moved out of the orbit of his concern with a long stride, saying, 'We've been out too long. They'll wonder what we've been up to.'

'Let them.' He invited her to smile like a conspirator, but she would not.

Faintly ruffled, he remembered something she had said about dances, about having a good time.

'I don't like dancing, anyhow,' he said aggrievedly as they strode along. 'It's like people have gone dance mad, since the war.'

'I love dancing,' she retorted. As if he didn't know. He felt a murderous hatred of the men who were her partners.

As they came out of the copse, he said, 'Tibby, think of all I've said.'

She stopped in her tracks. With a shift of perception, he thought: she is different too. Not quite the girl I remember. Changed. He couldn't quite define it.

'I loved Russell,' she said. 'You can't take his place, you know.'

He said, with increasing desperation, 'But you'll think of what I've said? Russell won't come back.'

# Twenty-Three

Before Donald's leave was finished he went to see his old professor at the university. Demobilisation couldn't be accomplished overnight and he had been warned it might be February or even March before he joined civilian ranks. But he wanted to get his plans sorted out. It seemed to him that if he did then he could impose a decision on Tibby, but although she had allowed him to take her out and sit with her in the garden of an evening, she was showing no inclination to rush matters. Quite the reverse.

'Your sort of restlessness is only too understandable,' said old Crombie.

'It isn't restlessness,' Donald argued.

'Changing horses midstream?' The wise old eyes tracked over the strained but still-youthful face before him. He'd had a procession of jittery, unsettled young men passing before him recently, unable to make up their minds what they wanted to do with the peace they'd fought for; some wanting action rather than the academic life; some justification for emigrating. 'You say your old firm want you back. I should think they do. There are not going to be many of your calibre available. It seems such a pity to pass all of that up, especially as you tell me you are hoping to marry and bring up a family.'

'I want into Divinity,' said Donald stubbornly. 'I thought if you backed me up—'

'Why can't you be in the Church as a lay member? An elder? Good works aplenty are there.'

'No.' Donald was looking almost alarmingly mutinous. Crombie remembered him at lectures before the war, tenacious to the point of bloody-mindedness in all his arguments. He gave in. 'I'll have a word,' he promised, sighing heavily at the responsibility. Afterwards the words *leadership material* came into his mind. There was something *imposing* about young Candlish. He was determined

189

to impose his views on Christianity on an unsuspecting citizenry, the old man added to himself, in his mischievous disrespectful coda. He'd seen many who felt called to such a role do possibly more harm than good. But he hadn't felt strong enough to fault Donald's argument that postwar reform had to start in the individual psyche, if there was such a thing. Aye, there's the rub, the old man thought. We think we can take total responsibility for our actions but really we are frail vessels, tossed about on a merciless sea called Fate, or heredity, or whatever. But he didn't want to get into metaphysics any more. These days he coasted close to the shore.

Donald saw the Divinity professor and came out into Gilmorehill still feeling vaguely dissatisfied. No one had promised anything. He wasn't greatly put off by this. Resistance only made him stronger. He knew they were bewildered by him back there. Same thing at home. He had caught his mother that very morning giving him one of her long, considering, brooding looks. Even he was bewildered at times. But not for long.

> *The padre had come into the room at Montreuil. He had been bad that morning, full of images of the court-martial and young Grieves and the devils of guilt that he, who was still alive, could somehow have prevented both deaths.*
>
> *The padre had looked at first an unprepossessing little man. Wispy-haired, light of voice. Yet he knew what Donald was talking about: he had seen it all, heard it all.*
>
> *Donald had been wrestling with the need for forgiveness. Why it was all mixed up with his mother's stony face and his father's upraised hand, with hellfire sermons back home in Perringhall Parish Church, he hadn't been able to explain. His mental suffering had thrust him deep into the trembling insecure recesses of his infancy. He had been convinced of his own wickedness.*

*'You're measuring God's love with human love,'* the padre had said in his light voice. *'His forgiveness with human forgiveness. His is illimitable. You don't have to earn it, though from the sound of it, that's what your mother taught you. It's just there. God's gift. You are loved whether you earn it or not.'*

*It had been like an explosion of light in his head, a loosing, an awakening. He hadn't found the words to express it yet without sounding maudlin. When the padre had gone he had wept. In fact, he had wept for several days and nights and then come out of that long tunnel of depression into daylight, plain and ordinary daylight, where things began to make some kind of sense again. But changed.* Converted. *Whether it embarrassed them or not. And he couldn't do anything about it.*

'Can you spare a copper for an ex-serviceman?' He had wandered into the park, where the last of the autumn flowers were freezing in their beds. A young man in ragged clothes stood before his park bench, blue-cold outstretched hand clothed in an unravelling woollen mitten. The eyes jerked about nervously in the dirty face, the shoulders twitched.

Donald dug into his pocket and brought out a shilling.

'Where?'

'Wypres.'

'Have you somewhere to go for the night?'

'Aye.' The figure shuffled, making strange, amused sounds.

'Where?'

'Under the hedge.'

'But—'

'Thanks for the bob. You're a gent.' The figure did not want to be catechised. It shuffled off, pleased with its booty, but Donald's imagination had already built a model lodging-house for him and his like, where they would get a hot meal, a change of clothes, a word of hope. He knew nothing would stop him. His Church would round up those ragged sheep.

When Donald had returned to his regiment, the two girls, Tibby and Belle, seemed drawn together as they had been when younger, both lonely and unsettled in these first days of peace. Each day Tibby left her own parents' home at the farm and brought her little girl to share dinner at Cullington Lodge. Sometimes she brought meat and vegetables, at other times she shared whatever was going. After lunch, Catriona and her grandmother slept in the parlour with the slatted blinds drawn and Belle and Tibby confided in each other in the kitchen while they washed up. It was a mutual support system they both seemed to need.

They had tried to get Belle to stay on at nursing, but after Russell's death she had turned savagely away from everything connected with the war. Now she was going in three times a week to the Public Secondary School at Perringhall, where most of the local children went till they left at fourteen and where she taught the girls hygiene and took choir practice.

It left her enough time to give her mother some help at home. That was supposed to be Kate's province but it was clear she had her hands full with the hen farm and with Wilfred, whose state of health was variable. What was happening more and more was that Kate and Wilfred led a separate life within the house, taking their meals on trays upstairs in their sitting-room.

Over the dishes, the big willow pattern soup plates and heavy dinner plates which they washed, dried and put away almost unthinkingly, in a pleasing, expert rhythm, Belle confided her reservations to Tibby.

'I might not want to stay on here. I might want to go away and make a life somewhere else altogether.' There was a kind of panicky defiance in her voice, for she had no idea as yet what her alternatives might be.

'What if Percy Barnett turns up?'

'What if he does?'

'What then?'

'He won't. He's either been killed or he's decided against seeing me again.'

'His letters might have gone missing. Been torpedoed. There's always that possibility.'

They had had this conversation, or a variation of it, several times in the past week. It was as though Belle was trying to feel her way into the future, but it was foggy and she kept coming up against this vague shape in the swirling mists, which represented the cairn of her feelings for Percy.

'Maybe you'll meet someone else,' offered Tibby, not very hopefully. They were both were aware of the preponderance of women there was going to be in the years ahead. Two million of them without husbands, one paper had said.

Belle folded her arms over her bosom, almost as though she were nursing an invisible child, and walked about the flagged kitchen floor with a kind of rocking motion.

'I'm not going to marry just anybody. You know Kirstie Anderson? Whose fiancée was killed at Armentiers? She's married an old widower farmer at Bowhill, one with six sons already and about six teeth in his head.'

'I'd heard.' Tibby put away the last of the cutlery and said with her usual cheeky bawdiness, 'Who wants an old man in her bed?'

'Kirstie Anderson, apparently,' said Belle drily and they both chose to laugh. 'But me, I'd rather be an old maid. There's dignity in that.'

Tibby looked at her wryly. 'And if there's one thing the Candlishes go in for, it's dignity.'

'What's wrong with that?' Belle demanded hotly. 'I couldn't live without mine. In a raggedy, smelly old shawl like some women, when they marry a man and fall for half a dozen children in as many years? You just need to go down the Rows and you'll see what I mean. The women are done for at thirty. I'd rather have my cambric nighties put away in lavender drawers, and time to play the piano—'

'And would you have had that, with Percy Barnett?' Tibby could not get a picture in her mind of this amorphous Englishman. All she had to go on with was the quick, merciless chime of longing that still lingered like a grace note when Belle spoke of him, the idea of some refinement, some courtliness she had not so far encountered in Scottish men.

'Time to play the piano?'

'You know what I mean.'

'There has to be some halfway house. Between being a man's slave and keeping something of yourself, for yourself.'

'There is,' said Tibby.

'What do you mean?'

There was an explicit silence while Tibby was busy with one of her favourite preoccupations, putting up her kinky, riotous hair into the black velvet rouleau that was supposed to restrain it and so seldom did.

'Do you mean French letters?' demanded Belle, at length. 'I know about them. I've been a nurse, you know.'

'Well, then.' Tibby gave her a quick grin. They were both embarrassed. They had been brought up to be embarrassed, after all, both mothers dragging them in off the streets if they so much as glimpsed a pregnant woman. It had been an uphill struggle to sort out what it was all about. Though not so much in Tibby's case, Belle thought now. Tibby had sorted it out at an early stage and because of Russell and little Catriona Belle was secretly glad of it. She was not sure of the situation between Tibby and Donald. Tibby had hinted he wanted to make love to her all the time and certainly when she was near he was passionately attentive.

'But Donald wouldn't – you know, before marriage,' Belle had said.

Tibby had said nothing. She had a way of straightening her lips which could look very bitter. But as for Belle, she still felt a certain repugnancy for 'all that'. Except for the time with Percy, which had surely been different from just 'doing it'. She could feel her mind creep back to what she had been talking about earlier – the pleasures of spinsterhood and clean linen. Maybe it was what she was cut out for, she realised. Then she saw that Tibby was looking at her with a strange expression, almost as though she were afraid of what she was going to say.

'What is it Tibby?' she faltered.

Tibby walked towards her and pinned her down with a resolute glare.

'You know about Donald wanting to marry me?'

'Yes.' They had been over this ground too, in the greatest confidence, already.

'And that I don't know what I want?'

'Yes.'

'Except . . . except . . . .' Tibby found she had lost the means of articulation.

Belle said almost gently, 'Except you want to enjoy yourself and be young.'

'You've said it! I know I've had Catriona, but it isn't the end of it, is it, of being young? I still want to go to dances and soirées—' As if to illustrate what she meant, Tibby grabbed her friend and they swanned up and down the kitchen in a tango, humming under their respective breaths, till they broke apart and fell into chairs, in mock exhaustion.

Then Tibby said in a great rush, 'What I've done, Belle, is rent a wee cottage, down Fell Street just beyond the school, the one the tailoress Mackinlay had before she came into her uncle's money. Two rooms and a kitchen. I want to be on my own. Tell Donald for me, for he won't like it, will he? He can still come round and see me.' She looked at Belle, pale-faced now as herself. 'All it means is I want a spell of independence. It's what we said about being your own woman.'

'He wants you to marry him soon,' said Belle, out of the family habit of putting Donald's wishes first.

'I know. But he also knows I won't be rushed.' There was an equal note of upbraiding in Tibby's voice and then a silence while they both digested what the other had opined.

Belle took a deep breath and said magnanimously, 'You

won't be far away. And it's a nice little house. I can see you there.'

'I've talked my father around. Mother's not so sure, but she's promised me a bed and a sofa and some rugs and I'll get a small allowance, though I'll maybe need to take in some sewing. I might even get some school cleaning.'

'Donald wouldn't like that.' Belle could feel primness well up in her.

'Well,' Tibby temporised. 'The idea is that Donald will take me as I am, or not at all.' She leaned forward and said relievedly, 'Gosh, I'm glad I told you Belle. I've been waiting for the chance.'

'You're a bit of a sly puss.'

'No one will be able to get on to me, you see. In my own place. At the moment, everybody does.'

'I know,' Belle acknowledged. Having your own place was an idea that had of course flitted in and out of her own mind. But girls in Perringhall generally stayed at home. What Tibby was doing was slightly scandalous and would revive the subject of Catriona's illegitimacy all over again as a subject for gossip. *Cambric and lavender*, Belle thought, half-wanting her own and the family dignity intact and sans the Tibby dimension. Except that beyond all criticism she liked Tibby. Belle felt sad and confused and restless, all at the same time. She went over and put her arm about Tibby's shoulder and, sharing their silent uncertainties about the future, each girl drew comfort from the other's quandaries.

# Twenty-Four

On Christmas Eve, the first Christmas after the war, Kate Chappell wrapped one of her husband's mufflers round her head and neck and battled against a stiff wind towards the hen-house. She had hot meal mixed with potato peelings which she spread out in the iron feeding troughs. She opened the hen-house doors and white, brown and speckled hens tumbled out and flew, clucking and pecking at rivals, towards their breakfast. The big crowing cock made a stabbing run at his benefactor, just to assert his authority. Kate enjoyed this procedure, the feeding hens, the more timorous young ones clucking round her feet, the rolling back of the morning skies, the beginning of a new day, the sense of not knowing what might happen next which was akin to a cautious optimism.

It had been a blow, losing the first lot of poultry to disease, but they were gradually building up again and orders for eggs and table fowl were coming in steadily. She collected what eggs there were, laying them gently in a wicker trug over one arm and none too quickly sauntering up towards the house, picking some kale for soup on the way. She felt like reflecting on the ebbing year, trying to get things into some kind of perspective and sorting out her feelings about the continued rebuffs from Tallie and Toby. Here was Christmas, New Year on its heels and after what they had all been through, they were still a divided family. Wilfred kept telling her she had to put the past behind her, but it was difficult. Her nagging sense of guilt made her feel alienated from Belle and Tibby and even little Catriona at times. They should all be together, if only for her mother's sake, but Wilfred said if it was not possible they should at least enjoy what they had as a twosome. *And she had him.* Coiling around her chest in a warm current was this bursting sense of gratitude that he had been spared to her. Frail he might be, but he was a man to whom good spirits and a positive attitude were inimical. He had taught her so much: to take each day as it came, to take pleasure in small delights, to be grateful for what they had. She saw how his philosophy worked, for his health was better in many ways than anyone could have expected, though with the coming of colder weather his injured leg was causing him a certain degree of pain and discomfort.

She smiled to herself as the strains of piano-playing waited from the house: Belle with her positive, thumping style, so disparate from her neat little figure, pounding out what every message boy had begun to whistle – 'I'm forever blowing bubbles'. After Russell's death, Janet Candlish had refused to allow anything but hymns to be played and these mostly her favourites. 'The Old Rugged Cross' and 'We Shall Gather at the River', but it seemed she had relented, maybe because a slightly moody Belle was herself in need of indulgence. As Kate passed through the hall on her way up to Wilfred she called in to the pianist, 'That was nice', but was rewarded by a dissatisfied grunt.

'Doesn't feel very Christmassy,' she grumbled to Wilfred as he handed her some hot cocoa, the milk and water for which he had heated on their little spirit stove.

'That's because Scots don't know how to celebrate Christmas,' he advised her.

'We used to hang up our stockings,' Kate protested. 'We got an apple and an orange and some sweeties in them.'

'That was all?' he mocked.

'Well, men had to work. The pit didn't close.' She remembered reading about real Dickensian Christmases when she was a little girl, Christmases with snowy streets and lighted trees and fat turkeys and blazing puddings, but it hadn't been like that in the Rows. Just the stockings and maybe a Sunday School soirée to look forward to, the steak pie and the black bun and the ginger cordial saved for the greater excesses at Hogmanay. She gave her husband a look of mock exasperation. 'We didn't go in for Sassenach over-indulgence.'

'Oh, we had presents,' he reminisced. 'Awkwardly, badly-wrapped presents, horrible scarves aunties had knitted and once I even had a toboggan from an uncle who was a joiner. They used to lie and taunt us from the top of the wardrobe, these presents, for weeks before. We had a tree from the market and a goose from Kent and mince pies—'

'Little gluttons!'

'And we went to the pantomime. Up in the gods. I thought the transformation scene was magic. It *was* a kind of magic. And we used to practise to go on the stage afterwards—'

Kate caved in. 'It must have been fun,' she said wistfully. 'Look at your face even now, when you talk about it.'

'Come here,' he bade her. She put down her cocoa and obeyed. His hands went round her waist.

'We'll spend Christmas Day together and that will make it wonderful. Won't it?'

'Have you got me a present?'

'I don't think I can afford it. Have you go one for me?'

'Same here. Too hard up.' She had squirrelled away a book, some toffee and a bottle of whisky. She hadn't been able to track down what he had been up to, if anything, but once or twice had surprised him looking unconvincingly innocent.

'I wish—' she began, but he put his hand to her mouth.

'No good wishing.' For Russell to be back with them. For Tallie to forgive them. Some shadows couldn't be wished away. Any more than the sense of deprivation and harshness from Kate's childhood could be rationalised. But he wouldn't allow her to mope and that night he insisted she hang up her stocking, one of her fine grey woollen ones, and he put up the longest sock he could find and averred Father Christmas would satisfy his long-held wish for a water-pistol and a tin clown banging cymbals. In this mood of indulgent silliness they went to bed.

Kate got up while it was still dark and thought it had been snowing. She threw a crocheted shawl over her flannel nightie and went over to the window, parting the half-drawn curtains wide. There were white dots all over the window and sitting, mysteriously shadowed in the deep window-sill recess, a small fir tree, decorated with red candles on silvery tin holders. At the foot of the tree lay a welter of small parcels, each shape odder than the rest and at its top there was a very fair cardboard fairy, with skirts made out of silver paper and wand from a pipe-cleaner. She looked more closely at the 'snow' and saw it was microscopic pieces of cotton wool stuck to the inside of the glass.

For a moment she did not move. The sight was so pretty, so disarming, she just wanted to let her eyes feast on it. She became aware of a pair of dark eyes watching her from the bed behind.

'So he's been,' said a voice. 'Father Christmas.'

'Wilf! How did you manage it?'

'With massive difficulty.' He sat up. 'Pass me up my stocking, woman.' She had put in knitted socks, a red and white hankie, an apple and an orange and some conversation lozenges. 'There's more to come,' she said, shyly.

'Just what I always wanted,' he said, blowing his nose on the hankie. 'Now yours.'

Her stocking had a lace-edged hankie, some saucy garters, a luckenbooth brooch wrapped in tissue paper, sweets and of course, an apple and an orange. 'You can't open the other presents till later,' he ordered. 'Did you like it, your Cockney Christmas?'

A new, emboldened Kate threw herself into bed beside him, smothering him with hugs and kisses till he protested. There was a knock at the door and Belle came in, bearing breakfast and a pretty card on a tray. 'Just this once,' she said. 'Since it's Christmas.'

They were like two children in that great untidy bed, she thought, going back downstairs to tell her mother about the tree and the snow and the stockings, her eyes full of stupid, jealous tears.

In the flat above the shop Tallie stood in her petticoat and chemise, washing hurriedly so she could gulp down a cup of tea then open up downstairs. Toby had tried to persuade her there was a case for closing, but she was of the opinion there might be more money about than on an ordinary day.

He had wanted to buy her something, but when he had tried to find out what she would like she had said presents were for children and she had everything she needed. He had dashed out the night before, nonetheless, and bought her a beautiful sealskin muff at Jean Simpson's, Gowns and Mantles. And he was thankful he had done, for in the event she had given him a handsome tiepin with a tiny diamond at the centre and they had exchanged shame-faced grins at the first light of day.

He sometimes thought he had a lifetime's work cut out, trying to understand the complex woman he'd married, but slowly he was learning to 'read' her. She was looking forward to the baby, he knew that. If only she would learn to take things more as they came. But she pushed herself. The house had been turned upside down, cleaned from top to bottom, for a Christmas they were not going out of their way to celebrate. Same with the shop. The window had been redecorated on Christmas Eve, the brass bell polished till it glittered, like the door handles. 'You want to get on, Toby, don't you?' she had reproached him, when he had counselled a more *laissez-faire* attitude. 'You want the best for the baby, don't you? And we want to get out of here soon.' He knew she had her mind set on a sandstone villa with a garden. But it was more than that, more than ambition. There was as restlessness in her that was putting a tarnish on things, like the gritty film that crept over the polished brass when sooty fog descended on main street. It stood to reason, he admitted. It must be hard for her to be estranged from her own mother and her elder sister. He would not allow himself to think of Wilfred Chappell. There was only so much a man could take. And if Tallie still had hankered after him, after all he, Toby, had been to her, then there was no hope for any of them. No wonder she polished brass till the shine exploded. No wonder she starched the life out of sheets and scrubbed the surface off the kitchen table till the wood all but sharded. In the midst of all this was Toby's love and pity for her. He wished now he had been more insistent about closing the shop.

He caught at Tallie's pinafore as she hurried past him.

'Oh, come *on*!' she cried, petulantly.

'Why don't we go up there tonight?' he said. The words came from out of nowhere.

'Up where?' She knew where. He watched the familiar closed-down expression tighten and alter her face.

'To your mother's. You know very well where.'

She snatched at the pinny he still held. 'Oh, come on, Toby. We've been over all this.'

'But it's Christmas,' he argued, helplessly. 'We could go up, take a bottle of whisky and some bun. Mend fences.'

She whirled on him. 'Mend fences? Do you not think it's up to her? To our Kate?' She spat out the name. 'She's the one who should be mending fences.'

'She has a sick man. But he's the root of it, isn't he?' said Toby painfully. 'Can you not find it in yourself to forget what happened, for all our sakes?'

The beautiful hazel eyes tracked his face. He had caught her unawares and now he could read the heights and depths of her hurt in one fleeting moment while her defences were down.

'That would be the answer, you know,' he said, with a quiet dignity and turned away from her. He had wanted to cry out, force the issue into the open. *Do you still love him?* But what was the use of that, when whatever the answer might be would take neither of them any further on. He thought of the brass filming over, dirtying till none of the intrinsic shine was left. He followed his wife down to the shop in time to hear the first customer bid her a merry Christmas.

Belle felt that the sole responsibility for making anything at all out of Christmas Day had fallen on her shoulders. Her mother, crabbed and pale, was sitting crocheting in the kitchen's chimney corner, her hands in black woollen mittens, not even offering help with chopping the vegetables for the soup. They were having cock-a-leekie to start, followed by chicken Kate had provided and a tongue that Belle had cooked the day before and which was now under the flat-iron in a pudding bowl. They would finish off with sherry trifle.

202

But tables did not lay themselves any more than cream thickened without somebody's hand at the beating. And those two were still behaving like two enamoured turtle doves in their dovecot upstairs. She had actually heard Kate shrieking like some wanton dairymaid and then the deep, low rumble of Wilfred's laughter.

Belle sighed for Tallie. She could always be relied upon to take her share of work. More than her share. Across Belle's mind flitted the shadow of a mild remorse that they had once all taken Tallie's presence at home for granted. It had been Wilfred who had fought for her freedom and she had thought he and Tallie would be together for always. Now look at him with Kate! If Belle wasn't careful, *she* was going to end up sacrificed to the household gods. And what about her music? What about ruining her hands! What about—

'Look! Look what I got!' The kitchen door clicked and Tibby and Catriona came in, the little girl bearing a doll almost as big as herself. 'I gotted this doll and she got socks and shoes.'

The china-headed doll with sleeping eyes and jointed limbs was duly admired. Then Janet suggested Tibby should take the new doll away from the child and substitute a rag one for everyday play. Tibby resisted. 'Let her enjoy it,' she said easily. 'If that's your philosophy, you'll never have anything decent,' said Janet snippily. If there was a chance of Tibby marrying Donald, Janet saw it as her duty to educate her out of her easy-going ways. She had already been down to the cottage to cast a disparaging eye over Tibby's attempts at independent housekeeping. Tibby let all criticism wash over her, saying nothing. She had found this worked best at the farm.

'You can't take the doll away from the child on Christmas Day,' Belle protested mildly.

'It's my doll,' stated Catriona irrefutably. She stood foursquare, her plump little face, so like her mother's, rosier than ever with excitement and defiance. 'Me keep it, G'anma.' Belle turned away to hide a smile. She felt her mother might have met her Waterloo.

Janet was irritable because her strict daily routine of dinner at one o'clock had not been adhered to, what with Kate and Wilfred coming down to join them, handing round little useless presents for everybody when they would have been better advised to save their money. It was Wilfred and his English ways, of course. She gave the bottle of lavender water they had given her a sour, ungrateful glare. What did they think she wanted with such fal-lals at her age?

Belle and Tibby served out the food. Belle was a fastidious cook and had carefully laid the most tenderly succulent chicken breast slices on her mother's plate, while Tibby made sure she had first serving of her vegetables and giblet gravy.

The trifle had been liberally laced with sherry. 'Did someone jog your elbow, Belle?' queried Wilfred straight-faced. After it, two bright red spots appeared on Janet's cheeks and she permitted Wilfred to pour her a glass of port wine when all the courses had been cleared away, which she sipped with a 'petticoat tail' of shortbread.

There were some glaring omissions from the conversation. Donald was mentioned, toasted and his determination to enter the ministry discussed with a thoroughness on all sides. Carefully after that Belle brought up Russell's name, choosing to evoke only happy memories, but she gave up when she saw the rigidity of Tibby's expression and a wetness on her mother's cheeks. The two people nobody mentioned were Tallie and Toby, until almost the end of the meal, when Tibby said, 'I was in Tallie's shop last night. She said they were opening today.' There was an explosive silence after this and a scraping back of chairs and the younger women made a thing of clearing the dishes and washing up.

Belle had tied sprigs of berried holly on to the tall plaster candlesticks in the parlour and with sparky logs in the piled grate the scene in there was one of almost inviting comfort, although Janet had the rigidly upholstered chairs and sofa smothered in antimacassars and Catriona well warned to keep sticky fingers away from any polished surfaces and not to touch the ornamental wax fruit.

In the middle of the afternoon Ernest Waters, the boarder, brought his fiancée, a plump and shabby-genteel little war widow, to meet the family and stay to tea, which was carraway sandwiches, seed cake and shortbread, as on Sundays. By this time Catriona was fractious and Kate suggested perhaps Belle should play the piano. They drew the curtains and lit the gas and the notes spilled out under Belle's agile fingers and presently she sang in accompaniment, her voice surprisingly full-bodied and confident. Why is it so unlike the diffident person, arms crossed in front of her body, that she presents to the world at large, Kate wondered.

'If you were the only girl in the world,' sang Belle, and 'Roses are blooming in Picardy', and the current favourite, 'I'm forever blowing bubbles', and then the one the troops had been singing as they left Flanders for home, 'Good-byeee'. At the end Belle looked weepy and emotional.

After this, Ernest, from a wish to impress his lady, volunteered to sing 'Dark Lochnagar' and finally Kate, prompted by Wilfred, 'Flow Gently, Sweet Afton', after which he kissed her cheek.

Janet had never relaxed her normal routine to mark Christmas Day in such a manner before – the Auld Kirk had never encouraged it – and by six o'clock she made it clear she had had enough. The engaged couple departed to visit more friends, Tibby took Catriona and the china doll home to the cottage and Belle wiped the piano keys with a chamois leather, on her mother's instructions, before turning down the lid.

'Do you want us to sit with you?' Kate asked Belle, when all the small tasks had been completed and Janet had retired early to bed.

'I'll be fine,' responded Belle off-handedly. 'I'll just read and think.'

'Are you sure?'

Belle nodded. It was as though a fine veil fell over her

features, rendering them void of response. Belle in her mulish mood, Kate thought, giving up. She wanted to be on her own with Wilfred, anyhow, as close as skin could be without melting. She wanted his voice in her ear, his breath on her cheek and for him to tell her once again why he had picked her, not Tallie, and hear the delight and wonder in his voice that it should be so.

## Twenty-Five

At Hogmanay, on the eve of the New Year which everyone was keen to welcome as a clean new page, free of the war in which they had all been mired for so long, Belle received a card of festive greetings from Percy Barnett and with it a long, rambling letter which she read over and over again.

She refused to reveal to her mother or Kate full details about the contents. 'He's been demobbed. He's been in hospital again, with his arm,' was all she would disclose. 'Yes, yes, he's all right. He's written, hasn't he?'

But when she was by herself she read the closely written pages over and over again, till she knew them almost off by heart.

'Dear Belle,' Percy had written. 'I know you must be wondering why you have not heard from me for so long. My bad arm has been troubling me and they took me into hospital at Tunbridge Wells where they almost decided to amputate. I've hung on to the blasted thing but it continues to give me quite a lot of trouble. This is one reason I haven't written but I know it isn't a good enough excuse. The thing is I got a bit down and there was a nurse, Julia Francis, at Tunbridge Wells, who was very kind to me. She was – is – a lovely girl, in spirit as well as form and I'm afraid the inevitable happened. Her husband, an army officer, was kept out in Flanders interminably – something to do with sorting out war graves – and she, like me, was lonely. I am afraid to say I thought for a time I was always going to be in love with her. This is making me very upset to write but I have to do you the honour of being absolutely truthful with you.

'Julia's husband came back and there was never any real doubt in the end but that she would make a life with him. He had been through a bloody awful time – as who hasn't – and she owed it to him to try and give him an heir, all that sort of stuff. I suppose I knew the outcome was inevitable but it didn't hurt any the less. I'm asking you to try and understand, dear Belle. I have been very unfair and unkind, a total cad, but it was just something that happened when I was at a nadir in my life and now it is over. It is a bit like getting over a sickness and you begin to see things straight once the fever's cleared.

'What I see straight now is that what I feel for you is still there. We had such a short time together and sometimes I can't put a face to the picture of you in my mind and at other times I see you so clearly I can almost put my hand out and touch you. I always hear your laugh, Belle. Did you know you have a lovely laugh? Is there any chance that we can get together again? I confess I'm shaken by what happened to me and I look back and think that the short, hectic, almost hallucinatory time we had together could have been a cruel delusion. But I hope so much that it wasn't, that something special happened to you then as it did to me.

'*Will* you write to me again, dear Belle? Please, please tell me all you have been doing and what has happened to Donald. I was shocked to hear about your other brother, Russell. I am going back next week to my job on the local paper but my ambitions are running higher now and I am for Fleet Street one day and a big paper like the *Express*. You remember you worried how I could type? I have become a one-arm wonder and the gammy arm's useful for tucking copy under! Belle, write soon and have the best possible happy New Year. I think of you. Yours truly, Percy.'

*I hate him*, she thought, every time she read the lines. And every time it was like being carried away on a high wind. I hate him and I hate her. Who did she think she was, a married woman, a woman with the name of Julia, a name I shall despise till I end my days, it is enough that it belongs to her; who did she think she was, to take someone else's dreams and trample them under her unthinking feet? She was lonely, was she? And what was I, what have I been, living a kind of half-life here, waiting to hear from him, watching the post day by day, looking at the mantelpiece every time I've been out, in case there's a letter with the familiar handwriting propped against the clock? What does she know about loving him, about really being lonely? When for me there was never remotely been anyone else. He was only a stopgap for her emotions, because he is young, and a bit immature for his years, at that: I know *all that* about him; and there is a gallantry about him, that would make him want to rescue a woman in distress. That was all it could have been: a wish on his part to help someone who was sad.

She always broke down at this part, which was why she had to read the letter always in private, for if that *had* been all why would 'the inevitable' have happened? Why would he have thought, if only for a time, that he was 'always going to be in love' with the woman of the abhorred and abhorrent name? No wonder he could not always put a face to Belle in his mind, for he had made her faceless, meaningless, expendable. So no, she would not write back. She always came to the same decision. She would do to him what he had done to her. Put him out of her life. Hate him. Abominate him. Die of this sickness before she would confess to an iota of remaining feeling for him.

Even her mother asked her what ailed her. Kate and Wilfred tried every means they knew to get her to confide in them, knowing full well the parchment-white face, the cried-out eyes, the plates pushed away at the table, had followed on the arrival of the card and letter. They had never been a family to talk about how they felt, so she knew of no way to break the mould now. You kept things to yourself. You let them boil and simmer. It was known as pride.

Tibby said, with a harshness that was threatening to become part of her since she had started her battle for independence, 'Nothing's as bad as losing your man in the war.' Her policy was the tough one she had been brought up with on the farm: when a member of the family had an emotional problem, you left them 'to hang as they grew' and eventually come out of it. She wouldn't push Belle to confide. If she wanted to, that would be a different matter. Tibby would have listened.

In the event, it was to Tallie that Belle took the ache that was threatening to distort her life completely and even put her teaching job at risk. In what she saw as a confession of defeat she pushed the offending letter across the kitchen table to Tallie, on a day when they had the flat above the shop to themselves, Toby having gone to the wholesaler's.

'Read it,' she commanded.

Tallie did, one hand resting on the mound of her stomach as if to quieten the now-kicking foetus. Her face turned as pale as Belle's own. At last she put the letter down and said quietly, 'The swine. You'll give him his marching orders, won't you?'

'I just won't write.'

'No. Why should you? I think he has a nerve.' She picked up the letter and threw it down again, cursorily, as if it were the very thought of Percy Barnett. 'He seems – almost proud of himself. I'm telling you, Belle, men can't be trusted.' And she heeled her own eyes as she saw Belle was weeping. 'Come on, Sis. I'll put the kettle on. I know how you're feeling. But you'll get on top of it. You must. Or it'll get on top of you.'

Belle hauled herself into the parlour for the tea, which Tallie had put on an enamelled wood tray with her best cups and with biscuits to accompany it, a signal that this was a day when you kept the flag flying. Belle felt as though she had been very ill and that she might be at the start of a long and not necessarily successful convalescence.

She knew then she had come to Tallie because they were now two of a wounded kind. It was the first relief she had known since the arrival of the New Year missive and it was a comfort to sit there while Tallie read the letter again and took it apart much as she had done, so many times, each time condemning Percy Barnett for his treachery and consigning the unknown woman called Julia to the flames.

After that, it was almost an article of faith for Belle to eat properly again, to take up her reluctant, recalcitrant pupils and make them get to grips with the rudiments of music. She would never write back to Percy. But she kept his letter. Tucked well at the back of her hankie drawer, under the lining paper with the smaller of her two Bibles on top.

By the time Donald came home for good, Wilfred had started teaching again at Perringhall Academy; by agreement, only two days a week to start with. The headmaster was desperate for staff of a decent calibre and Kate could see her husband needed some kind of intellectual challenge and boost to his self-confidence. To start with he came home exhausted but after a couple of weeks became caught up in what he was doing and determined to stay.

Kate did not feel the need to go back to teaching herself – or at least, if she did, it was only intermittently. With Wilfred to talk to about every subject under the sun, she felt her intellectual vigour increasing and a kind of bliss at the idea of the books and ideas they could share.

She had embarked on a study course on her favourite subject, psychology, reading everything she could lay her hands on and becoming more and more caught up in it by the day. She had never been much in favour of poetry, but Wilfred insisted she read the war poets, Sassoon, Owen, Brooke, Thomas and her consciousnes began to expand beyond the mere preoccupation of what had happened to her, in her own little wheel of existence.

They decided to scale down the hen farm a little. They

bought no more pullets, as last year's began at last to lay with a commendable regularity, and employed a boy from the village to come in to help. Davie Dunnett enjoyed hammering in stabs and moving the wire netting when the hen's enclosures were moved and for all his awkward adolescent presence was gentle with both fowl and eggs. Soon Belle was annexing him for the odd morning errand, feeding him soup and Paris buns at the kitchen door when her mother wasn't looking. He said he was fourteen, but they suspected he was younger. Maybe only twelve, but taken away from school to help out, however modestly at home. Both girls encouraged him to express his opinion, which he did vividly but coarsely. Kate corrected his grammar and Belle taught him manners such as wiping his nose on a hankie she provided. It was surrogate mothering which all parties found pleasing.

Donald was to start his Divinity course in the autumn and meantime lost no time in setting up an ex-serviceman's club affiliated to the parish church. Soon war widows as well as ex-soldiers were coming to him with their problems over money, rent and needy children and he began a fund-raising assault on the local conscience, taking in decent clothing and half-worn boots from those who wanted to help fiscally but had no spare cash and groceries and home-baking from anybody to feed those who had fallen into the direst circumstances.

Sometimes, despite what he had said to Tibby about not emulating the street-corner 'God-man', he took to preaching to the shopping crowds in Perringhall and even Hamilton and Glasgow on Friday or Saturday nights.

He and a band of the more evangelical church workers of both sexes were set on a crusade to bring the war-disaffected back into the churches. If this meant climbing up on to a soap box and competing on occasions with Socialist tub-thumpers Donald was prepared to do it. In fact he found that he had something of a gift for turning popular preoccupations into the subject of his mini-sermons and for catching the passing ear with some pawky piece of observation or humour. How his popular soubriquet sprang into being was never quite explained. Some unknown wit, seeing how he popped up from place to place, often in the twilit hour before the leeries had been round to light the gas-lamps, nicknamed him Shadow Jack. He had a certain amount of innocent fun with the name when he found out about it, but he knew its usefulness and did not mind it. Shadow Jack began to be mentioned on the local weekly newspaper and even in the *Times*, *News* and *Citizen* in Glasgow. The better he became known, the more likely people were to listen.

The public persona was punchy, positive, uplifting. It was only those at home who saw the hollow-eyed look and who suffered when he got over-tired and over-stretched from the backward-glancing bouts of imperious bad temper.

Janet was in two minds about her son. If he had to be a minister, she would rather he would be one of the old, remote, Fear-of-God sort, handing out a corrosive Gospel from a high Sunday pulpit and accessible only in a dim, book-lined study in a forbidding manse on weekdays.

She wasn't sure about Donald, who didn't care what he wore – decent cast-offs if need be – and who liked nothing better than a chat with the local Catholic priest if they met in the main street. Should the kirk be on nodding terms with the confessional? Donald told her they had all had the same God in the trenches. That might well be, but *she* wore her best for church on Sunday and the local Catholics didn't seem to mind if they went in their old shawls. It was because Donald laughed when she pointed this out that Janet remained in two minds about her son.

Belle moved in and out of both camps, sometimes feeling the evangelical approach was the right one, sometimes feeling that sitting upright in a polished pew for an hour on Sunday, one's mind only part taken up with the proceedings, was as much as she could expect from herself. Kate and Wilfred were not churchgoers because Kate averred Wilfred needed to take the day of rest literally.

A bit cautiously at first Tibby allowed herself to be swept along by Donald's enthusiasm. As the mother of an illegitimate child she felt she should work towards grace and restitution but a much larger part of her was more taken up with the idea of soirées, dances and concerts – any means of having a legitimate good time – to raise funds. She didn't mind doing what she could in the way of baking cakes, making costumes for children's shows, even singing in the choir, if she could let herself go occasionally in the tango and quickstep. She sometimes felt she only really came alive when dancing and loved everything about it: the careful wash beforehand, the guilty face-powdering, the shorter skirts, the strappy shoes, the head-bands, the quick, fleeting touch of men's cheeks against hers and their big hands in the small of her back.

Donald danced with her. There were some of Perringhall who said he should not come down to the level of local lads, not when he was intended for the ministry, but he wouldn't stay out of anything. He said Christ was everywhere. He wasn't a bad dancer and he took up lasses like Mary Hunter with the ferocious squint and Emily Stewart who never looked you in the face, but Tibby preferred Alec Swann from the bus garage or Tug Fleming from Over Farm, because they were more with you in the rhythm. They were more with you entirely. She could feel the sweat of their palms mingling with hers and the confluence of their strong bodies with hers at the height of the tango melodies. She loved that, loved telling them 'Phul-Nana' when they asked if she was wearing scent, loved their sighs in her ear when she stumbled occasionally and her soft bosomy front collided with their broad and muscly chests. Donald never sweated. His hand was firm and cool.

When it became general knowledge that Donald Candlish was courting Tibby Robertson there were two schools of opinion. One was that he should not be doing it because Tibby had been as good as married to his brother. The other school argued why not? From all accounts he could have been the baby's father anyhow.

The serious scandalmongers knew it for a fact that Donald was a frequent visitor to Tibby's cottage. Always openly and in the daytime, though he didn't stay long and they couldn't be, well, up to anything, because her dressmaking customers were liable to come and go all day long. But some thought more clandestine visits were probably made, in the dark, and Ruby Macdougall, an experienced curtain-twitcher who lived nearby, swore to at least one dawn departure, though admitted under duress it could have been the milk-cart and not Tibby's gate that she heard clanging.

Tibby was holding Donald at arm's length. Belle knew very well the game that was being played and urged Donald to force her to a decision or to give her up.

'I can't do that,' Donald argued, when they sat in the kitchen one evening when the others had all gone to bed. There was only the light from the fire and confidences were easier.

'There might be someone else just waiting for you,' Belle pointed out quietly. She did not feel she was being treacherous towards Tibby, rather that she was trying to protect Donald, to whom she had transferred some of the feeling she had once had for Russell. She did not know quite how to put it, even to herself, but Donald since the war had become a much more vulnerable and therefore lovable man. She did not want Tibby hurting him. And Belle had been observing Tibby closely. Her visits to Glasgow, on her own; the new dresses, the way she took hemlines up faster than anyone else, the way she went on at dances, even her laughter. She did not behave the way a prospective minister's wife should behave. The wildness was surfacing again, almost as if Tibby couldn't help it.

'It's Tibby I want,' said Donald stubbornly, into the shadowy dark.

'But why, Donald? I sometimes think she's not right for you.'

'There's no explaining these things.' He could not talk about physical attraction to reserved, easily-scandalised

Belle. Since the day in the wood he had made love to Tibby maybe half a dozen times. It was playing with fire, he knew. He could have given her a child each time. Yet that had been part of the madness. He would not let himself examine it. It was something between them, a wild adventuring and each time Tibby had been willing to go just as far as he did.

Belle poked the last glowing embers of the fire. 'I must go up to bed,' she said sheepishly. 'But try and pin Tibby down. That's my advice. Marry her and stop up the gossiping mouths.'

It was the second shop Donald has been into that morning where he had been met with sidelong looks and the statement that he had been missed at the church dance.

'I had business in Glasgow,' he informed Gertie Mason. 'How did it go?' he enquired. He knew Gertie was going to tell him anyhow.

Gertie had inherited the tablet shop from her late, grubby-pinafored mother and with it the recipes for the best sugar tablet and toffee balls in the West of Scotland. He was buying some of her cough candy for his mother.

'Tibby had a great time of it,' said Gertie slyly. She was holding back, not too sure how far she should go. Donald had helped her sister fight for her war widow's pension and with his education was entitled to a certain amount of respect.

'I'm sure she did. I *hope* she did,' said Donald, his expression forbidding.

'Quite the belle of the ball,' said Gertie blithely. 'Her dress had pointy bits all round the hem. Great for the dancing. Tug Fleming couldn't leave her alone.'

'I don't know what you're trying to say, Gertie,' said Donald, with an assumed mildness. 'But I hope you'll bear in mind what the Bible says about gossip.' He couldn't for the life of him remember the relevant text. His mouth was drying out and there was taut feeling below his ribs.

Gertie was known for her touch-paper fieriness.

'It's no' just gossip. The other one was all over her, too, and you couldn't say but she didn't encourage him.' Gertie had decided to be bold as she liked.

'The other one?'

'Aye. Alec Swann from the garage. She went away early with him. He would be seeing her home, like enough. I hope he wasn't seeing her up a close.' The local euphemism for a man trying to have his way with a girl. Close-mouths offered a privacy the bare streets did not.

'That was commendable of him.' The words came out of his mouth like marbles. 'You're aware, Gertie, aren't you, that Miss Robertson is a free agent and entitled to be seen home by whomever she likes?'

'I was only saying . . .'

'I know what you were only saying and I'd advise you to pull one lip down over the other and say nothing,' said Donald savagely. He threw the money for the cough candy on to the battered counter. 'I'll bid you good-day.'

Outside on the pavement he stood for a moment, so shaken with anger – and something else – that he couldn't move. Only when Gertie's face swam like a pale enquiring moon above the greasy shop window curtain did he gather his wits and move on.


# Twenty-Six


Old Andy Johnstone and his apprentices had laboured hard on the war memorial which was to be erected at the entrance to the proposed new public park in Perringhall. There was a lengthy list of names on it, in the centre of which was that of his only son, Benjamin. The plinth, partly because the whole thing had been greatly hurried, was simple but dignified. No soldier with head bent over his rifle, no angel with outspread wings. Just the names and a wreath of poppies at the base. To most people, that seemed enough.

Janet Candlish went with Belle to look at Russell's name. Belle could not believe that the letters gouged out of the harsh stone were all that were left of her brother's memory. Any moment, she expected to hear his shout, inviting her to come and join in some childish game, and see his grubby form come tearing round the corner, a tear at his trouser bottom, his bootlaces undone. She seemed to see him in every dishevelled urchin spinning a top or hurling an iron hoop at the end of a cleat. But of course he had died as a man and there was a robust little girl playing her own games in a cottage in Fell Street to prove it. Belle sighed. Russell's death had left a tangled emotional situation between Tibby and Donald. To put it at its mildest. Belle had stretched both mind and heart to try to understand it, but she still did not know how it was going to sort itself out.

'She is still getting over Russell,' she had tried to tell Donald on the night he had come in distraught over the remarks by Gertie Mason in the tablet shop.

He wouldn't have that. 'The way she's going on?' he'd demanded. 'You don't go out dancing dressed like that – like a—' He had been going to say 'dressed like a whore', when Belle's furious admonitory gaze had stopped him. Certainly she herself had seen the flash of Tibby's rosette-finished pink garters and had only with difficulty dissuaded her from rolling down her silk stockings below her knee, as some did. Even putting rouge on their knees if they felt like it. But it was only silliness, Belle knew. Only what a lot of young girls did to shock their elders and Tibby was still young. It did not necessarily indicate a life of total depravity.

'There's still his picture above her mantelpiece,' Belle reminded Donald. 'She told me the other day she'll never take it down.'

'She will one day,' said Donald grimly. 'Even if I've to do it myself.'

'Don't force the pace,' Belle pleaded. But Donald had refused to discuss matters any further, raging out of the room with a face that would have frightened the Kaiser and Belle had been visited by a feeling of being powerless in the eye of a life-threatening storm.

After the unveiling of the war memorial there had been a special church service at which Donald had been invited to preach the sermon. It had been a powerfully-felt affair and people had come out from it dabbing at red eyes. He had preached of war and the horror of war, of the need for reconciliation and forgiveness and for starting again, cleansed, as it were, by suffering.

Janet Candlish had felt something more than pride that day. She had always known her first-born was destined for significance but even she had been surprised by his ability to hold the congregation in the palm of his hand, chiding, uplifting, comforting.

Normally she went to church because it was part of keeping a respectable status and although she enjoyed the theological argument she had always been a sceptical rather than a convinced Christian. Today her son, using the powers of his considerable intellect, had refined the Gospel message so that the feeblest, most wavering heart had been touched. She was able to conceive, if but dimly, what the war had wrought in her son and through him begin to let go of the sorrow and anger she felt over her younger one.

'Belle.' She clung to her youngest child as her faltering steps took her up the churchyard afterwards. 'Belle, I've not always been a good mother, have I?'

Belle put away her hankie and sniffed. 'You have,' she said stoutly. 'You've done your best.'

Janet shook her head. 'At times I've been hard. At times I've been partial.' Her rheumy pale eyes pleaded for understanding. 'I always saw Donald would be something special. He is, isn't he? There's no getting away from it. But Russell was my bairn too—'

'And you'll always love and miss him,' put in Belle quickly, before they should both be swamped by the emotion that threatened to overtake them. 'He was a scamp,' she said fondly. 'A lovable scamp,' and into her mind unbidden came the image of him at the river on the day of the picnic, in those sunlit days that now belonged to Before the War, poised naked and beautiful for the dive into the pool and Tibby looking at him as though she could never take her eyes away.

'He could always get away with more than the rest of you,' said her mother. 'He made me laugh. No' a bad way to remember somebody, is it? To say he made you laugh?'

'I thought Tallie might have been at the service,' said Belle, as they went through the church gates and started the walk home, arm-in-arm. 'Her and Toby.'

'Too near her time.'

Belle looked at her parent quickly. She had not been sure how aware her mother was of the date of the expected birth.

'If she had been there, would you have spoken?' asked Belle timidly.

Her mother's features almost automatically took on the old harsh resolute cast but she said nothing. They stepped out, the brae rising and through the fine covert stuff of her mother's coat she could feel the ageing body bracing itself for the effort. At length Janet said evenly, 'She knows where I am. I'll not turn her away if she comes to me.'

*But you could go to her* Belle wanted to argue. You know you'll regret it if this estrangement goes on. You are the mother. But she knew very well from her own somewhat rigid nature that it was much more difficult for some than for others to change, to make gestures, to be magnanimous. Her mother was what she was. Despite what Donald had said in the pulpit back there. And he was what he was and had no business to be so helplessly caught up with Tibby . . .

They were nearing Cullington Lodge. Even in the sunlight, the grey stone looked as though it would never warm up. Belle thought of the mellow old houses she had seen in southern England on her way to the front, even of the houses in the French villages that had survived bombardment. They had sat more easily in their respective landscapes. *Unfreeze*, she thought. Houses and people. We need to unfreeze, though how grey stone could do that, she did not know.

'There's somebody up at the house,' said Janet.

'Who are we expecting?'

'Nobody. It looks like a stranger.'

They pushed through the gate, Janet first and Belle looked without any great surge of curiosity at the man in the brown and beige checked suit with the brown bowler. Someone looking for Donald, no doubt. Donald was away for a few days. Nothing to do with her. Then as the figure turned round on hearing them she felt a great swooping movement in her pulse and saw that it was none other than Percy Barnett, looking as frightened and hesitant as she was dumbfounded.

She hadn't known what to do or say. Through lips that had suddenly seemed made out of frilly paper she had introduced Percy to her mother, who mercifully had taken command, pushed the two of them through the front door and into the parlour and brought out the Madeira wine and seed cake.

'I was up this way,' Percy had babbled, 'and thought I would just call in and see how you were getting on.' There had been more in this disjointed vein, talk about a week at Oban and looking up an old friend in Greenock, until Janet had said decisively 'I must see about the supper' and left the pair of them to it, closing the door behind her as she went. Belle fought down an uprush of panic.

But she was angry too. Quite detachedly, part of her mind was noting that anger had been the first thing she had felt on seeing him. At this effrontery, not only now, but when he had written to her. Expecting to be forgiven. There were other emotions, admittedly. Some kind of pleased acknowledgment at seeing he hadn't changed, that despite the somewhat loud (if stylish) suit and longer hair, he did not look any less handsome than he had done in uniform, and Belle had noted this was not always so. There was confusion, too, confusion over who she was – Belle who had been settling into being Miss Candlish, spinster of this parish and teacher of music, or Belle, distrait hoydenish creature who wanted to rush upstairs and do her hair, change into brighter clothes than those she'd worn for the service and who wasn't making sense, any kind of sense, out of anything she said.

With a mighty effort, Belle pulled herself together. He would have to take her as she was. It did not greatly matter either way, though as she began to regain her calm she admitted to herself that her church-going dark clothes set off her pink-and-white complexion and fair hair rather well.

With some composure, she finally managed to ask him, 'And what has really brought you here then? To see me?'

'You didn't answer my letter.'

'There was nothing to say.'

'None of it meant anything then? Back there in Montreuil? I thought it had meant a great deal.'

The colour mounted her face, but she grasped one hand with the other and said straight-backed, 'It wasn't I who reneged on what we said then.'

He had the grace to look away. 'No,' he admitted. 'But I've been hoping against hope you might find it in your heart to forgive me.' He stood up and came towards her, then impulsively went down on one knee in front of her. She saw he could not use the bad arm to steady himself. She made a little fluttering movement to indicate he shouldn't abase himself, but he remained where he was, his gaze riveted on her face.

'I was in a bad way in the hospital. Sometimes you take the only road out – when you're desperate, I mean. And Julia took compassion on me—'

'I don't want to hear of Julia.'

'No,' he agreed. 'Julia's in the past. Now I'm here, with you.' His mouth began to quirk. 'And you're even prettier than I remember.' His good hand rested on her left knee, smoothing the stuff of her dress. He went on quickly, 'And I'm going to make a go of things, Belle. I can offer you a home. I have a legacy from an uncle. Please let's go back to what it was all about in Montreuil. Let's get married and be with each other. Isn't it what you want, too?'

She would not give him any kind of answer that evening. Her mind was too full of reproaches and she had no wish to do anything but confront him with his behaviour in the hospital at Tunbridge Wells. Her mother came in with a tray of tea and biscuits, saw the two faces absorbed in argument and went out again. Later still, she came in to light the gas and suggest to Belle it was getting on, maybe it was time the young man took his departure.

'Can I see you again?' he asked miserably, as Belle saw him to the door.

'I can't see any point.'

'I'll put up in the village. Meet me there tomorrow. Please. Even if it's just for old time's sake.'

He stayed for three more days. By day two they were beginning to feel more at ease with each other, less like strangers, though she had not given an inch. And having got over the shock of his sudden appearance, she had mustered the true gravamen of her case. The Bruce Arms Hotel had laid on a majestic high tea but she ignored the cake-stand with its bounteous offerings and went straight to the heart of the matter.

'Don't you see? What you're offering me now is second best. If – if *the woman* you met at the hospital had been free, you would have married her.'

'Not fair!' he reprimanded.

She would not listen. 'I don't think I like being second best, Percy. So there's no use us going round and round the mulberry bush.'

'You're letting pride get in the way of everything,' he protested miserably.

'Maybe I am. Maybe her pride is all a woman's got. I certainly intend to hang on to mine.' The temperature in the musty hotel seemed to be mounting dangerously, so they continued the wrangling outside till parting in acrimony and despair.

On the third day he turned up at the house at ten o'clock.

'Oh no, not you again!' said Kate wearily, answering the door. To Belle, loitering behind her, he said shortly, 'Coming for a walk?' and she snatched a coat and went without demur.

'Second best, eh?' he said, belligerently when they were out of earshot. 'I lay on that damned lumpy hotel bed and thought of what you said, all night.'

'Good,' she said, with equal temper. 'You were meant to.'

'Second best! Even allowing for such an outrageous judgement, have you ever thought of the people who came out of the war who will only ever have a hundredth best for the rest of their lives? The blinded, the legless, the widows, the women who'll never get a man? What's so special about Belle Candlish, that life should award her the pink rosette? I was a bloody war casualty in that hospital. Taken out of my depth. I thought I was going to lose my arm and even my life.'

She had gone white at the force of his vehemence. 'Now who's being unfair!' She wept out of vexation as much as anything else. 'You're playing on my sympathy.'

'No.' He had, in fact ironed all emotion from his voice, which had a kind of flatness that frightened her. 'I didn't come here on a whim. I came here because I was drinking, Belle, and in danger of messing up everything I came out with, including my job, which matters to me. I had a long talk with my editor. He's a really good sort. He convinced me I should have one last try to sort things out with you.'

'Drinking?' She put her hand up to her mouth.

'I can get on top of it, but I need you to help me.'

She looked at him aghast. Drink in her mind was inextricably linked with her father's brutal behaviour when he took it.

'Drinking,' she said again. 'I can't cope with that, Percy. You might as well know.'

223

'Please, Belle. I won't give in to it. But help me.' He looked at her beseechingly. 'Look, haven't I been honest with you? We've had this – this closeness since the day we met. You're like the other half of me, the better half . . .'

'I don't want to be somebody's prop. I don't want to be the monitor of your actions.'

'What kind of world do you want to live in, then?' he responded, almost viciously. 'One where nobody fails, nobody gets sick, nobody needs anybody else? A half-world?'

She wanted to run away from him then. She felt like he had stuck a knife into her heart and then turned it, so that the pain was excruciating. For she had suffered too. Just because you knew how to put a face on it, did not mean you were not part of the real world, the hard unrelenting place where failure and lack of charity faced you at every turn.

There was the homely sound of a horse on the quiet road and a farmer passed them in his jaunting cart and bid them a cheery good-morning.

'Go away,' she said, as the clip-clop of the horse's light hooves faded. 'I can't take any more of you, Percy Barnett. Just go away and leave me alone.'

She thought she wouldn't forget the look he gave her then. If she had been paper it would have scorched her up without trace. He turned on his heel and left her, walking up the middle of the narrow road with his head down.

She knew she had done the right thing. If you kept yourself to yourself, as her mother had always advised them, then you did not suffer the same slings and arrows as the importunate, the feckless. It was a policy that had served her quite well up till now and it had a lot going for it.

Then why were her feet dragging her slowly after him? Why was she remembering how his right arm went out to protect the gammy one, how he didn't get the parting quite right on his thick hair because you maybe needed two hands to get that right, how he still bit his lip and blinked a lot although he assured her the physical pain from his injury had gone?

He needed a warmer scarf. Somebody to brush his shoes properly. Suddenly she knew she had enough will-power for both of them. She loved and wanted him so she would have all the strength she ever needed and if their joint strength was not enough she would put her arms around him and comfort him.

'Percy!' she called after him. He heard her, but he did not turn round. 'Percy!' she called again and this time he did turn and waited patiently for her to come to him.


## Twenty-Seven


'Never thought to see that back on your finger,' said Tallie drily, looking at the signet ring with its small winking diamond which Belle had retrieved from the depths of her stocking drawer and which Percy had put back on her finger before he left for Oban.

'Nor did I,' Belle admitted soberly, 'but I do love him, Tallie, and I'm going back south with him when he gets back from seeing his friends. There's an aunt of his I can stay with till we get married.'

'How are *they* taking it?' Tallie did not have to mention Cullington Lodge.

'Kate is for it. Mother makes doom-laden noises, but I just ignore them.' Belle stared at her sister defensively. 'Once you've left home, you know how to be your own woman.' She changed tack swiftly. 'When are you going to make it up with them? I'd feel better about going away if you did.'

Tallie never answered nowadays when Belle harped on this theme. She went instead to a drawer and took out a carefully wrapped parcel, kissing Belle as she handed it over. 'Best wishes to you both from Toby and myself.'

'What is it?'

'A lace-edged tablecloth and napkins.'

'That'll be really useful. I mean to entertain a bit,' said Belle importantly. She sat down, suddenly pink-faced and tearful. 'I wish I were going to be here for the birth. Make sure Toby telegraphs me the minute he can.'

'Of course.'

Tallie felt Belle's departure more than she would admit. The last days of her pregnancy began to seem interminable and she was now so big she refused to serve in the shop. Everything was ready. She had scrubbed and polished and finished off the last of the little knitted things for the baby, so she did not know what to do with herself except stare out of the window with her hands folded over her vastly-extended stomach. That, and sigh.

Her mother-in-law had just left one afternoon after checking all was well when she began to feel the first pains. It was Toby's day for visiting the warehouse in Glasgow and he would not be back for several hours. All she had to do was call Sally who was helping out in the shop downstairs and Jeannette would come galloping back, full of wise saws and reassurances. Tallie did not want any of that until she was ready for it. Stoically she sat out the increasing pangs till Toby returned. One look at her crumpled face sent him galloping off for the midwife, Mrs Gallacher.

'Och, she's doing fine,' said that comfortable matron, accepting a slice of sultana cake and a cup of tea. 'First babies are never in a hurry. I've got another one, just round the corner, Mary Stoner's girl Maggie, a bit further on than you. I'll just see to her and be back to you in a wee while.' She patted Tallie's hand. 'Get your man to rub your back. That'll ease things a bit.'

It was several hours before she returned, apologising that matters had taken a bit longer than she imagined. In the meantime, Toby had fetched his mother who laboriously checked on all Tallie's preparations and kept replenishing the big brown teapot.

'Should things not be happening now?' Toby demanded

226

of the midwife. He had peremptorily ushered her from the bedroom while an increasingly worn-looking Tallie rested from her last bout of pains. 'Do you think I should get the doctor?'

Mrs Gallacher was not a young woman and beginning to show the strains of a long day, but she shook her head. 'Not just yet. He doesn't like coming out unless it's really necessary.'

'But she can't go on and on like this,' Toby protested.

'She'll be fine,' said the midwife automatically. But the brief hesitation before she answered was all Toby needed. He was off for Dr Macarthur, who promised to come when he had finished his meal. He had been out all day on calls resulting from the latest wave of influenza. Macarthur was a newcomer to Perringhall, a youngish and likeable man who nonetheless already had a reputation for liking a drink. Toby suspected he might have been indulging that evening. He said sharply, 'Don't be long. My wife is exhausted.'

The long night began. Tallie's narrow build was operating against her and the baby. She was fighting as hard as she could and making a considerable noise in the process. Summarily she sent poor Jeannette away from her bedside and in the end told Toby to get to hell out of it too. Pale-faced he suffered his excommunication, knowing that in full possession of herself Tallie never used bad language.

'Get her mother,' said Jeannette.

Toby gave her a shocked, astounded look. Jeanette repeated her order. 'Get her mother down here.' Toby was at the point of desperation where he would have climbed mountains, swum rivers. He almost dragged his mother-in-law from her home, but noted she made no demur when he issued his initial request.

The midwife and doctor were sweatily working on either side of Tallie as Janet Candlish removed her second-best navy coat and smoothing down her hair walked into the bedroom. She took in the forceps in the doctor's hands and the wet tangled hair on Tallie's pillow before she moved to the top of the bed and took her daughter's hand. Tallie's eyes opened once in her hot face before they closed again in frenzied agony and she issued a yell that could have taken the roof off.

'Steady,' said Janet, her grip tightening. 'You're nearly there.'

'Don't go,' ordered Tallie. She grabbed her mother's arm and hung on to it like someone hanging on to a low tree branch overhanging a river torrent. Bent over his task, the doctor applied his forceps to the baby's reluctantly emerging head. He was thinking there should have been a Caesarean. This poor girl – and the baby too – could be reaching the end of endurance. He knew from her restless uneasy stance that Mrs Gallacher was sharing his doubts now about a viable birth.

'Mother, don't go!' cried Tallie again. 'Mother.'

'Once more,' said Janet calmly, 'and you're there.' Her fierce gaze steadied the tired doctor and calmed and rallied the midwife.

Tallie's nails sank unrelentingly into her mother's forearm. With another uncharacteristic oath and with all her remaining strength she pushed a mighty push at the end of which she gave a rending cry. From the door Toby watched the tableau round his wife's bed and wept without knowing it. And then when desperation had reached its pitch, there was in the end a gentle kind of shooshing sound and the faint, protesting yelp of a new human being entering the world.

More activity. The doctor busy with Tallie. Her mother wiping her brow. The midwife lifting the baby high by its heels, the beginning of a smile on her face and calling to Toby, 'It's a wee girl. A fine, bonnie wee girl.'

Toby focused on his wife's white, exhausted face. He wanted to rush in and restore her, take away this maternity that had so threatened and engulfed her, revoke the love-making that had brought it about. But his gaze was drawn to the baby, the little mewling, protesting thing that by its spasmodic movements was declaring life, independence, recognition. His daughter. Some of the terror was ebbing away now and rapture invaded.

Tallie was saying something. 'Rowena,' she said faintly, as though in recognition. 'It's Rowena.' And he could see the same rapture in her: before his very eyes he could see happiness and accomplishment knit up the ravages of the previous hours, though her spent matchstick arms on the coverlet told him the physical cost. When the midwife placed the infant, wrapped in its soft shawl, in the crook of Tallie's arm, she looked first at the baby and then at him and he felt some compact sealed between them, something neither time nor causality could alter.

It was Jeannette's turn to come into her own now, with tea for everybody and a drop of brandy for those who needed it. Toby took his mother-in-law home. In the dark she clung to his arm for support and he could hear her breathy wheeze as they climbed the brae. They did not say anything but when she had let herself into the house he thanked her formally.

Going down the hill again, Toby felt the night was like Prospero's island, full of soft airs and mystery, to which every nerve and fibre of him responded. He tried to let his mind run ahead in the speculation of what life might be like for his child, but could not. She was his and not his. Her life would be her own and that was a sobering thought, that his intervention could only be partial.

The three of them. Him. Tallie. Rowena. He felt like the first man who had ever fathered. He felt like howling to the moon. He flet like knocking on doors and handing out cigars. He felt like the first man on earth. And he knew love was illimitable.

'Look at her,' said Donald approvingly. 'She's a model infant.' He tugged at the cord which set Rowena's crib a-rocking – the crib that had been Toby's before her – and smiled at the pink, satin-rimmed face doing its best to focus back at him. As she'd just recently been fed and was regurgitating slightly. Rowena wasn't finding the task all that easy.

Tallie bent and wiped the baby's mouth, rewarded by a

windy, toothless smile and a waving of hands. Three months after the birth, Donald thought his sister had never looked more comely, her angular figure softened by the contours of motherhood, her expression one of fulfilment and content.

With his confidante Belle gone (and quietly wed in the south in a register office ceremony to Percy) he found he was dropping in on Tallie more and more often. Sometimes he was the emissary between her and their mother, for Janet Candlish had not been back since the night of the birth because of a chesty condition and Tallie still would not go to Cullington Lodge in case she saw Kate. That was one relationship that had not softened one iota with Rowena's birth. Donald had chewed round the edges of the topic with both sisters but had not got anywhere. When the family dropped off to sleep he tried again.

'Do you think Kate and Wilfred would like a family?' he offered, noting how Tallie's back appeared to stiffen at the very mention of the names.

'How would I know?' she answered unresponsively.

He ploughed on in what he realised was a clumsy, amateur-psychologist way, 'Do you think she would like to be upsides with you? I mean, she must have heard all about Rowena from Mother.'

What had he been thinking only a moment ago, about how the sunnier side of Tallie's nature had recently asserted itself? It certainly wasn't in evidence as she rounded on him and said abruptly, 'I wish you would all accept one thing: I want to live my life without any reference to Kate. Or her husband.'

He looked down at his hands. What he really wanted to talk about was his own deep misery, his sense of disorientation since the war and need to have what Toby and Tallie seemed now to take so much for granted: a home and a spouse and the start of a family. He had thought his work might be all-embracing, all-rewarding, but although it was often both of these things, there were times at the end of the day when he needed creature comforts like the rest. And his mother, with the constant smell of camphorated oil in the house, her home-made onion-and-sugar cough cure, even the constant rattling around of striped peppermint balls in her mouth to try and stop the irritable, hacking cough sessions, or her eggcups full of whisky and water for the same purpose – his mother, poor soul that she was, irritated the life out of him with her dark-eyed reproachful stare at his own inability to sort his life out properly. What would some of the more ardent admirers of Shadow Jack think of that? It was a lot easier, he'd found, to preach than to practise.

Still, he was prepared to try again with Tallie and the subject of Kate. It would take his mind off the all-pervasive matter of his obsession with Tibby. He knew he'd tried everybody's patience to the limit over that and still Tibby would neither be hurried nor harried.

He put forward one of his favourite gambits. 'What did you learn from the war, Tallie?'

She looked at him blank-faced.

'That big sores build up from little ones. That we can't put the new world to rights, till we put our own personal lives right.'

She gave him an unbelieving, scornful smile. 'You'd know about that, would you?'

'I *try*,' he said patiently.

'Maybe you should try leaving Tibby alone. You're in danger of making a right fool of yourself over her.'

'I love Tibby.'

'And what would you know about love? It's wanting the best for the other person, isn't it?'

'Of course it is.'

'And giving them time to know their own mind. Not forcing them into decisions they're not ready to make.'

'You can't lecture me about love,' he said, calmly, 'while you shut out your own sister and her man.'

The toffee-coloured eyes were level with his own now, their gaze almost luminous with hurt.

'You know what she did?' she stated. 'She stole the

man—' She stopped, her eyes flying to the cradle where the baby stirred and then said, a little more calmly, 'She stole – she stole Wilfred.'

'But you've got Toby. And now the baby. Time to forgive, Tallie. You know it.'

'Never.' Her lips closed down hard in the line that was so familiar from their mother.

'You must learn to put it behind you,' he said relentlessly. 'It was the war, Tallie, that put all our lives out of true and now we have to put the war in perspective and start binding up all sorts of wounds.'

'The war doesn't excuse what Kate did to me. She always had it in for me.'

'You know what you sound like? You sound like some child who's been done out of her turn with the skipping rope.'

'Don't worry! She did me out of that, too. She never let me have anything!'

'Listen to yourself! You are being incredibly childish. And you a mother!'

'It doesn't go away, does it?' She rounded on him, her eyes vivid with subdued fury. 'What people did to you when you were young? You all thought I was there to be taken advantage of. With you it was "Wash my socks, run my bath". With Kate it was "Don't think your opinions matter". And Wilfred came along and made me see I did matter. Wilfred stood up for me, got me my freedom, helped me to be a nurse. That was why I thought the world of him. And if you want the truth, I still do. I should be there, nursing him back to health. She usurped me and I can't forgive her for it.'

Tallie had begun to weep half way through this diatribe and Donald, alarmed at what he had set in motion, stood up and made quietening motions with his hands. Then he put an arm round Tallie and gave her an awkward sort of hug.

'You have to let it go,' he urged quietly. 'What can't be cured has to be endured. I think you've idealised Wilfred more than a bit. Don't pass up the substance for the shadow.'

'You're a fine one to talk,' she said, more calmly.

'I'm a mess,' he confessed.

Close to him as she was, she could feel the fine nervous tremor of his body. 'Maybe a fresh start somewhere else would be the thing for you,' she offered impetuously. 'You're guddling about in too small a pond.' Her voice levelled with him. 'Because of Tibby.'

'Change the subject,' he said. 'Will you and Toby come to the Victory Ball?'

'You know what I think of such things. What have we got to celebrate? Russell's dead. How many others? You can't go into Glasgow without seeing an army of one-legged ex-soldiers dot-and-carry one along the gutter with tin mugs out for pennies—'

'It's over. Isn't it enough? I couldn't help being roped in for the ball. Kate and Wilfred are going, with other masters and their wives from the Academy.'

'Then we'll certainly not be there.'

'Think how it would silence the wagging tongues if you got dolled up in your best frock and came too. Toby came through unscathed, after all. That's something to celebrate.'

'No chance,' she said dismissively.

'I'm hoping it will be the night Tibby finally says yes.'

She gave him a pitying glance. 'Donald—' she began.

'Don't say a word.' He made for the door, glancing into the cradle as he went. 'Madam's waking up. I'll go before she screeches.'

# Twenty-Eight

It looked for a time as if the fate of the Victory Ball was in the balance.

There had always been some criticism of it from those who had lost family members in the war, criticism which the fact that all proceeds would go to help ex-servicemen and their families did nothing to stifle. Then as the third wave of influenza took a grip, people began to doubt the wisdom of large public gatherings anyhow. After all, in London they were boarding buses wearing face masks. Flu wasn't something that anyone could afford to take lightly.

'The parish hall is big and airy enough,' Donald argued with detractors. 'People won't want to dance if they're sick. If we give in to every ailment that's going the rounds' – he was thinking particularly of the tuberculosis that had taken a hold in the miners' rows – 'we might as well shut up shop altogether. We'll take all necessary precautions and go ahead.'

In the end, Tallie and Toby went after all, with Jeannette and 'Daddy' Wilson. Kate had succumbed to the influenza epidemic and although recovering would not be well enough to attend and Wilfred would not go without her. With a new dress in palest eau-de-Nil lace with a satin underslip, pale stockings, flirty shoes and a diamante bandeau for her hair, Tallie felt she was stepping away from the iron bonds of early motherhood and back into some kind of selfhood. Toby's dark eyes studied her as she swung the white rabbit-fur cape over her outfit before they set out. 'You look like a princess,' he said gravely, holding out an arm.

'I love to dance,' said Tallie, almost as though surprised by the fact, as she and Toby sallied through the heavy doors of the parish hall and they heard the spirited strains of the evening's band. She wondered at this capacity for light-headedness, the readiness to whirl so mindlessly in the reels and respond to the breathy foreign rhythms of the tango. Even after the news that Wilfred had been presumed killed, she remembered now that even then the response had not been extinguished in her. Strange!

But she felt welcome relief at the uplifting of her spirits alongside a determination to keep an eye on Donald. Since his demob she had felt mainly a guilty irritation towards him. Remembering his lordliness at Cullington Lodge when they had all been growing up together, his harsh selfishness when she'd made a bid to be something other than the family maid-of-all-work, she'd taken his postwar assumption of saintliness with more than a pinch of salt.

But since the baby's birth and Belle's departure she had seen a different Donald, one who had been coming more and more often to her and Toby as though their little home and family offered him some kind of stability and re-assurance lacking in his own life. (Why did she think in the same breath, as it were, of the night of Rowena's birth and how she herself had hung on for dear life to her mother's arm?) She had made up her mind after Belle left that she would map out her own life with Toby and Rowena and now it seemed as though the family, the first family, the Cullington Lodge family was reasserting itself and she would never be able to cut herself off from its obligations.

She'd tried to say some of this to Toby and he'd said that was life; it got more and not less complicated and he'd been glad of her mother when Rowena was born.

She wasn't going to allow herself to get too soft over Donald, but as she and Toby had listened to him go over some of his trench warfare experiences she had begun to think that in his mind he was still stumbling from shell-hole to shell-hole, looking for a place where the guns would be silenced. In his preaching he could sound confident, a man reborn. To her and to Toby only, it seemed, he could reveal the mental scars and spiritual wounds that were still in the process of mending – or perhaps not mending. He said he couldn't talk to Kate or Wilfred. He and Wilfred had more of an accommodation of opinion these days but could still

235

needle and goad each other. Besides, Kate seemed to want to keep Wilfred all to herself.

Whirling into the first dance in Toby's arms, Tallie prodded that area of consciousness concerning Kate and Wilfred and felt the same sick bile rise up in her. If the network of her emotional concern could spread to Donald nowadays – and it did – couldn't she, as everyone urged, also try to mend fences with her sister and her husband? Always she came up against the same blank negative. She knew she meditated on the situation – brooded might be a better word – and that if she were not careful the hurt, the need to get back somehow at Kate, could take over her life again as painfully as it had done at the start of her marriage. She tried to think of all the positive and good things she had going for her – Toby, whose health had improved dramatically since he had left his mother's coddling concern; the baby; the business; even the fact that the basic, necessary relationship between herself and her mother had been restored.

Sometimes it all seemed to come together and she was, not happy exactly, but conscious of a way forward where happiness could be achieved. Sometimes – just sometimes – she heard herself and Toby laughing over something the baby had done and she was able to savour the moment as true, like the ring from pinging a finger off an unchipped china cup. No flaw. But then some idle comment would set her off and she would know the hard, dangerous anger again, coupled with the longing for and loving of a form she no longer put the name of Wilfred to; could not allow herself to call Wilfred, because he belonged to Kate. And it was as though she was outside the little house in the Rows in her cold childhood, the one who had to work harder than the rest for attention. The one who had tried so hard to be good. And found it led only to exploitation and the rage that exploitation set up in her.

In the mêlée of the dance floor another couple bumped into them and jogged Tallie out of her reverie and back into the present. Donald and Tibby grinned at them and as the music finished for the moment they moved as a foursome off the floor to share a table set with a huge jug of still lemonade and four tumblers. Donald poured everyone some liquid and sat back to survey the scene.

'You look lovely, Tibby,' owned Tallie, feeling her own costume dimmed by the radiance of Tibby's paillette-encrusted cream gown with matching headband. She looked like something straight out of a musical comedy, bursting with a creamy luminosity her red-gold hair did nothing to dim. She wore a gold slave bracelet on her upper left arm and diamante ear-rings sparkled and swung with a gay insouciance from her pink lobes. Donald kept stealing glances at her like a little boy outside a toy shop.

Oh, God, Tallie found herself appealing silently to her deity, don't let something terrible happen between these two. She did not know what the something terrible might be, just that she could feel the weight of Donald's adoration and possessive need alongside something she could only define as a kind of rejecting insouciance in Tibby.

Of course like everybody else in Perringhall she had heard the rumours about Tibby. That she was meeting Alec Swann, going to dances elsewhere with him and that Tug Fleming took her presents of eggs and fowl from his farm. Who did she meet when she went off to Glasgow? She told nobody anything, keeping them all guessing with a defiant smile and a tiny lift of her fine eyebrows. Sometimes little Catriona stayed the night with her grandmother Janet and Tibby would accompany Donald to the pictures or some civic or church event. Tallie knew Donald had a house in mind, a rather fine detached greystone villa, which he would be able to rent without too much difficulty if only Tibby would accept his proposal to settle down together. But blandly following her own line Tibby stuck to the little house in Fell Street, with its dressmaker's pins all over the place, its rustling tissue paper patterns and half-finished garments and, in the spaces in between, Catriona's armless dolls and broken abacus frames.

Something has to give, Tallie thought grimly. She's

237

making an ass of him. He should see sense. He should know the best of her went to Russell. But when did anyone 'see sense' when it came to the person they loved? This much she knew: the heart had its own indelible, crazy, irrational, irrefutable reasons. Or maybe it wasn't the heart. Maybe it was something darker, stronger, like the blood, like the sexual tides that rocked and loosened and carried you away out of your depth. She didn't know any more. She was only taking in familial sensations about her brother, sensing in an almost psychic way a dangerous pain in him that was seeking outlet.

'Maybe he feels, like I do, guilty for being alive,' Toby had said to her once. 'Maybe he's trying to live Russell's life as well as his own.'

'But that's senseless, useless,' she had argued.

'Maybe. But we do feel guilt. Those of us who came through.' And Toby had given her a strange, naked, suffering look that had made her think she did not know her husband at all.

'May I have the pleasure?' Willie Stanton, a dapper master grocer who was a close friend of the Wilson family, bowed by Tallie's side and extended a hand to take her up for the next dance, a waltz. Decorously and mindlessly Tallie circled half-listening to her partner's easy pleasantries, her thoughts centred on some fathomless level of panic over Donald.

From the corner of her eye she saw Donald stand in front of Tibby and try to sidetrack her away from the main body of dancers, as though he wanted a private word. Once more round the crowded floor and she saw they were arguing, quite heatedly to judge from their faces though they were obviously trying to keep their voices down.

When Willie returned her to Toby she saw Tibby was dancing with Tug Fleming, the big rugged farmer who wore green tweeds even to an event like this.

'It's all right.' Somehow Toby had absorbed her alarm. 'I'll get him a drink.'

'One only. He's got to make a speech at suppertime.'

But by suppertime it was clear Donald had had more than one whisky. Nobody minded very much that his speech was rambling, but Tallie felt naked relief when he sat down. Although Tibby had been his supper partner, she was soon off again with a variety of dancing partners, seemingly indefatigable. Tired out after the rigours of a Dashing White Sergeant, Tallie and Toby found themselves back at the first table they had occupied earlier in the evening, with a morose and uncommunicative Donald now well gone in drink.

'Where is she?' he demanded at intervals. He did his best to be sociable, even jocular, with the people who stopped by to chat to them but relapsed into silence as they moved on.

It was not an event of great sophistication, Tallie thought. She had been to county affairs and dinners connected with the master grocers and they had their own stiff-necked sense of propriety. But although county names were here tonight and a strong scattering of professional people, the preponderance were from the rumbustious farming community and the Miners' Rows and they hadn't paid out good money for tickets without intending to let their hair down and have a good time.

The men had not been obvious in their drinking but had got down to it nevertheless with a degree of seriousness that was beginning to show in red faces and discarded jackets. As the music grew ever more syrupy and nostalgic, amorousness broke out. There was a lot of dancing cheek-to-cheek and hasty departures for dark corners outside where more urgent sensations could be explored.

Tallie had seen Tibby retreat at one point with Alec Swann, the bus-garage owner, and then return to the dancing without, thankfully, Donald spotting it. Then, just before the last dance, she saw Swann take Tibby by the arm in proprietorial fashion and lead her towards the cloak-rooms. Two minutes later they made a swift exit, wrapping up swiftly against the night air.

Her consternation had somehow been communicated to

Donald, who roused himself from some interior dialogue in time to see the departure of Swann and Tibby. Without a word he rose and followed them.

'Go after him.' Tallie pleaded with Toby.

'I don't think so.' Toby was not used to whisky and after three of the unaccustomed drinks was gazing owlishly at his wife. 'I want to dance the last dance with you and then go home. You are the most beautiful woman in this hall tonight.'

Tallie hesitated. She did not want to create a fuss and she remembered Donald's temper from old. With any luck, Tibby and her companion would have got well away and Donald would just have to take another knock to his pride and would then hopefully have the sense to go home.

She danced the last waltz with Toby for propriety's sake and then in a fever of impatience dashed to the cloakroom for her fur cape. She had worn it earlier with such pride and now it somehow seemed shabby and irrelevant. In the exiting crowd outside she looked around for her brother but he was nowhere to be seen.

She wanted to reproach Toby for not going after him, but he was bidding a protracted and voluble goodnight to his grocer friends and his parents, who despite their years had danced almost ever dance and were now in an advanced state of exhaustion.

Tallie bit her lip then thought of the baby, who had recently gone on the bottle but might not take it from baby-sitter Sally. She should, really, go home, but she was full of foreboding and a terrible sense of helplessness.

'You're trembling,' Toby commented as he took her arm. He thought it was from the cold.

'Let's go home past Cullington Lodge,' Tallie pleaded.

'Whatever for?'

'To see if Donald has got home all right.'

'How would we know that?'

'There'll be a light on downstairs.'

It took them a bit out of their way but the night air was pleasant after the heat of the dance floor. As they approached the Lodge, Tallie was first to spot a motor vehicle standing outside. There were lights on all over the house.

'Something's up,' she cried, in alarm. 'That's the doctor's motor-car.'

'I thought he had a pony and trap.'

'No. He's just bought the car. I recognise it.'

They stood hesitating on the pavement.

'Perhaps you mother's ill,' suggested Toby.

'Or something has happened to Donald,' she said fearfully.

'You have to go in.'

She stood, her body juddering with apprehension, her teeth chattering. Despite the rapprochement between herself and her mother, she had not been able to bring herself to visit. Even now, she knew if Kate answered the door she would not be able to speak to her.

'I'll go round the back,' she decided, 'and see if Mother's in the kitchen.'

Her instinct had been right. Through the kitchen windows she could see her mother pour hot liquid from kettle to teapot. Janet's keen ears had detected the sound of footsteps and alarm gave way to relief as she identified Tallie and her husband.

'What's up?' Tallie demanded urgently.

'It's Wilfred. His turn for the influenza. He's pretty bad.'

Tallie could feel something like a butterfly flutter in her throat. She tried to clear it and it came out like a cry. Toby touched her arm reassuringly.

'It must be bad, for the doctor to come out at this hour,' she said.

Her mother's look confirmed this once again. 'Kate's in a right state,' she said. 'She's not over the flu herself yet. She's not fit to look after him, but who else is there?'

'Where's Donald?' Tallie demanded wildly. 'He said nothing about any of this.'

'He doesn't know,' said Janet. 'He's been away

overnight in Glasgow and went straight to the Victory Ball. He took his dress clothes with him.'

'But he's not come home?'

'Not yet. What is it?' Janet asked quickly.

'We thought he might have had a touch too much to drink,' Toby interposed. 'I expect he's sobering up somewhere before he faces you.'

Janet looked hard at her daughter, seeing for the first time the strain and perturbation in her white face. She said, with an unaccustomed softness of tone, 'Come in to the fire, lassie. Sit yourself down and get warm. You'll have some tea?'

Tallie, nodding, did as she was told. She was cold all through, but it was something to be back at her mother's kitchen at last. Familiar items leapt out to greet her. The steady ticking of the old wag-at-the-wa' clock sounded in her ears.

But she could summon up no answer when her mother demanded hoarsely, 'What do you think has happened to Donald, then?' She could only look mutely from her mother to Toby.

'We don't know,' said Toby.

# Twenty-Nine

He was losing control. He knew that. It had been his responsibility as chief organiser of the ball to see off the civic dignitaries and lock up the hall and he had just left everything. He did not do that kind of thing. He was a punctilious man who thanked everybody, down to the ladies in charge of the cloakroom tickets. And he had just blundered out after Tibby and Alec Swann and when he had seen no sign of them had set out for Fell Street.

Halfway there he had taken a gulp of air and realised what he was actually doing, how it must look to the people left behind. He had thought he must go back, wash his face and put on some kind of display of normality after the playing of the last waltz and the National Anthem. *Then* he could think about Tibby and Swann and sort out in his mind what could be done. But he had ignored this last flash of common-sense and kept on stumbling towards Tibby's cottage. This was how he knew he was out of control. There was even a mad kind of peace to it. Going too far meant there was no going back. He was going to make Tibby see what he wanted, once and for all. Once she did, she would have no option but to comply and that would be that. 'There is a consummation devoutly to be wished', he heard himself saying to the night air. So he was drunk, he was far gone, he was out of control. Good old him. A man could only take so much.

He was well along the main street before he realised he must have missed the turning for Fell Street while he argued with himself. Turning, half-thinking he might still go back to the parish hall if Tibby would get out of his mind – Tibby with the red-gold hair on her arms and the way of giving all of herself in the act of love-making – and how many did that, even then? – Tibby with her dancing feet and slow, man-slaying smile – but she wouldn't, she wouldn't relinquish her hold on him and so the parish hall dwindled and fell away and the music faded from his mind.

Turning, he fell over. Once you started to stagger, he found, you couldn't stop and it took a shop door to stop his momentum. Once there he allowed himself to remain on the ground, to hunker down as they had done in the trenches and he found himself staring up at stars as though he had never seen them before. But he had. Over there. All the time.

He could almost imagine he was back in Flanders, propped upright with his rifle at the ready but half-asleep as the enemy guns crumped interminably. Gutless and pitiful he'd been half of the time. He could hear the echoes of voices, mates who'd faded into the mists of time, died with their boots on and he could almost smell the rotting, creeping, evil miasma that crept over from No Man's Land, the mixture of mud, gunshot, rotting animal carcass and gas, the stench that even now had not entirely fled his nostrils.

'Who is it?' Three faces were peering into the shop door, two men and a woman who must have been going home from the dance, judging from the scent of the woman's face powder and the fur he could just determine round her shoulders.

'Are you all right, fella?' asked one of the men. He came in and tried to hoist Donald to his feet.

'Good God, it's the preacher!' cried the woman. 'It's Shadow Jack, so it is.' She began to dust him down, peering incredulously into his face to reinforce the identification. 'Whatever are you doing here?'

'Whew!' said the second man. 'I think he's a drink taken. Or two.' He began to laugh. Just shows you, doesn't it, Maggie? This one hasn't stuck to holy water!'

The first rounded on him. 'You wer'nae at Wypres, Bernie. I was. So was he. So chuck the insults will you?' Almost tenderly he said to Donald, 'Never mind, old son. We'll get you on your feet. Feeling a bit off, were you? It can happen to the best of us.'

'I'm all right.' Donald put out a hand to steady himself. He had a feeling there was some sensation that should be registering with him, like shame, like disgust, but it wasn't quite getting through. What was registering was the woman's softness, the blur of her rounded outline, her fur, the rustling of her dress. And he knew he still had to get to Tibby.

'Where are you going?' asked the man who had picked him up. 'Can we take you there, fella?'

'I'm all right,' said Donald again.

'Do you know where he lives?' the man asked the others. They shook their heads.

'Fell Street,' said Donald clearly. 'That's where I'm going.'

244

They walked him to the corner of Fell Street and the exercise and fresh air restored him enough for them to leave him there. He was still a bit unsteady on his pins but they were anxious to get home and could not spend all night trying to elicit from him exactly where he wanted to go.

He patted the gate to Tibby's cottage gratefully and suddenly more sober knocked on the door. It was Alec Swann who answered with Tibby peering fearfully behind him.

'What do you want?' demanded Swann.

Donald ignored him and spoke directly to Tibby. 'I'm coming in, we've something to settle.'

'On your way,' said Swann.

'Tibby,' he appealed once again. 'You don't mean what you said, do you?'

'I've told you, Donald, it's all over. Why won't you believe me?'

'Because it can't be. I love you.'

'I don't love you.'

'You heard me,' said Swann, evenly. He bared his teeth under a rust-coloured moustache.

Donald's right arm shot out and grabbed Swann's shoulder, pulling him through the doorway like an arm through its sleeve. His left fist connected with the other's chin with a crack like a basin falling and his right knee came up into the other's stomach. Swann was almost a head shorter but thickset and well nourished after a war spent on the home front. He doubled up in pain, gasping, but fury brought his head forward like a bullet into Donald's groin and above his arms windmilled into his opponent with all the ferocity he could muster.

'No! Don't!' Tibby was screeching helplessly as the two men refused to break apart. In front of the lighted doorway they scuffed and kicked in the light gravel, squashing pansies and roses in the flower border.

After the first instinctive blows, Donald's co-ordination had gone again but he held on to the top of Swann's trousers

245

like a terrier with a rat, while Swann dodged and kicked like a manic spider, wild oaths spewing into the night.

Tibby had picked up a walking stick from the hall and now came at Donald, thwacking it across his back with such ferocious strength he was obliged to release his spastic-like grip and send Swann spluttering into the border.

'Get out! Get out of my life!' Tibby screeched at Donald. 'I never want to see you again.' She darted forward and grabbing the bloody-faced Swann dragged him through the door, closing it with a reverberating bang that shook the inset glass.

Donald picked up the iron foot-scraper and stove it through the glass.

'Jezebel!' he shouted. 'Jezebel! Trollop! Tell him about the times you went with me!'

The door remained shut and he retreated down the path. There was a bleeding graze on his forehead where Swann had head-butted him and his back ached from the unerring blows of the heavy stick. He was sobbing in his rage and betrayal and determined somehow to return to the attack, but he could not think how. Instead he swore and cursed and pulled up the silent mute plants he stumbled alongside by their flower heads.

'S'gone,' he heard him say to himself. But he didn't know what had gone. He was in too much pain. It wasn't just in his body but all through his mind, like a great crushing thresher. There was no escape from it. He stumbled back down the length of Fell Street, unaware of bedroom curtains twitching, in some cases quite brazenly pulled back. He was roaring like a stuck bull and anything liftable he came across, he threw – milk-cans on doorsteps, flower pots on window-sills, stones in the gutter.

In his confusion he thought he was back on the battlefield and that the enemy were all around him. He could hear the pitiless crack of the guns again in his head and see bodies disintegrate in the air with mud and shrapnel. 'Bastards!' he cried. 'Who brought this on us?'

He got to the Mercat Cross, stumbling towards it as

though it were some omen that would yield sense. He wound his arms around it and wept. Some of the physical pain ebbed but the cold night air remorselessly fought off a hoped-for oblivion.

S'gone, he thought again. This time he knew what it was. Any possibility of redemption. They would know him for what he was now. And Tibby would never make those reparations possible, would never knit up his hurts with her harvesting arms. Tibby had never been a real option. Tibby had been a vision, a delusion, conjured up by his infatuated need.

Dimly he saw his early desertion of her had made her what she was – a woman who would never be able to decide which man she wanted or what she wanted from him, because at base she trusted none of them.

That was the sort of man he was. A betrayer. And he would not, could not, let the thought through of the worst betrayal of them all. The time he had pinned a white cloth to a man's heart and seen him shot in cold blood. Always, the blink of the corporal's eyes would follow him. Seemed to follow him now.

He let out a bellow that seemed a compound of his pain and his guilt, his sorrow that the world had turned out the way it had for him. He had never understood why his own father had behaved the way he did when in drink, but now of course he knew, not intellectually, but viscerally, knew it had all come from some pain inflicted on *him* and so it would all go on till the world ended.

'Mr Candlish, sir, is it you?'

Through the tangle of his hair Donald looked down and saw Perringhall's police constable, Walter Blessup, looking up at him. The man had been dragged from his bed and a section of his pyjama jacket stuck out from underneath his tunic.

'See the names, here, Constable? Some missing, y'know.'

'Aye, sir, you can tell me about that later. We'll see you home to your bed now.'

247

'Some ran. They were just flesh and blood, y'see. Reared on their mothers' milk. Human.'

'True, sir, so come on down out of there.' The constable took hold of Donald's arm and dragged him to the solid bench set up by some benefactor nearby, so that people could be near the memorial and reflect.

'I'll be all right,' Donald mumbled. He decided he did not like the blue serge feeling of the law. They'd all been terrified of a cuff from Blessup when they were children. The man had twisted their cold ears or hit them with the hard edge of his hand.

'We'll get you home now, sir,' the constable repeated. Donald made a mighty effort to assert his will.

'I'll just rest a bit then get on my way.'

'See you do. I don't want to lock you up. Not a man like yourself, sir.'

The ageing constable could feel the cold seep up through his boots and knew he would be in for a bout of bronchitis if he hung about. There was also an urgent need in him to pee.

'You going to be all right?' The climb to Cullingford Lodge to deliver Donald to the arms of that harpy, Janet Candlish, seemed a less and less desirable course. 'You'll quieten down, mind? Behave yourself?'

'Certainly, Constable. You go on home.' Donald sounded almost benevolent.

He must have slept for a short while after that and when he woke he was violently sick over the edge of the seat. Everything began to come back to him, then, with a dreadful, heightened clarity. Had he really been cautioned by the old policeman, ordered home like a miscreant apple scrumper? Had he really thumped Alec Swann so mercilessly, thrown that scraper through Tibby's front door and gone up Fell Street afterwards like the wrath of God? And this was the man who was supposed to minister eventually to a congregation, who was supposed to be an example to others, to bind up their wounds?

He was sick again, at the growing, emerging disgust at his

own behaviour. How could he have drunk so much? How could he face the town when tomorrow his escapades would be the talk of every street corner coterie?

He got up from the bench as the first indication of dawn was no more than a faint bleaching of the sky's palette. His thought was that he should get away. The trouble was he felt weaker than he realised and certainly very cold.

He'd seen tramps, hadn't he, criss-crossing the country with the same weary, sluggish trudge he employed now. One foot in front of the other. What had happened to them to separate them from people who slept in houses with blankets to cover them at night? Was it also happening to him? He felt divided, not just from his family, not just from Tibby, but from the world at large. Very cold. Very tired. Very alienated.

He turned up a narrow country lane. It didn't make much sense to do so. But he might find an isolated ploughman's cottage or a farm. Didn't matter, did it? What could he say when he got there? 'I am someone fallen from grace, fallen a great way?' Couldn't. Couldn't. He was the one who helped the fallen.

He had veered off the path on to the lush green verge bordering hawthorn hedges. As he thought the word 'fallen' he began the physical act of keeling over. It seemed in slow motion, while his mind struggled to find ways to avert it, but it was remorseless. He went into the green, feral thickness of the hedge and it scratched his face and the hands he put out to save himself. Then a grey wave came at him and he went out, far out, where nothing touched him and as dawn came up the dew turned to rain and washed away the green stains of grass and hedge, as well as the blood and tears, from his face.

# Thirty

There was a small scrabbling sound and then the door to the kitchen at Cullington Lodge opened and Kate stood there, pale as a wraith in her long white nightgown and washed-out blue dressing-gown. She had long since grown her hair again after that far-off day of rebellion and it hung in short plaits to below her shoulders.

'The doctor is going.' She addressed her mother, Janet rose and went in the hall, where Macarthur took his shambling goodnight without looking her in the face.

'What did he say?' Janet demanded.

Kate said nothing at first, then shook her head slowly.

'To be frank, he doesn't hold out very much hope.' Her head came up and she gazed directly at Tallie. 'I suppose you'll say it's no more than I deserve,' she added harshly.

'Now, wait a minute, Kate,' Toby protested. 'You've no right to say such things.'

'Don't.' Tallie intervened, her voice sharp. She went over to her sister and led her to the chair by the fire. She knelt beside her and said urgently, 'What is it? Pneumonia?'

'Pleurisy. His poor lungs. He's too sick even to be moved to the hospital. Macarthur's coming back in the morning. What are *you* doing here?' There was no vestige of warmth in her voice.

'Donald's no' come home,' said her mother. 'And he's been at the drinking.'

'That's all we need.' Kate's head drooped into her hand. Tallie noted the skin was paper-white, the fine blue veins visible like tracery on a map. She could see her sister was not recovered from her own bout of influenza and a concern she had not known was in her made her say anxiously, 'Are you up to nursing him? Wilfred, I mean.' There, she had said his name.

For answer, Kate lay back in her chair with her eyes closed.

'No, she's not,' Janet answered for her. 'Get her some brandy,' she ordered Toby. 'Over there on the dresser.' She held the small tot of brandy to her daughter's lips. Kate took a sip and fell limply back again.

'I'll go up to him.' The words came of their own volition from Tallie's lips.

'Wait a minute,' Toby temporised. 'You haven't had the flu. You don't want to catch it. And what about the baby?'

But Tallie was not looking at him, although she took in what he was saying. She was staring at Kate, whose dark blue eyes had opened in that face that looked as though it had been made up of crushed butterfly wings and her expression was not pleading, but imploring.

She did not even stop to think. 'Take the baby to you mother,' she said with a gentle urgency to Toby. 'And don't worry about me. I don't catch things. I've built up a nurse's immunity, and the baby shares it.'

'No, go home to your baby,' said Kate, through pallid lips. 'Toby's right.'

'Then who will take care of the pair of you?' Tallie demanded impatiently. 'I've been exposed to germs in the shop. I'm sure at the start of the flu epidemic I had a mild dose. You remember, Toby?' she quizzed her husband. 'I was off colour for a week.'

She was starting up the stairs when Toby pulled her back once again.

'Think what you're doing,' he said soberly.

'I'm a nurse. I've got to help. You see the state that Kate is in. She's in total exhaustion.'

'Tallie!'

'Trust me.' She suddenly came back down the last few steps and kissed him full on the lips. 'I do know what I'm doing. I'd never forgive myself if I didn't do something.'

He was about to remind her she had said often enough she would never forgive Kate, but he saw she was incandescent with a kind of messianic energy and he suddenly understood what her vocation had been about. Being a nurse was being Tallie at her most fulfilled and he loved her too much to deny her.

He pulled her into his arms and held her wordlessly. 'The baby'll be all right. I'll look after her myself,' he heard himself saying. 'But come home as soon as you can.'

She tiptoed into the sickroom. The gas mantle had been extinguished and the only light was from a small paraffin lamp at one side of the double bed. This was the big room where Wilfred and Kate conducted a large part of their lives, eating, sleeping, reading. It was filled with the paraphernalia of the mental life they shared – books and prints and paintings and on a bamboo table by the window a large new gramophone with a horn. There was the sickly smell associated with illness – camphor, lemon, lavender water.

She should see his head on the lace-edged pillow, the dark hair she had once touched. She remembered the gesture of his hand up to move it off his brow. Now he lay on his side, and even from the door she could hear his laboured, stentorian breathing.

She went over and with her light, experienced touch felt his brow and cheek. He was burning up. There was water in a little copper kettle standing on a paraffin ring, possibly heated for a drink of some kind and it was still warm enough for her to pour into the basin on the marble wash-stand and to begin sponging him with a clean face flannel.

He moved restlessly in his fever and his eyes opened but did not register her presence. She opened the neck of his pyjama jacket and sponged his sweat-soaked neck and chest, drying them with a careful professional tenderness.

As her eyes became accustomed to the dim light, she saw how sunken his cheeks were and how the dark hair was streaked with white and grey. She could even see the scar where they had operated and inserted the steel plate. It could have affected his speech and his intellectual capacity but it had done neither. Belatedly, she put up a prayer of thankfulness that this was so. She could do this because there were just the two of them and in this curious bubble of time, in a strange undeniable way, he belonged to her.

All her antennae as a woman and a nurse were working at full stretch. She did not know – had never tried to analyse – what had put her ahead of others in her profession. It hadn't anything to do with the rules or even experience. It was more that right from the start she had had an unerring instinct about what might work for a particular patient, coupled with meticulous powers of observation. But it was more, even, than that. It was a kind of sixth sense about the possibility of recovery and it had to do with the very spirit of the sick person. Somehow at a vital point she tuned in to the will that was there and it was in harness that patient and nurse battled towards getting better.

Tonight she waited for something: some sign that the embattled spirit in the bed had not been totally vanquished. But it did not come. She had known death's shadow many times and she knew it was waiting in the dim recesses where the light did not reach.

The door opened and Kate came slowly in, drawing her robe about her with a shivering movement.

She came over to the bed and looked down at her husband. Her gaze absorbed rather than saw. Then she sat down on a chair and held his unresisting hand.

'I've sponged him,' Tallie whispered. 'Have you poulticed his chest recently, with kaolin?'

Kate shook her head. 'The doctor thought the effort might be too much for him.'

Tallie said, 'I think I could do it, so it wouldn't take up his strength.'

'Are you sure?' Kate's eyes glowed like dull, half-extinguished lamps. Tallie had seen the same look in sick and dying animals.

'Kate,' she ordered with a lift of alarm, 'lie down and try and rest.' She led her sister's unresisting form over to the *chaise-longue* that had been made up with pillows and blankets previously. She lifted the weary feet and tucked them in, then pulled the covers over Kate's upper body. Kate's eyes closed as though they could not help it.

Tallie began to work then with a calm concentration. The white kaolin paste had to be heated and then spread on a gauze pad with a spatula. It had to be hot enough for the warmth to permeate to the pleura and yet not so hot as to burn the sensitive and delicate skin, tender and pink from previous applications. Somehow when the pad was ready she slid it into place, lifting the skinny body just sufficiently to make her task possible.

Then once again she sponged Wilfred's body. The face, she thought, had altered since those times before the war when she had lain against it and felt his laughing breath against her cheek. Yet people did not essentially change. The same Wilfred was still there in the moulding of the mouth and chin. Here was a man who had responded to life not just through the intellect but with his heart. Who had seen, when no one else did, how she had been quietly draining away her youth in domestic drudgery when her talents lay elsewhere. Who had given her full accreditation as a human being. No wonder she had loved him. Still did. She was not going to let him go without a fight. They were not going to have him, the forces of evil, the cruel wounds from the war and the sly scourging germs of this killer epidemic that had followed relentlessly in the battle's wake.

She felt his pulse, slow and reluctant. Again she sponged, and again. With a corner of a clean towel she moistened his cracking lips.

And still she waited, for some sign, some indication that they could take up the fight together. Kate slept. In the shadows, it seemed to Tallie that Death again rustled his wings. She was not aware of how time passed, only that in the spaces between watching Wilfred's face, sponging him, moistening his lips and tongue, the clock's tick impinged on her consciousness with a savage dolour against which she wanted to appeal.

Toby came into her mind, and the baby. The thought of

her husband was like some balm and she marvelled at his goodness and at the way he was somehow in the room there with her in spirit, commending her. She let him go again, him and the baby, and began again the tiny useless ministrations that she somehow hoped would get through to Wilfred. She was aware of being worn down, of rash hope seeping away to be replaced by a silent, wild desperation.

'God wants him for His own,' said Kate at her side. She had risen so silently from the couch that Tallie had not been aware of her. Now the two sisters found their hands entwining as they looked down at the figure in the bed and the dramatic Biblical statement did not seem in any way extravagant.

'I know you loved him too,' said Kate. 'But I couldn't let him go.'

The words rose up in Tallie's breast and she almost said them. *And now you'll have to*. But instead she turned her sister's head into her shoulder and stroked her hair. Instead of anger she could feel only a great compassion, one that took her beyond all hatred. She felt in that moment she was being shown what love was, and it was never selfish, or full of self-regard.

'Will it soon be morning?' asked Kate, sounding like a piteous child.

'Not long,' said Tallie. 'Not long now.' She wrapped a quilt around Kate as she sat on one side of Wilfred and then took up her own position on the other side. The dawn was coming up, like the melting of the borders between sleep and waking, between dream and reality. She had known many mornings like this on the wards, touched with some curious quality she could only think of as miraculous. Falling in love with Wilfred had been like that, something that had gone beyond the bounds of the ordinary and been touched by a quenchless magic. She didn't pretend to understand. She only knew she had to use the gift, somehow, to enrich her life ahead.

*

'Come on, son. Come *on*. What brought you here?'

Donald opened first one eye and then the other, closing them both again immediately. He thought he had just seen a small, round face with silver-rimmed glasses and a clerical collar. Something sharp, admonitory, hit his cheek, like a cold hand. If he had not been mistaken, the face belonged to Perringhall's only Catholic priest, Dennis Hanlon. He tried to make some connection between the fact that he was lying back against a hedge and Hanlon was saying irritably, 'Sharpen up, man. Get on your feet,' and failed. 'Where am I?' he tried, half-groaning at the predictability of it.

'For Jesus' sake,' said the priest. 'You're halfway up a hellish lane to a farm cottage, where I've just given a poor old labouring sort the Last Rites. Sure it's a miracle I managed up here on my bike. You could have lain for days else, with nobody near you.'

Donald groaned again. 'You could have died from exposure,' the priest continued to scold, 'except you had this thick hedge for an overcoat. Look at you! Can you not stand?'

Donald tried. He felt as though some process had been at work on his body overnight, turning everything to granite stone, except that stone could not ache the way he did. With a mighty effort he straightened, then staggered. The priest gripped his arm. 'Can you walk back to the cottage? I'll get the old woman to make you some tea.'

The corpse of the old farm labourer was laid out in simple dignity in a set-in bed. The new widow, after she had obediently made the tea required of her by the priest, softly keened to herself by the fire, her black shawl almost covering her features.

'I'd had too much of the fiery stuff,' Donald confessed miserably, as the hot, sweet liquid took effect. He looked obliquely at the severe, spinisterish little Irishman opposite him. They knew each other and observed the usual courtesies when they met in Perringhall.

'You had a bad war,' said Dennis Hanlon, un-equivocally.

'How do you know?' Donald demanded truculent.

'I know. I was out there too.'

'Where?'

'The Somme, Ypres. Passchendaele. God saved me.' He gave a brief, spare smile that somehow illuminated the pink, androgynous features.

'I don't go over the war,' said Donald. 'I try to put the war behind me.'

'Won't be left behind though, will it?'

'Wasn't the war, last night. It was a woman. And what would you know about that?'

He saw a spasm of plain hurt cross the other man's face and tried to make immediate reparation. 'I didn't mean to offend. But she's cost me everything. I can't go back there now— ' He jerked his head in the direction of the town. 'I've made too much of a bloody fool of myself.' To his chagrin, Donald's body began to jerk in gasping spasms and he was sobbing uncontrollably. 'She's humbled me. And a man is nothing without his – his dignity.'

'Are you strong enough to walk back?' The priest saw the old woman was being affected by Donald's outburst. He thanked her for the tea and pushing his bicycle accompanied Donald back down the lane towards the main road towards Perringhall. It was a slow progress.

'You know as well as I,' he offered, 'the Lord wants a humble and a contrite heart. You're not of my Church, man, but I've heard of the good you've done for a lot of people, including some in my own flock.'

'Do you miss women?' Donald demanded bluntly. Once again he saw hurt and embarrassment on the other's face, but Dennis Hanlon simply said, 'I minister to women every day of my life.'

'I mean—'

'I know what you mean,' said the priest with some belated authority. 'I am not troubled in that respect.' He looked consideringly at Donald. 'Are you going to be all right? In control of yourself?' They were getting near to the town. 'You can come and talk to me, you know. Any time.'

He gripped Donald's hand and his gaze, direct and innocent, lingered on the other's haggard features, then his tone softened. 'We've been there, haven't we? We've seen what man can do to man. In some ways I'll never get over it, any more than you will.' And Donald felt the hand in his tremble.

Once the priest had cycled off, Donald made his way along the main street, glad at least that his overcoat covered his evening clothes and that a comb hastily borrowed from Father Hanlon had tamed his hair. It was still early and there were not many people about.

Passing the corner of Fell Street, he could feel something almost like a physical tug in the direction of Tibby's cottage. But he knew it was the end if he ever gave in to the destructive impulses that made him want to appeal to her one more time. How he was going to get the strength to turn his life around again, he did not know. He began to climb the brae towards Cullington Lodge and found that his physical stamina was returning. That was something. He thought he could smell bacon frying in one of the nearby houses and the juices ran unbidden into his mouth.

He didn't know why he thought of Browning, but he did. Just the lines: 'I was ever a fighter, so – one fight more'. He couldn't even remember which poem it was from, but it lifted his head as he walked on, and thought of breakfast and smelled the damp, fresh morning air.


When the birds had stirred, making the sleepy indistinguishable sounds they made before they found the place in their song-books, Tallie had thought they had lost him. She had felt for Wilfred's pulse and could not decide whether she detected anything.

Kate had looked at her and she had given her head an almost imperceptible shake.

'Kate,' she had said brokenly, 'there is nothing more we can do.'

They had held each other and wept and tried to dry each other's tears and then she had detected a tiny movement in

258

the bed and had felt for the pulse again and found it, faint but unmistakably there.

It was another twenty-four hours, however, before she saw it: the look she had waited for, as Wilfred finally opened his eyes, identified her and gave her the ghost of a weak, acknowledging smile.

She knew then they were hooked into real hope, together, nurse and patient. She had fought for the lives of men in the delirium of typhoid, after all, and for children gasping in the throes of diphtheria. Nothing but her and her skill between them and that old shadow who had folded his wings and crept away with the daylight. She wouldn't let him back. She wouldn't.

It was a week before she and Kate stood, nonetheless, with their arms about each other's waists, looking down at the patient who was undeniably on the road to recovery.

'How can we thank her, Katie?' he asked.

Kate said nothing. Her large, eloquent eyes said it all for her.

Tallie squeezed her waist, thinking about the mystery of sisterhood. Family bonds, she thought, they loosen and slacken and now in some strange way, it was what Kate and she had between them that mattered. Undeniably it was bound up with what they both felt about Wilfred.

She could not sort it all out in her mind, it was too complex and mysterious but she felt it was to do with the sharing of love. She knew, also, that all-unconsciously during the last few months she had been learning new lessons from her husband and baby. About generosity of spirit from Toby and the miracle of uncomplicated responses from Rowena.

Maybe, she thought, I am really growing up and into family life. Maybe I can help Donald and maybe Toby and I will soon have another baby. I'd like that. For I love and trust him totally, she thought, feeling, with a start of surprise, the need to be with him, to hold and be held.

To Wilfred she said, 'There is nothing to thank me for. Don't forget, you started me on the road to adulthood. You made it possible for me to be a nurse. And I'll always be grateful to you for that.'

Without letting go of her sister's hand, she leaned over and kissed him. It felt, she thought, as all the old miseries fell away, a bit like winning a war.

# Jean Chapman
## The Bellmakers

Forced to take on her pedlar grandfather's tally round and sell stockings to save her family from starvation, Leah Dexter is unprepared for the abuse and prejudice she encounters travelling alone on the new railway. And when she arrives at the village of Soston just as brothers Ben and Nat are reclaiming the cursed Monk's Bell, the superstitious local folk take her appearance as an evil omen.

When Ben intervenes to save her he wins Leah's everlasting gratitude and heart. But prejudice, superstition and the unbridled lust of the squire's son still threaten the proud and beautiful pedlar girl and those she loves . . .

# Mary Williams
# The Bridge Between

From the moment she arrives in the tiny Cornish fishing village of Port Todric in 1904, Julia Kerr loves the place. Through the ups and downs of her own writing career and her marriage to a man who always puts his painting first, she draws strength and encouragement from the unchanging rhythm of village life.

Julia's daughter Sarah, while very different from her mother, shares the same passionate wilfulness. Will she break Julia's heart by continuing to estrange herself from her family after a quarrel? Or will their shared love for the village bring about a reconciliation?

A warm and realistic love story with a lovingly rendered Cornish background, *The Bridge Between* is a book to touch the heart.

# Rose Boucheron
## Promise of Summer

It is 1939 and despite the threat of war the future is bright for three South London girls. While Sarah's dreams of fame propel her into a world far removed from her family and friends, her schoolfriend Julie stays closer to home, taking a clerical job in a paper factory. There she soon wins a new admirer Andrew, a RAF pilot officer and the boss's son.

Andrew's sister Olivia is also in love – with a married man – and is forced to conceal her true feelings and agree to her lover's demand for secrecy. But can she really be content to win her own happiness at the expense of another woman's?

A rich and satisfying story woven from the lives of three very different girls, hoping to secure love and futures for themselves despite the heartbreak of war.

# June Barraclough
## Time Will Tell

Susan, Miriam, Lally and Gillian have grown up together in the Yorkshire village of Eastcliff with their close friends Tom, Nick and Gabriel. *Time Will Tell* is the story, told by Gillian, of the intertwined adult lives of these seven very different friends. Will anyone stay on in the village now? Will they all marry and have children?

As their lives unfold it becomes clear that while some of them will make their mark in the world, not all of them will find happiness. Even far from Eastcliff, childhood events and attachments continue to cast shadows over their lives until the friends come to see all their pasts, including Gillian's own, in a new light.

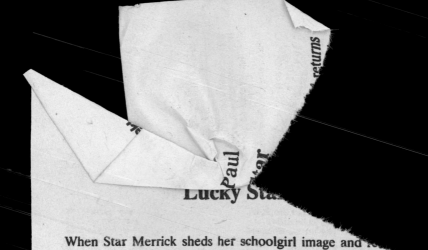

# Lucky Star

When Star Merrick sheds her schoolgirl image and home a lovely and sophisticated young woman, her mother is far from pleased. Glamorous but fading soap star Laura Denning will not tolerate a rival – even her own daughter.

To make matters worse, Laura has moved a new man into the house, Max Macdonald, a ghost writer working on her autobiography. Star finds him disturbingly attractive though he is obviously concealing something in his past. She struggles to keep her distance but the chemistry between them is too powerful – until Laura spitefully reveals what Star least wants to hear . . .

The prices shown below were correct at the time of going to press.

## Fiction

...prices at short notice. ...may differ from those

| | | | |
|---|---|---|---|
| | | in the Sun | Nina Lambert £1.99 |
| | | Bellmakers | Jean Chapman £1.99 |
| | | The Bridge Between | Mary Williams £1.99 |
| | 1 86056 015 6 | Promise of Summer | Rose Boucheron £1.99 |
| □ | 1 86056 020 2 | Tallie's War | Jan Webster £1.99 |
| □ | 1 86056 025 3 | Time Will Tell | June Barraclough £1.99 |
| □ | 1 86056 021 0 | Lucky Star | Betty Paul £1.99 |
| □ | 1 86056 055 5 | With This Ring | Jean Saunders £1.99 |
| □ | 1 86056 065 2 | A Captain's Lady | Jennifer Wray Bowie £1.99 |
| □ | 1 86056 060 1 | Lily's Daughter | Diana Raymond £1.99 |

All these books are available at your bookshop or newsagent, or can be ordered direct from the address below. Just tick the titles you want and fill in the form below.

Cash Sales Department, PO Box 5, Rushden, Northants NN10 6YX.
Fax: 0933 414000 : Phone 0933 414047.

Please send cheque, payable to 'Reed Book Services Ltd', or postal order for purchase price quoted and allow the following for postage and packing:

£1.00 for the first book: £1.50 for two books or more per order.

NAME (Block letters) .................................................................................................................

ADDRESS .....................................................................................................................................

............................................................................................... Postcode...............................

□ I enclose my remittance for £.......................

□ I wish to pay by Access/Visa Card Number

Expiry Date

□ If you do not wish your name to be used by other carefully selected organisations for promotional purposes please tick this box.

Signature .....................................................................
Please quote our reference: 3 503 500 C

Orders are normally dispatched within five working days, but please allow up to twenty days for delivery.

Registered office: Michelin House, 81 Fulham Road, London SW3 6RB

Registered in England. No. 1974080